VARNISHED FACES

Books by David Blixt

The Star-Cross'd Series
The Master Of Verona
Voice Of The Falconer
Fortune's Fool
The Prince's Doom
Varnished Faces: Star-Cross'd Short Stories

Will & Kit
Her Majesty's Will

The Colossus Series
Colossus: Stone & Steel
Colossus: The Four Emperors

Nellie Bly
What Girls Are Good For – A Novel
Charity Girl – A Novelette
Clever Girl – A Novella

Eve of Ides—A Play

Non-Fiction
Shakespeare's Secrets: Romeo & Juliet
Shakespeare's Secrets: Macbeth (with Janice L Blixt)
Fighting Words (with Kirby, Leoni, & Gerard)

Visit www.davidblixt.com

VARNISHED FACES

STAR-CROSS'D SHORT STORIES

DAVID BLIXT

English language excerpts of Dante Alighieri's L'INFERNO, PURGATORIO, and PARADISO that appear in this novel are from, or adapted from, translations of each text by Robert Hollander and Jean Hollander (Doubleday).

HEART'S EASE is from SHAKESPEARE'S SONGBOOK
by Ross W. Duffin, published by Norton.

English language excerpts of THE BALLAD OF VERONA by Manuello Giudio are from, or adapted from, a translation by Rita Severi.

Varnished Faces

ISBN-13: 978-1944540128
ISBN-10: 1944540121

www.davidblixt.com

Published by Sordelet Ink
www.sordeletink.com

For Janice Lee

My Heart's Ease

CONTENTS

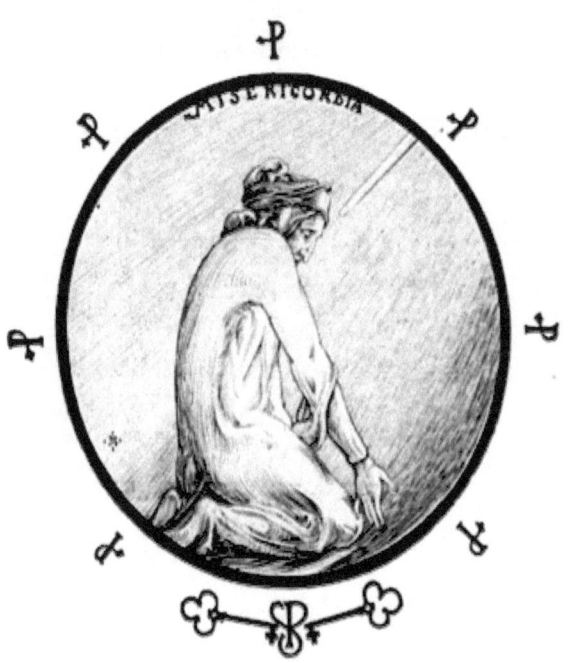

FOREWORD

I HAVE TOO MANY STORIES.
   Now, that's not generally a problem. An excess of ideas is far better than the alternative. So I'm not complaining.

   My trouble is that many of my stories don't fit in a novel, don't serve its arc, don't help to push through to the finish. I come from a theatre background. One of my favourite directors to work for is Kevin Theis, because among his many directorial dictums is this gem: "Get on with it! We can smell the ending!"

   It may not seem so judging from the size of my novels, but I always have that in mind, both on stage and on paper. While I tend to write these massive tomes, I really do have an eye always on the question of, *Does this move the story along?* Even as I lay groundwork for future stories, balancing that against the ongoing action, I look for places where I, as the reader, would be saying, "Get on with it! We can smell the ending!"

   This leaves me with stories that don't fit in the novel—if I tried sticking them in, they would each become a huge digression, detracting from the narrative push.

   But they're good stories. And they do impact future events. Be a shame to lose them. Hence, this volume.

   You may notice a few threads linking some stories—death, roses, prophecies, and even bees. But the strongest thread, the most prominent one, is the city of Venice. That's deliberate. For though the story VARNISHED FACES takes place in Padua, the line comes from *The Merchant Of Venice*. Again and again, as I looked at the pieces I had for this, Venice was there, lurking in the shadows, hovering in the mist, her fingers reaching out to wrap around each tale's tail and pull.

   Thanks are due to Constance Cedras, Marina Bonomi, Judith Testa, and, of course, my wife Jan, as well as the casts of every Shakespeare play I've filched lines from. This book also relies greatly on the Dante scholarship of Robert Hollander.

   So here they are, rescued from or inspired by THE MASTER OF VERONA, VOICE OF THE FALCONER, FORTUNE'S FOOL, and THE PRINCE'S DOOM. Enjoy!

A Poet's Nightmare
Part One

"FINISH IT."
    "I don't—"
"Finish it."
"—appreciate—"
"Finish it."
"—your tone."
"Finish it."
Silence.
"Finish it."
Silence.
"Finish it."
"SILENCE!"
Beat.
"Finish it."
"Pietro! Can you please curb your—!"
"He's out. Finish it."
"I will."
"You won't."
"I will."
"You say it but you won't do it. Do it now."
"Brat. Go away."
"When you finish it."
"It will take me a year at least!"
"Then you should start."
"Wretched boy!"
"Names can't hurt me. Finish it."
"I will!"
"You never finish anything."

"I certainly—"

"*De Vulgari Eloquentia, Convivio*..."

"I was interrupted."

"By what?"

"An annoying child."

"I wasn't even born."

"Ah! But you admit you're annoying."

"They stopped paying you, didn't they?"

"Who?"

"The professors at Bologna. They stopped paying, so you—"

"It was a series of... no! I'm not explaining myself to a six year-old! Go away! Leave me in peace."

"Fine. If you won't, I will."

"You will what?"

"Finish it."

"Oh ho. The stripling thinks he understands *tirza rima*?"

"Better than you!"

"I invented it!"

"Just tell me what happens and I'll write it for you."

"O God, I despair! Fine. See? I'm picking up the quill."

"Good. I'll fetch some water to dissolve the ink."

"Bring me some wine while you're at it. Wretched child."

"You'll thank me one day, old man."

"You should live so long, boy."

—Dante & Cesco

SAN BONIFACIO'S CURSE

FOR MARINA BONOMI

"The Count is neither sad, nor sicke, nor merry, nor well;
but civil, Count, civil as an Orange,
and something of that jealous complexion."

—Beatrice
Much Ado About Nothing
ACT II SCENE I

ACT THE FIRST

WHEREIN THE BRAVE COUNT IS STARTLED BY AN OMEN

"FIRE THEM UP."

With a patter of running feet, the order was repeated. Through dusk's fading light, signal torches blazed to echo the changing sky. The ramparts were transformed to a dancing line of flames atop the ancient walls.

A moment later those selfsame walls were shaken by thunderous hoof beats below. Knights and mounted soldiers spurred through the gate, across the great Ponte Molino that spanned the Bacchiglione River. Following the curving road west over a second bridge, past the churches of San Giacomo and San Leonardo, the riders then wheeled north.

Two men on horseback, unfortunate enough to be coming in the opposite direction, were lost in the tumultuous mass of horseflesh and steel. One threw himself from the bridge to save his life. The other was knocked from his mount and trampled past recognition.

High above, a lone evening star winked down the history of the days ahead. A strange code, light against darkness, God's own plan manifest to those who could decipher it.

Count Vinciguerra of San Bonifacio had no key to the stars. Nor did he care. The wealthy exile stood on the tower above the Ponte Molino, and though his deceptively cheerful eyes were fixed on the single star, his thoughts were of more practical affairs—the disposition of men, the supply lines, the weather. Another hot day, even this late in the year. The Count mopped his forehead in disgust. Even if secrecy had not been vital to their enterprise, he was glad of the night march. A large man, he was embarrassed at how freely he sweat.

As he shifted to replace his handkerchief—a new custom, making him quite *a la mode*—the setting sun caught the finish of the polished helmet under his arm. Momentarily dazzled, the Count frowned—a comical sight, his visage not being built for it. His was the face of a happy, fat friar, not a knight and soldier.

Yet soldier he was. Across his ample chest he wore his *petta*, the breastplate with his family crest lightly etched in acid—two stars in opposition, and two branches of different plants, bound together at the base. Occasionally Vinciguerra wondered about the plants, but he was no herbalist. It was the crest of a noble line.

Now nearly extinct, thought the Count.

"Well, the die is cast," muttered the Count's companion. Just a few months ago, Ponzino de' Ponzoni had been an official of Cremona, far from the politics and wars of the Feltro. Padua had a long tradition of giving military and civil command to foreigners, as no one trusted a native not to use that power to establish permanent rule. Thus the *Anziani* of Padua had elected this Cremonese fop as Podestà of Padua. They were already ruing their decision.

"My lord Podestà?" Waiting a few paces behind them, Ponzoni's page sounded excited.

Ponzoni did not answer, gazing instead at the same evening star the Count had ignored. "A clear night."

"Too clear," grunted the Count. "We could use more clouds."

"They say the stars are always clearest on the eve of a great victory," replied Ponzoni.

"They hold our future, you think?" Vinciguerra's voice was wry.

But the other man nodded soberly. "Victory. Defeat. Glory. Ruin. Fame Eternal. Insignificance. All these lie in our stars."

Fool, thought Vinciguerra. *A man makes his own fate.* The Count was far from convinced that this forty year-old intellectual from Cremona could pull off this night's coup. Which was why he planned to be close at hand through it all.

Aloud he said gruffly, "It's a good plan." It was—he had devised it.

"What do you think of our numbers?"

The Count's mouth turned down. *A child needs less approval.* "Thank God for the Venetians, is what I say." A full quarter of the troops, Dutch mercenaries, had been supplied by Venice. That stinking lagoon had a more than passing interest in the outcome of this war.

Hearing gruffness in the Count's voice, Ponzoni misinterpreted it and clapped Vinciguerra on the shoulder. "Cheer up, my friend! By tomorrow, I'll be free to send soldiers to retake your castle!"

Incompetent dolt, was the Count's savagely repressed answer. Aloud he said, "In due time. Let's be sure he's well and truly crushed."

Nodding gravely, Ponzoni turned to address his page. "My horse is ready? Then let us descend." The page raced to the steps along the inner wall.

Ponzoni took a few steps. When the Count did not follow, he said, "Are you coming?"

"I'll be right along." Vinciguerra smelled a speech coming, and he had no use for them. Were this his army, he would already be in the saddle, riding with the vanguard. *Generals lead from the front, not the rear.*

As Ponzoni vanished below the wall, the Count gazed over the rampart at the knights flowing across the bridge below. He spied the crimson plumed helms of the della Torri, a minor house from Milan, famous for its warlike bishop rather than proper soldiers. Such undistinguished knights would be lodged at the back, which meant the horse soldiers were almost past. The foot would follow, while the supplies were taken through the Ponte dei Tadi along the southwest wall.

Logistically, Ponzoni should have sent the foot out the gates first. But no noble would allow the rabble to take the vanguard. The laws of war often had less to do with good sense than politics and manners. *Manners! Must observe the niceties!* Vinciguerra knew what *he* would have done had this army belonged to him, niceties be damned.

Not that he would ever be trusted with a Paduan army. Not even if they succeeded. *Especially* not then.

Still, Ponzoni is correct in one thing. The die is cast. With these numbers— yes, we should so it. Even with a fool in command, we should do it. Provided luck is with us. Vinciguerra might sneer at augers and soothsayers, but it was a poor soldier who did not believe in luck.

Below and behind him, he heard Ponzoni launch into his first speech of the night. His audience was comprised of the noble lords chosen by the Anziani to ride with the Podestà, to confer on the plans for the assault—and to second guess their foreign commander. The city would never invest full authority in one man, no matter how trustworthy.

Indeed, that was the ultimate point. This evening's undertaking was to ensure that no one man ever would—ever *could*—rule the Lombard League.

Of course, murmured a voice deep within the Count, *if it's the right man…* But there was time enough for that.

Ponzoni's oration began: "Friends! Noble citizens of the Commune of Padua! Tonight we reclaim what rightfully belongs to us! For over a hundred years, the city of Vicenza has been within the Paduan sphere of influence. But four years ago a handful of Imperial puppets handed the stewardship over to…"

Mind wandering, the Count let the words fall over him, the retelling of history so well known it was taken for granted. Emperors and popes, fighting wars over who held what legal right. The noble Guelphs, supporters of the pope, against the wretched Ghibellines, tools of the empire. The name of Padua seemed to creep into the tale more than by rights it should. No doubt the speech would invoke *patavinitas*, the curiously boastful Paduan honour that seemed to rule every waking moment in this benighted city. The fact that the Count had been forced to live here for so long only made such pride stick in his craw.

But overweening pride was the style of the day. In that respect their enemy—the Pup, as the Count liked to call him—was the worst offender of all. Mythic title indeed! If Vinciguerra owned little use for astrology, he had even less for prophecy. He felt it in his bones—there was no Greyhound.

From somewhere in the night, out of a nearby house, a child cried out, audible even above Ponzoni's oration. Not a cry of hunger, nor of pain, but a joyful squeal of delight.

At the sound, a shiver ran down the Count's spine, and he could not help wondering, *Why?* The Count had found reason to like children of late. Perhaps he was softening in his dotage.

Below, Padua's Podestà gave his final cry: "*Muson, Mons, Athes, Mare Certos Dant Michi Fines!*" This ancient Latin phrase literally defined the city—'The Musone River, Mountains, the Adige, the Sea Give Me Definite Boundaries.'

The assembled citizens cheered back, wafting their firebrands high into the air. *Time to go, then.*

Turning, the Count saw a woman all in white who seemed to float in the air. In fact, she was standing on a darkened balcony. Dressed for mourning, her pale clothes seemed to glow, and Vinciguerra was intrigued to see the sheen of refined silk. The failure of the last Crusade had closed the Silk Road, making the material quite expensive. Yet this gown was newly made. Signifying a new loss.

Her face was hidden in shadow, and her shape was lost in the folds of the garment. But Vinciguerra could see a bundle in her arms. She was likely mourning the child's father. *Poor lass.*

While he gazed at her, the Count again heard the laugh. It seemed that the swaddled babe delighted in the running horses, normally a sound to frighten the tamest of children.

But the joy in the infant's wail was quite inhuman, as if, hearing the thundering call to war, he was answering mirthfully. The Count, who had waited his whole life to hear a child of his own laugh like that, shivered again.

The torches lowered, and mother and child disappeared into darkness. No light came from within the house. It was as if they had never been.

Sixty-three years of age, a man tried in bloody war and bloodier politics, Vinciguerra da San Bonifacio was not a man to quail in the face of any threat. Yet he was unaccountably eager to be away from this place. Away from that woman. Away from the horrible, mocking infant she had birthed.

He descended using the crafty gait he'd devised over the years to cover the limp from a badly healed broken leg. Once below the line of turrets, he walked to where the assembled nobles were readying to ride.

His path took him past a juniper bush outside the house of mourning. Torches burned at the front gate, and in their light he saw the device engraved on the wall—a common symbol of commerce, the staff called the *virga*, what the Greeks called the *caduceus*. Twin snakes embraced atop a cross, their bodies entwined all the way to the tail. The sign of the Messenger of the Gods.

For a man who disbelieved in the power of Fate and the stars, Vinciguerra bitterly resented the small internal voice that asked, *What message does he bring?*

Shaking his head as if to fend off a gnat, the Count banished all thought of the mourning house bearing Mercury's message. Instead he focused upon this night's mission—to bring down the Pup once and for all.

Entering the cobbled yard where the army's nominal leaders prepared to depart, he found his horse ready, attended by his young groom. *They're all young. And getting younger.* Quickly he mounted, settling in to the well-worn saddle.

Briefly he scanned the others. Among the scores of knights and nobles, two stood out: Il Grande da Carrara and his nephew, Marsilio. Richer than God, they were also the best that Padua had to offer. In Il Grande's case, that wasn't bad at all. He was a nobleman in the vein of the Romans of old—a true patrician gentleman. His nephew, on the other hand, was a hotheaded preening princox. But then, weren't all young men? The Count snorted. *At least those of any value.*

Already mounted, young Carrara was gazing warily back at Vinciguerra. The lad was certain that any Veronese was born spinning deceit, and he'd made clear his objection to the Count's presence. Indeed, his very existence. Knowing that amusement drove the young man to distraction, the Count chuckled and turned away.

Ponzoni was in the process of mounting, gripping the wooden horn on the first *arcione* with his groom near at hand to assist as needed. The Count saw the impending disaster an instant before it happened. The groom was holding his torch high to give his master illumination, but stood too close to the horse. Unnerved by fire inches from its face, the horse shied and stepped sideways. Half in the saddle, Ponzoni lost the stirrup. Weighted down by armour, his body slipped. The Podestà made a mumbled exclamation, half a curse, half a cry for help. The groom moved forward, but again the horse turned from the light, dragging Ponzoni around with him. In a moment he would be under the horse.

The Count wanted to laugh. *A marvelous end to this great campaign, over before it begins!*

The nobles shifted in their saddles, looking for an opening to assist. It was the Carrara boy who kicked forward and seized the bobbing mane firmly without spooking the horse further. Carrara held the mount while Ponzoni clambered the rest of the way into the saddle.

There were disgruntled murmurs all around. The Count listened in disgust. *Oh, the idiots. A bit of poor handling, and they think it's a bad omen!*

Ponzoni's foot rediscovered the lost stirrup, the right foot followed suit, and he settled himself into place. "Thank you, Ser Carrara. Let us hope that is as much excitement as the night affords. Come, friends—Vicenza awaits!"

They cheered, if halfheartedly, and began their quick journey to the Ponte Molino to follow their army.

The Count paused as he passed Ponzoni's groom. Flicking a heel at the boy, he rowled his long golden spur across the boy's nose, slicing it neatly in two. "Watch your torch near the next animal, or you'll find yourself victim of a meaner kick."

With that, the Count of San Bonifacio spurred after the Paduan nobility, advancing two wars—Padua's, and his own.

ACT THE SECOND

WHEREIN THE NOBLE COUNT RECOLLECTS OLD WOUNDS

THEY OVERTOOK THE LEAD ELEMENTS of the army four miles up the road, crossing the new canal between the Brenta and the Bacchiglione.

Here they met the commander of the foot soldiers. Vanni Scorigiani by birth, he was known to friend and foe alike as Asdente, meaning the Toothless Master—a fitting title, as he'd had his teeth shattered by a sword-stroke from the Pup himself. Asdente was perhaps the fiercest warrior the Paduans owned.

They discovered him busily ushering the last of the mounted force out of the way of his beloved 'groundlings', who had a wearying trek ahead—twenty miles to cover between sun down and sun up.

For all their thunderous exit of the city, the army was remaining remarkably quiet. This was entirely due to Asdente's presence. He could have made a fortune hiring himself out as a *condottiero*, leading mercenaries into battle for a different prince each season, wintering in the south with all the wine and women he could manage. But gruff and bluff as he was, Asdente was a patriot. Padua was lucky to have him, the Count knew. And, as often happened, Padua was ungrateful for their good fortune.

Vinciguerra watched as the Podestà greeted Asdente in cool tones. The older and viscerally martial Asdente seemed to know Ponzoni's every insecurity, and relished each opportunity to rub his nose in them.

"Any trouble?" asked the Podestà.

"I had to get rough with a few of the Dutch knights to get them to stop their wretched singing," growled Asdente genially. "The rest fell in line."

"How rough?"

Asdente's twisted grin looked like the rictus of a corpse. "Battle hasn't started, and we've got casualties." Noting Ponzoni's hardening look, he shrugged. "They'll live to complain."

The Count watched Ponzoni stifle a rebuke. Good. Padua needed Asdente, or someone very like him. The only pity was that Asdente knew it.

Seeing Ponzoni's face, the elder Carrara arrived decided to intervene. "No sign of spies?"

"Haven't seen a soul," replied Asdente, his lack of teeth making these words a momentary puzzle. "They're lazy after that scare they gave us last month. Think we'll hole up until Spring."

Ponzoni's relief was evident. "Then this surprise will work."

"It better. Vicenza belongs to us," added Asdente.

That was almost laughable. Vinciguerra made a point to study the road ahead. An educated man, the irony of this war was not lost on him. In opposition to historical precedent, a minor war had grown out of a larger one. All over one small city, the Commune of Vicenza.

A hundred years before, the Holy Roman Emperor Henry VI had declared his right to rule the lands of central Italy—Tuscany, Umbria, Romagna and the marches thereabouts. These had been ceded to Henry's father, Frederick Barbarossa, by a duke named Welf VI. Before Henry pressed the claim, these lands had always been under the influence of the papacy.

Henry hadn't owned sufficient political might to enforce his aspiration, but his successor, Otto IV, had. A condition of Otto being offered the imperial throne was his renunciation of all rights to these fertile lands. Otto had agreed and, immediately following his coronation in Rome, done just the opposite. Assuming (correctly) that they faced less interference from an Emperor in Germany than a pope in Rome, the central states flocked to Otto's banner under the cry of "Welf! Welf!"

Meanwhile, opposition among the northern states solidified behind another German faction, the Waiblingens, who devoutly supported, not the papacy, but the rights of another German ruling house, the Hohenstaufen. When Otto died, he was succeeded by the Hohenstaufen ruler Frederick II. In a twist of irony, the Welfs chose to side with their former enemy, the Papacy, against the Waiblingens.

Adopting this very Germanic fight for their own, the Italians naturally changed the names of the parties. Welf, a hard sound, had become Guelph, and Waiblingen had transmogrified somehow into Ghibelline.

And so the lines had been drawn. Padua supported the Guelph cause, harrying each new Emperor in favour of papal rights. Though Vicenza was nominally an independent state, Padua had long viewed it as within the *padovano*, the Paduan sphere of influence.

Two years ago, Vicenza had bucked Paduan authority, declaring itself for Emperor Henry VII by voting the Pup into office as the Imperial representative. Padua had been incensed. Vicenza was theirs! Vehement protests to Venice and Florence proving fruitless, the Paduans had decided upon force to prove it.

Why Padua hadn't won in that first year was probably a mystery to Ponzoni, listening to reports from his comfortable home in Cremona. They had done well in the field, with battle after battle a Paduan victory. Asdente in particular had distinguished himself, bravely riding into every engagement. "I eat steel for breakfast!" he was often heard to roar, the disfigurement slurring his softer sounds.

But the war had dragged on, and it seemed only the Count understood why. The Pup had a streak of immortality, of puffed-up grandeur that made him seem larger than life. It didn't hurt that a Florentine poet had hinted at some prophecy surrounding *Il Veltro*, one of the Pup's many names. With the story of Dante's journey into Hell being read aloud and even sung by everyone from the nobility to the lowest serf (a clever consequence of writing in Italian, not Latin), everyone was coming around to the view that the Pup was this invincible Greyhound of legend.

Thus, regardless of Paduan bravery or victory, they never seemed to be able to weaken the enemy spirits enough to retake their lost city. Nor were they ever able to catch the enemy general in the field. The Pup was wily, from clever and dangerous stock.

No one knew the family better than the Count. The blame for his family's exile lay at their door. Inside the Count burned an injustice as old as the Guelph-Ghibelline feud, a hatred so long-lived had to be tended, stoked, carefully nursed, lest it burn itself out.

THE ROAD TO VERONA
5 NOVEMBER 1259

"WE ARE ALMOST HOME." Vinciguerra's father, the Count, pulled his horse alongside the wagon bearing his son and a few family trunks.

The father clearly expected his son to share in his delight. But the ten year-old surprised him by saying, "Is he truly dead?" The boy was staring at the trees lining the road as if the Tyrant would leap out from behind them and behead them all. In the last thirty years, Romano the Tyrant had become the nighttime dread of every child in Italy.

Vinciguerra's father laughed with real pleasure—not at his son's fear, but at the question. "There's no doubt! Leaders of three factions slew him and chopped him to pieces. Oh, how I wish I had been there!" The old man clenched his fists on the reins. "Still, there is the Montecchio clan to be dealt with." The Count looked sharply at his only son. "Tell me why they must be destroyed."

Dismissing his fears, young Vinciguerra sat upright on a trunk and recited from memory, "Because when the Tyrant drove our family out of Verona, he was aided by the Montecchi."

"And who are they?"

"A bunch of horse-thieves turned noble," parroted Vinciguerra, to his father's approval.

"Yes. Just like the Romani—they, too, took their names from estates stolen from true Veronese. And what did they used to be called?"

"The Onara," said Vinciguerra instantly.

His father nodded. "Never forget it. Names matter, boy. We need to remember who we've been to know what we will become. Prove to me that you know the tale—tell me, where did it begin?"

"Vicenza."

"And when."

"Forty-nine years ago," said Vinciguerra with utter certainty. These facts had been drilled into him before even his letters. "Out of revenge for us exiling them from Verona, the Romani usurped our control of Vicenza and used it to wage a feud against us. Great-grandfather fought bravely—"

"Names, boy! Names!"

"Bonifacio di San Bonifacio," said Vinciguerra quickly. "He fought valiantly to hold off the Romani. But he died, leaving two children, a son and a daughter, to carry on our line. Grandfather—Rizardo di San Bonifacio—carried on the fight for ten more years. Then God came to the Romano lord—"

"Or the Devil," interposed the Count, as he had a hundred times before, "to give him a well-deserved fright from Hell."

"Yes. Romano made peace with grandfather Rizardo by offering his daughter in marriage. In return, grandfather gave his twin sister Tilde to Romano's son. Romano gave up his possessions, retired from public life, and lived out his days in a monastery a broken man."

"Leaving us no quarrel with him," said the Count. "He repented his bad deeds. God has forgiven him, and so must we." Vinciguerra's father did not sound as if he truly believed the words, learned at his own father's knee.

"But he failed!" protested little Vinciguerra. "His son, married to your aunt, made war against us again! He united with the Montecchi to throw us out of our lands and take over Verona!"

"Don't forget the final offense," chided the Count. "My father was the Podestà of Verona at the time. Ezzelino da Romano had a puppet, Leo delle Carceri, whom he declared *Capitanus Veronae*. The title itself is an insult— the Tyrant created the Captainship to supersede the Podestà.

"But Ezzelino III's reign was proof that we were in the right, boy. The blood that flowed over the Feltro ruptured the Lombard League. I hear that when the Tyrant finally gasped his last, he begged like a dog. It gives me heart. There is justice in the universe. No stone marks the grave of that enemy of God and mankind. I only wish my father was alive to see this day—for today, my son, the San Bonifacii return to our rightful home, our rightful throne. Verona is leaderless. We shall ride through the gates and be hailed as saviours."

He did not say so, but little Vinciguerra wished they had marked the Tyrant's grave somehow. It frightened him to think that such a man's spirit might be rooted anywhere at all, that one might stand on the patch of unhallowed ground and not know it.

Seeing his son's anxious look, the father chuckled. "Don't be concerned. They know we're coming. I sent word. Now, prove to me you know the value of names—recite the family tree."

Vinciguerra did not sigh as another boy might have done when asked to recite the Christian names of a family line stretching back six hundred years to the days of Emperor Charlemagne, who had installed a man called Milo to rule Verona in his stead. No, Vinciguerra merely furrowed his brow as he worked his way from Milo, the very first Count of San Bonifacio, to the present one—his father.

But before he reached the recitation's conclusion, his father cut across him. "Look, boy. There it is. Verona."

Young Vinciguerra twisted about in the wagon to look past the driver at the city rising into view. His father's city. *His* city. "The towers! Oh father! Look at all the towers!"

"Yes, son. And we shall build more, to honour our family. More and more, until the city is a forest of towers, looking down on the rest of the world. Under our rule, Verona will become the new *Caput Mundi*."

"My lord," called one of their men-at-arms. "There is a mounted party on the road."

The Count turned to his son. "Come, get on your horse and follow me. You must meet your subjects properly."

Vinciguerra's horse was brought and he followed his father to the front of the procession of their worldly goods, riding right alongside the men-at-arms and knights in the employ of San Bonifacio.

The waiting party of riders were equally numerous, armed and armoured. At their center were three men, dressed in finer mail than all the rest. One was broader than a bear, with a chest-plate so wide and deep that Vinciguerra could have used it for a winter sledge. Next to him was a tall man, rail-thin, with close-cropped hair and cheekbones so sharp his skin seemed in danger of being cut. The third wore a helmet, a massive helm with a snarling mastiff leaping from the crown.

The other pair appeared apprehensive, but this man was perfectly still in his saddle. That stillness made him fearsome, and for a wild moment Vinciguerra imagined that the tyrant Romano had risen from the grave to bar their path. He looked to his father, who was scowling. "Who are they?"

"The big one is Nogarola. The others, I'm not sure—though the thin one looks like Ongarello. He was from a family of carpenters, though they climbed the ladder of their own name and stepped into some little power."

"Are they here to welcome us?"

The Count waved the question off. "Wait here, boy." Nodding for his guards to accompany him, Vinciguerra's father rode boldly forward.

There followed words that young Vinciguerra could not make out. But the shaking of his father's fist was clear enough. So too the laughter from inside the hound helmet. Relaxed. Easy. Scornful.

They were denying him! As Vinciguerra realized this, he fully expected his father's great sword to be drawn, hacking at these pitiful fools who barred passage to their rightful realm. He ignored the anxious looks passing between the men-at-arms, ignored the assembled pikes and crossbows that faced them, ignored everything but his father.

Who grew very still. Who said nothing. Who—

Who turned and rode back. Away from Verona. Away from their home.

When his father reached him, Vinciguerra saw a face flushed with anger, hard with sour rage. But more, it was older. It was weak. And it was shy of meeting Vinciguerra's gaze.

"Father, what–?"

"Not now." The Count began issuing curt orders for the wagons to be turned about.

Vinciguerra twisted in his child's saddle and looked murder at the man in the snarling helmet. Then his eyes traveled up to the towers rising, it seemed, from the waters of the river Adige itself. Then the order was given and the future Count of San Bonifacio rode away from the city of Verona—*his* city.

In that moment, Vinciguerra swore he would kill the men who had destroyed his father's dream.

THAT HAD BEEN THE FIRST and only time the Count had seen his homeland. Oh, he'd raided his family's former holdings in San Bonifacio and Montecchio, but never Verona herself. Nor had he ever again seen the man inside that snarling helm. Mastino, his name had been. He'd died, murdered in the street, and his brother Alberto had taken the mantle.

Then Alberto's sons, the last of whom now wore the Houndshelm.

Vinciguerra's father had died of a broken heart not long after. Inheriting the grand but empty title, Vinciguerra swore to bring down anyone of the Scaliger or Nogarola name.

Tonight's venture pleased him for two reasons. First, in taking Vicenza he was reducing the two Nogarolese yet living, sons of the man who had faced his father on the road that fateful day. Secondly, a surprise attack on Vicenza over a hundred years before had been the beginning of the bad times for his family. Poetic justice, then, that Vicenza was the key to restoring the San Bonifacio fortunes.

From Vicenza, he would urge the Paduans to take Montecchio, followed by the castle at Illasi and his own hereditary estate to the south. Then on to Verona itself. In two months, the Pup and his allies would be licking their wounds on the far side of the Alps. Or in their graves.

But that meant treading carefully, leading these fools to triumph without ever letting them think they were his pawns.

ONCE ACROSS THE CANAL, the army covered the next ten miles quickly. They were now past the border of Paduan lands, into the rocky terrain that had seen so many of these wars. The horsemen spread out in small clusters, ready to chase any peasant or traveler who started an alarum.

At midnight they reached Camisano, a castle just down the road from Vicenza. Here Ponzoni ordered the men to leave the road, instead following a cattle track to remain out of sight of the guard-towers.

It was a nerve-wracking two hours as the entire body of men moved silently past the enemy-held fortress. Properly, Ponzoni held the ground a mile from Camisano, directing the troops. The Count stayed close by in case he was needed but, to his surprised satisfaction, the general seemed to have things well in hand.

After the bulk of the foot had passed, the Podestà rode up the length of his forces to the front line, leaving young Carrara to finish directing the last two hundred soldiers straggling behind. An older man would handle it better, but Ponzoni couldn't deny Carrara the right of his station. *Manners.*

Once past Camisano, the men moved faster, eager to pass through Vicenza's gates and sweep through the city like an inferno. The garrison would be killed before they could unsheathe their swords. For the glory of Padua, of course. *What does it matter the cause,* thought the Count, *so long as the deed is done.*

The army kept away from the roads entirely now, following the Bacchiglione until it met the Astico River coming down from the Alps. Here Ponzoni was faced with a decision, and the Count was at his elbow the moment they reached the water's edge.

"Reports vary on the fordability of the river," said the Podestà. "You know these parts as well as any. What do you say? Should we trace the Astico up to the road to the bridge, or can we ford here and continue following the Bacchiglione?"

"The Tesina bridge is the compulsory passage to and from Padua," replied the Count. "It's fortified by the *Visentini* population. You may have heard, it was the site of fierce fighting last year."

"Yes," replied Ponzoni. "I understand that the towers guarding the bridge were completely razed."

"Which ensures that someone is watching the bridge. The river here may not look it, but it is shallow enough."

Ponzoni looked to the elder Carrara, who shrugged. "I bow to his superior knowledge of the terrain."

Fortunately young Carrara was nowhere in sight—he would certainly have objected to any scheme proposed by the Count.

"Ford the Astico it is." Ponzoni issued orders, and Asdente took charge of the logistics, using the remaining fifty-two Flemish knights to form a wall of horses that would keep back the waters while the bulk of the army crossed. There were hissed curses and protests in Dutch as Asdente enforced his command with fists cloaked in mail gloves, with spurred heels, and elbows with spikes on the armour-joints. Two more mercenaries fell before the group moved to obey.

When the first man hit the ground, Ponzoni reached for his reins. Vinciguerra reached out a restraining hand. "Don't."

"I have to stop this," the younger man said. "That's not the way a *cavaliere* treats his men."

"It is if he wants them to fight." The Count shrugged, then jerked his wobbly chin. "Look at them."

Ponzoni did, and saw grins on the faces of the Dutch knights—not all soldiers respected respectful treatment. Disgusted, the Podestà spurred away. The Count wondered if the fellow would be any use at all in a real crisis. Not that it mattered. It was old soldiers like Asdente who really ran armies. Generals were for speeches and plans.

Warfare was for warriors.

THE VILLAGE OF QUARTESOLO DERIVED its name from the Latin *quartum milium solum*, meaning 'fourth mile'. It stood four miles from Vicenza's gates, down the ancient Roman *via Emilia* which linked Vicenza and Padua. The Roman mile measured 1477 meters, the equivalent of 1500 Roman soldier paces, exactly one quarter the distance from this spot to Vicenza.

The small hamlet was asleep, and therefore easily subdued. Ponzoni gave strict orders against pillaging. The men of the Paduan army were being well paid, he argued. There was no need for plunder.

Manners. Vinciguerra knew the Podestà longed to be welcomed into Vicenza with open arms. If he forbade the unsavoury behaviour knights were notorious for, made them behave as knights ought, perhaps he could win over the people. It was admirable, if foolish. But for the moment it harmed nothing, so the Count remained silent.

After taking Quartesolo, they waited for the return of their scouting party, led by young Carrara. They were back in less than an hour. Scouting was for youthful bones.

The Count spied a spring in the young man's step as he dismounted, and his impression was confirmed as Carrara reported. "There's no guard. None. The outer walls around San Pietro are completely unguarded. The double gates are shut, but that's all."

The Count was surprised at that, for once sharing a sentiment with Ponzoni, who was wide-eyed. It was the elder Carrara who answered. "Can it be a ruse? Do they have an army inside?"

"They can't, Uncle," replied his cocky nephew. "We rode on the hill to the north of the suburb. There's nowhere for an army to be hiding."

"What about the main city gates?" asked Asdente.

"Too far to see without being spotted." He frowned. "I did suggest we climb the walls and take a look, but I was outvoted. I thought Florence was the only working democracy," he muttered.

Asdente snorted. "Democracy doesn't work. One look at Florence would tell you that."

But Vinciguerra had latched on to something Carrara had said. "The walls aren't manned at all?"

Disliking being addressed by someone he considered a traitor, young Carrara answered with heavy scorn. "I said so, didn't I?"

"Entirely?" asked the Count.

Carrara coloured. "There are three men parading around every quarter of an hour. Hardly a guard."

"And hardly unguarded, either," said the Count archly.

Before the youth could challenge the Count to the duel he clearly longed for, his uncle intervened. "What do you have in mind, my lord Count?"

It only took the Count a few moments to outline his new plan. As he finished, a smile crossed the elder Carrara's lips. "I like it."

"I don't," his nephew objected. "It could be a trap. He could be handing us over to the Scaliger." But no one paid him any heed, which seemed the best way to deal with the boy.

But young Carrara was not the only one who objected. Ponzoni was frowning, but in concern. "You're not serious. The soldiers could have those gates down in an hour." He waved his hand at his army.

The Count merely smiled. "I'll have them open for you in half that."

ACT THE THIRD

WHEREIN THE DARING COUNT IMPLEMENTS HIS SCHEME

RELIEVED OF HIS HEREDITARY ARMOUR, the Count eased himself into the moat, his eyes fixed on the wall across the murky water. He was flanked by a pair of Paduans—Asdente and young Carrara. The former he had asked to come, and the latter had insisted on being at hand for every moment, lest the wily Count somehow betray them. Behind them a dozen more volunteers, equally armourless, slithered across the open ground to wade in with them.

Like every modern city, Vicenza was a bull's eye target, a series of concentric rings. Those walled rings provided an ever-increasing degree of protection against invaders. The outer-most circles protected the suburbs where dwelled the poorer classes, with the less essential commodities. Then another set of walls for the middle class. The final set of walls enclosed the city itself.

With the outer walls all but unguarded, the Count's intent was to infiltrate the suburb of San Pietro, so dubbed for its church. Once inside, they would open the gates and ride the bulk of the army through to assault the inner walls.

Vinciguerra cast off and swam, keeping his head above the filthy water. Though the river was near, Vicenza's waterway was not as efficient as Padua's. Refuse and nightsoil lingered before floating off down river.

It was only a matter of yards to the wall, and though the stink offended his nostrils, the Count was across and scrambling for a handhold within moments.

Unslinging the rope from his shoulder, he held the grapple loosely as he waited for the younger men to reach him. Deep down, the Count knew he shouldn't have come. These were the kinds of assignments on which a good commander sent able but expendable men. Yet something deeper insisted he lead this foray. Was that superstition? Or pride? Whichever, the Count had been compelled to come. He could not sit back and do nothing. Perhaps that was his curse. Let Ponzoni and Il Grande lead the Paduan army through the gates once the signal was given. It was up to the Count to give that signal.

A signal which would only be sent if they could maintain their secrecy. In warfare, the element of surprise was everything.

The others were present, dripping but eager. Crouching low, feeling the aches of decades spent in a military saddle, the Count gave the silent order. As one, the soldiers threw their grapples. Some fell back to earth, but most caught—caught with a terrible scraping of metal talons on rock, producing a clamour that was sure would bring a thousand spears hurtling down.

Nothing. No voices raised in alarum. Not even a murmur.

Already the Count was hauling on the rope, heaving his great frame up, hand over hand, using the porous rock of the walls for toeholds. Rather than throw again, those who had missed their first attempt waited to follow on another's rope.

The Count was quickest to the top, surprising everyone. Including himself. Swinging his bulk over the crenellated turret, he drew his longsword. Young Carrara was next over, with Asdente scrabbling up third. Next came Carrara's cousin Ubertino, and the poet Mussato. Ser della Torre almost fell over, and the others had to catch him.

They all looked around for the guards. Not a soul.

Heart racing, the Count was deeply uneasy. *It has to be harder than this!* He waited with Carrara, Asdente and the others for the rest of their tiny invasion force to reach the top. Then, stationing a few men behind to signal the waiting army, they began the descent to the gatehouse.

Creeping along the wall in darkness, the Count heard young Carrara whisper, "I'm right behind you. Just in case."

More rage than sense, that was young Carrara. None of his uncle's forethought. If the impudent youngster were to be cut down in the next few minutes, the Count decided he would not be missed.

Down the wide stone steps, hugging the deepest shadows of this shadowy night, the cluster of men behind the Count moved as silently as they were able. Still no one stirred. The Count's heart was ready to burst from his chest. It was impossible. It couldn't be this easy!

Five minutes after cresting the wall, Vinciguerra reached the guardhouse. He was actually glad to see guards here. Three men slept in chairs, one more snored under a table among the straw rushes. A flagon of wine, stained at the lip, sat beside one prone figure.

Ticking off the seconds on his upheld fingers, the Count dropped his hand like a blade in signal. Asdente flung wide the door and the Count burst in, the others directly behind. Bleary eyes opened, but before the drunken garrison could do more than fall off their chairs, the struggle was over.

Taking all the necessary keys and tools, the invaders departed, leaving the four corpses soiling the rushes.

Still the Count fretted. A canny general would sacrifice four men to draw an enemy into a deadly trap. And the Pup was unquestionably canny.

The hair was standing up on the back of Vinciguerra's neck as he moved to open the gates. He could see his own suspicions reflected in the faces of the men around him. It was all too easy. But the gates were swinging open, and in minutes the whole Paduan army would be streaming into San Pietro, the first objective achieved.

It was the opening of the gates that woke the populace to the fact that they had been invaded. There was a bell attached to the pulley which none of the Paduans noticed until it began to clamour.

"Silence that!" growled the Count, already feeling Carrara's furious glare.

Too late. Hearing the tramp of feet behind him, the Count turned, expecting to see the Pup's men springing from the earth like the army of the dragon's teeth.

But these were mere citizens, sleepy men pushed out of their homes by their wives to see what the matter was. Upon sighting the soldiers, the men shoved their women back inside to bar the doors.

"I said it was a trap!" hissed Marsilio furiously.

"If it were a trap, boy," Asdente shot back, "there'd be soldiers waiting, not citizens. Besides, it's too late. Look."

By now both the inner and the outer gates under the arch were open, and the torches ready along the ramparts to signal the full army to ride in. But the Count did not give the order to light them.

"What are you waiting for?" demanded young Carrara. Furious, the knight turned to shout up to the waiting men on the ramparts to light the torches.

The Count grabbed his and roughly covered the Paduan's mouth. "Fool boy!" Carrara struggled, certain of betrayal—until he felt himself being grasped by more hands. Asdente and Mussato had hold of his arms.

Swiftly the Count explained. "It will be another ten minutes before the bulk of the army arrives to cross the bridge. If we show fear now, these people will have us dead and the gates closed in half that time. No," he finished briskly, removing his hand from Carrara's mouth, "now is the time for diplomacy. Someone fetch me a torch. Asdente, a word."

Sheathing his sword, he took the Toothless Master aside for a few quick orders. A torch was brought, lit from a taper in the guardhouse. Taking it, the Count slipped his baldric from his shoulder and handed it off. Unarmed, he left the protective knot of Paduans to advance on the gathering crowd. He wished now that he had his full armour—not for protection, but for the air of authority it bestowed.

The crowd was muttering, fearful. Certainly someone had gone to wake the men at the next ring of walls. But that was a problem for the future. The immediate concern was holding San Pietro.

The Count scanned the faces of the citizenry. All it would take was one voice raised to have them charging forward, and the Count would be dead, the gates resealed. He had to get in first. But what to say?

He cleared his throat and spoke boldly. "My name is Vinciguerra, Count of San Bonifacio. I have brought an army of liberation to free the noble city of Vicenza from the Scaliger dog!"

If he had hoped for a cheer, he was disappointed. But the muttering died away, turning to pure silence.

Having begun, he plowed on. "The commander of this army of liberation, Lord Ponzoni de' Ponzoni of Cremona, gives you his word as a knight and a gentleman that there will be no plundering of person or property! It is his wish to accomplish this peacefully!" So far he had neglected to say from whence the army had come. Instinct told him that the name Padua would not help his cause. Instead he took a step, reaching out with his free hand as if inviting an embrace. "Come, friends! You know me, my family. You knew my father, and his father before him. We have been neighbors for hundreds of years. I come now, not in armour, but in this humble shift, having crawled through ignominy to plead with you. But this present shame is nothing to the ignominy I have felt these many years, apart from the land I love. Come friends! Take me as I am, here, naked and unarmed. Embrace me! Renew your ties with San Bonifacio, and together we shall live and prosper! Throw out the dog, and together we will regain our lost pride! We shall live as men ought, free to be what God ordains, not what Verona demands! We shall live as free men!"

Another silence. The Count willed himself not to look at the gate. This tension couldn't last much longer. A decision had to be made. If the crowd turned, he would be the first to die at its hands. A horrible death, not on the field, but torn apart by people who should have revered him.

Suddenly the silence was broken by a shout. It started from somewhere to his left—the sinister side. The crowd advanced. The Count girded himself for the end.

Then he heard the voices. "Bonifacio! Bonifacio!" Suddenly Vinciguerra was swept up in offers of gifts—food, wine, beer, gold, someone's daughter, someone's wife. Behind him Asdente was laughing as Carrara ordered the torches lit at last.

When Ponzoni and the elder Carrara crossed the bridge at the head of their army, they rode through the gates to a glorious reception. Freeing himself from the admiring throng, the Count of San Bonifacio waved to them. "San Pietro is ours."

"So I see," laughed Ponzoni in delight. "Well done!"

The Count bowed, then fell back against the wall as the riders passed to stake out the next set of walls. His page arrived and together they stepped into guardhouse to shift his filthy clothes and re-suit the armour.

Asdente was already within, stripped naked and wadding up his disgusting hose. "Well done," he said, unconsciously echoing the Podestà.

"Well done yourself," replied the Count. "Your men started cheering at just the right moment."

Asdente shrugged. "Aw, the crowd was wavering. All it took was a little nudge in the correct direction. Sheep, Count! *Visentini* are sheep!"

Vinciguerra chuckled. "Nevertheless, give them my thanks. It must have been difficult mingling with the crowd—especially smelling like this!" he added, throwing off his befouled tunic.

"Let's hope it will all be this easy," said Asdente, rubbing at some filth with a handful of straw.

Minutes later, standing on the ramparts and gazing at the next set of walls, the Count reflected on that statement. It had been easy. Perhaps God had willed it to be so. Or perhaps Luck had abandoned the Pup, switching sides like the traitorous da Lozzo. Or perhaps the stars had smiled upon them. Whatever the reason, the Count hoped his father's spirit was resting a little easier this night.

Thinking of dead spirits, the Count recollected the child whose laugh had begun the evening, and of the sign of Mercury behind which he lived. Mercury was the harbinger of death and destruction—not only of men, but of dreams.

The practical Count indulged in uncharacteristic fantasy, if only for a moment. *The little child of Mercury was an omen. He was the destruction of the della Scala family. He was the ruin of Verona. He was the death of a dream. From the ashes of that dream, a new Verona would emerge and lead Italy—nay, the world!—into a new dawn.*

Vinciguerra heard these thoughts as if they had been spoken aloud. But they were so far from any thought he'd ever had, so unlike him, that he tried to wash the words from his mind. They made him unspeakably uneasy.

Why? Because the child's laugh tonight had been too much like that of the long-ago knight in the Houndshelm. He felt certain that laughter was aimed at him, just as it had once mocked his father. Mercury brought death, and death was indiscriminate.

I am old. If Mercury wants me, I cannot stop him. But perhaps before I die I can pierce the Pup's sense of inviolability.

He shook off such grim thoughts. It was not he but the Pup who would suffer Mercury's message.

Yes, if I were a fanciful man, one who believed in omens and stars and such rot, I would say that Mercury is coming for Cangrande della Scala. If I had the power to make it so…

Shaking off such nonsense, the Count of San Bonifacio returned to the war.

HOURS LATER, AFTER THE DEFEAT, after the rout, after the utter humiliation of having lost so many men to a handful of rabblement, after having abandoned his armour and his pride in order to save his life, Vinciguerra fled back past Quartesolo with the Pup's joyful laughter in his ears and the terrifying certainty in his heart that no, Mercury was not coming for Cangrande.

At least, not today.

ACT THE FOURTH

WHEREIN THE CHASTENED COUNT LICKS HIS WOUNDS

DAYS LATER, THE TOWER OF the Ponte Molino shook under a thunderous sky. It was wet, and it was cold. Not that the Count cared a fig about rain. He had been cold before.

No, it was the chill in his heart that was new.

It was five days since Vinciguerra had returned to Padua in headlong flight from the Battle of Vicenza. Vinciguerra wasn't shamed by the fear that had caused him to run with the rest of the Paduan army. It was only practical. Let other men worry about honour and such nonsense. For example, the two Carrarese hadn't run, more fool they. *With any luck, Il Grande and Marsilio will be forced to ruin themselves by paying their ransoms.*

Common sense told Vinciguerra that when the army had broken, it was best to live on and fight another day. Vinciguerra was a man who could listen to reason.

What did hurt the Count was that he'd lost his father's armour, which he would now never pass on to his heir. *My heir...* The chill grew worse, made him shiver.

Returning to Padua at the head of a broken army, he'd seen the fear on the faces of the people, waiting for the thunder of Scaligeri hooves.

Thunder had come, not from the roads, but from the skies. The downpour was greeted with tentative cheers, growing louder every hour it continued. The moats swelled, the paths to Padua turned to mud, and still there was no sign of Verona's army. With the aid of fickle Fortune, the city had been fortified against an attack that now seemed unlikely to come.

The threat past, a defeated Ponzoni dei' Ponzoni had given the *Anziani* his resignation, then climbed into a wagon back to Cremona. Watching him leave, Vinciguerra thought, *He's spent, and awed. I understand. This is not his fight. Whereas I will never tire of this war. And it will take more than a chance victory to awe me.*

Yet he had learned something. He saw now that military might alone could not attain victory. Not against the Pup. *No, there has to be something more personal. I have to find the man's weakness, an Achilles' heel to exploit— then I can use Padua's army to strike.*

But there were other matters to attend to first. With both Ponzoni and Carrara gone, Vinciguerra saw his chance for advancement. He attended the Paduan *Anziani*'s meetings, listened to their petty squabbling, heard their panic and their fear, and plotted to wrest control from these complacent couch generals. With the right bit of timing, with the correct words, he might actually gain enough of their trust for them to grant him soldiers.

The day before, he had been at one of these meetings, considering how best to begin, when his steward had approached trembling hands and ashen face to deliver a note. Annoyed, the Count had taken it up and unfurled it.

It had contained only three words: *She has fallen.*

To the amazement of the *Anziani*, Vinciguerra had risen and fled the chamber. It had started a fresh panic that spread like wildfire across the city and had everyone manning the walls, looking for Verona's soldiers.

The Count did not care. Suddenly his schemes and plots meant nothing. Not compared to this.

He dashed for a house near the Chiesa degli Eremitani as swiftly as his age and size allowed. Racing through his door and up the stairs, he burst into the salon to find a parcel of women, but no doctors. After just five minutes kneeling and whispering comfort, he was off again, making the rounds to the city's physicians, inviting them to his house—by swordpoint, if necessary.

They all came, and in the end they all said the same thing. "My lord, recovery lies in the stars."

Chasing them from the house, Vinciguerra cursed all doctors. Then he set up a long vigil by the sickbed and waited.

A day passed without a change. This morning he'd paced in the hall outside her door—silently, lest he disturb her. He had never been patient for illness. And they had been through this before, many times—though never so close to crisis. She owned a high-strung nature, alternately loud and silent, active and inert. But always she vibrated, even when still, full of a humming passion that put even his to shame. These passions led to bouts of illness that no doctor could fathom beyond "*an imbalance of the humours.*"

But it was not an illness to love, to rage. She shared his desires, longed to fight for them with all the vigour in her soul. In so many ways she was his other self. She burned. Like her name, she was ever on fire. His Fiametta.

He was well aware of the irony of his love. Not noble. Not even legitimate. And from a family he had cause to despise. Yet such was love. It flouted reason, drawing two people who by rights should detest each other into a life-long embrace. *Love and loathing—twin sides to a single coin. Flip it into the air and see where it falls.*

It had fallen on him, complicating his life to no end. She had given him all he could desire from a woman, and he could offer nothing in return. Not lands, not fortune, not even status. He would be mocked for their union, a figure of ridicule, undermining all he had striven for. Not until the time he had won his rights. Then he would bring her to Verona in triumph, and make her the princess she deserved to be. Until that day, she had to remain secret.

Yet, if he could not claim her openly, he could at least see to her care. This house was his, a stone's throw from his own official dwelling. Likewise the servants—cooks, maids, steward, nurse—all bought with his purse. They knew better than to gossip, recognizing the happy visage as but a masque for a hard and relentless man who had just one weakness, known only to the secret inhabitants of this house.

The waiting was unbearable. Finally he threw on a cloak and pushed past the porter, whom he gave strict instructions. "If there is any change—*any*—find me!" Then he stalked into the rain-filled streets.

This is the Pup's fault. If not for the war, if not for the stress… Vinciguerra considered himself a fair man. A part of him was aware that the Pup had nothing at all to do with Fiametta's spells. Yet his reason could not quell the shattering rage within him. *If we had our rights, if she had been at my estate and not in this mud-hole of a town, this would never have happened!* Soaked to the bone, the rain could do nothing to quell his fury. Vinciguerra's hatred grew, transcending reason, transcending time, growing to titanic proportions.

Yet even now his exterior remained deceptively friendly. People smiled at him as they passed, and though he paid them no attention, they felt warmed by the sight of his wide, comic face.

Eventually he came to a halt here, where the invasion had been launched less than a week before. *A week! So much changed, so much lost. Months of planning, scores of lives. And my father's armour…*

The rage fled, replaced by a despairing fatigue. Not a man prone to tears, he did not weep. He merely sagged, feeling the weight of all the years of rage and fury, imagining the fraying of his bones such emotions had wrought. What the Paduan loss had not done, Fiametta's illness had. The Count felt weak.

Through the curtains of rain, a flash of lightning lit the street, and Vinciguerra saw the house with the *caduceus* engraved on the outer wall. This was the mansion that housed the mourning mother and devilish son who had so disturbed him at the army's exodus.

Squinting at the carved snakes entwined in stone, he understood what death they foretold. The death of dreams. His father's dream.

Perhaps I am accursed, he thought. Cursed by that dream, *destined to labour forever, like Sisyphus and his boulder, to please my father's ghost. There is nothing worse than the expectations of the dead weighing upon the living.*

Nonsense, he told himself gruffly. *You're getting old, and old men grow superstitious. There is no significance to this house, or to that child. Your future is bright, your legacy assured. You just have to survive long enough to grasp it.*

Turning his back once more on prophecy and portents, he sloshed off through the streets of Padua as the clouds overhead ripped wide with thunder.

Act the Fifth

Wherein the Wrathful Count Lays New Plots

JUST AS VINCIGUERRA WAS BEGINNING to consider returning home, he heard the patter of running feet in the wet alleyway. Turning, he saw his steward sprinting towards him, breathless and red in the face. The fellow slipped in the rain, toppling to the cobblestones.

Rushing forward, Vinciguerra almost broke the man's shoulders, so violently did he grasp him. Entirely unconcerned for the man himself, he demanded, "What is it, man? Is she dead? Tell me!"

Wincing, the steward shook his head violently. "No, no! Lord! No!"

"What, then? What?!"

"You—you have—have a visitor, my lord."

Throwing the steward aside, the Count stalked to his own house, separate from Fiametta's abode, though close by. Approaching his door, he took a moment compose himself—if it was a representative of the Anziani, he couldn't risk being ill-tempered. It was his good fortune that he had a phlegmatic temperament, and his features always created a jolly façade, whatever his mood.

He was met at the door by servants, and Vinciguerra allowed them to remove his outer garments and sodden boots. "Sergio has fallen in the street," he told them before climbing the stairs. "Find him, make certain he is able to continue his duties." The servants dispersed in absolute silence, having long since discovered the deceptive nature of the Count's visage.

He took time to dress in dry garments, then walked through the rushes to his study. It was not until he entering room that he discovered the identity of his visitor. Not a Paduan at all, but one of his paid scoundrels from Vicenza. "What the devil happened to you? You look like a drowned rat."

"My lord, I came as quick as the roads allowed," said the man unctuously. "I have news."

The Count stilled. "The Pup is coming."

"No, my lord. He is not. Definitely not. He is preoccupied. With his heir," he added.

The Count almost staggered. "Giovanna di Svevia has given him a son? I was not aware she was with child."

"No more was she, lord," replied the man with a knowing glint. "This son is a bastard."

The Count frowned. "A bastard? Why is that important? He has at least two others, if rumours are to be believed." *They are a family of bastards,* he did not say.

"Yes, lord. But this one he treats different. He has taken it in, given it to his sister to foster. Claims it's not his, but everyone knows."

The Count sank into a cushioned seat. "He truly has an heir?" The visitor nodded. "Tell me all of it, from the beginning. Leave nothing out."

Vinciguerra listened to the rest of the man's story—of how the Pup had refrained from attacking Padua so that he might slip off and bring back the child from whoever the mother might be. "You have no idea who the lady is?"

"None, my lord. There are many speculations, but no one has seen a pregnant lady of birth of late."

The Count gazed at his guest. "Speak of this to no one. You have done me a great service. You have no idea how great. I will reward you." Withdrawing a key from his desk, he opened a small chest and withdrew a bag of silver, and one of gold. He tossed the first to his visitor. "This is for your upkeep. Go clean yourself up, and let me know how to reach you." He hefted the second bag. "This, and more like it, you will get when the child is here, in my possession, and alive. Alive, do you hear me? It must be kept alive. She would never allow—" He was thinking aloud, an unusual happening. He realized it and stopped at once. It never did to share one's thoughts with inferiors. "Do nothing else until you hear from me."

Hungrily eyeing the bag of gold in the Count's grip, the spy allowed himself to be led to the door, and so out. After he was gone, Vinciguerra sat down heavily on a stool. His hands gripped his knees, and he stared into the middle distance.

After some time his steward Sergio knocked upon the door. "Yes."

"My lord," said the man, wincing as he entered. "She is awake, and asking for you."

The Count nodded and rose, though he refrained from running as he exited his house. Entering the one by the Church of the Hermits, he climbed the stairs and entered the master bedroom as noiselessly as he could manage. Crossing to the bed, he knelt down and put a hand out. "You're back."

A thin hand grasped it. "So are you."

"You have no right to frighten me so."

"I have every right," she told him.

It made him laugh. "Don't talk, my flame. Gather your strength."

"I am stronger for seeing you. And my other visitors were here a few minutes ago. Have you seen them? Or my brother?" He shook his head. "You should, you know."

"I know. But I was hoping to have better news to give them. And you." She stroked his wide hand. "Have you found it? Your father's armour?"

"No. It is lost."

"Then I shall have new ones made. With the crest all in gold." She saw through his happy expression to the thoughts within. "Something has happened. Tell."

He shook his head. "Now is not the moment."

She sat up at once, flinging her body carelessly as her thin arms grasped his bulky ones. "Tell me at once. What is it?"

Keeping it from her would only drive her back into illness—though he feared this news might well do the same. "The Pup has taken in a bastard heir."

Her arms dropped, but already he could see the vibrations as these words sank beneath her skin. "He has acknowledged it?"

The Count shook his head. "It appears not. He has given it to his sister to raise."

"We cannot kill it."

"I have already given that order. But if we were to snatch it away…"

Her eyes began to glow. "Yes. Oh yes, my love. That is the way! Oh, what does your father's armour matter, when we are given such a gift?! Oh, forgive me, love. I was weak, I doubted! I feared the loss would break you. That in this war you would not win. But I see now that God loves you, and me, for He gave me to you! What would break lesser beings only makes us burn brighter!"

"The only loss that would break me would be losing you, my flame."

"No fear of that," she said, trembling. "We shall emerge victorious, and curse their line down to the thirteenth generation." She flung back the blankets covering her legs. "O, kiss me! Kiss me, love! I burn for you!"

With that, he forgot her delicate nature, pressing his lips to hers.

It was in the arms of his beloved that he realized whom he could call upon for help. The perfect foe, the strangest of bedfellows. For his flame had inspired him. No, his father's dream was not a curse. It was a calling. He would curse this line of Scaligeri down through the ages.

Especially this little bastard heir. *Il veltro del Veltro*. He would forever feel the curse of San Bonifacio.

AUTHOR'S NOTE TO SAN BONIFACIO'S CURSE

As I was trimming and honing the text of THE MASTER OF VERONA, I debated long and hard on the action that should begin the novel. Eventually I settled upon the murderer Ciolo and his attempt upon the infant Cesco's life.

But that wasn't the original beginning. Being a reader of adventure stories and faithful watcher of action films, I first intended to start my tale with the Count of San Bonifacio and his part in the assault on Vicenza. Begin with the villain, say I, and let the hero rise from the pack.

Eventually I concluded that, while exciting, the Paduan assault on Vicenza didn't have enough to do with the overall story. Still, I so enjoyed writing the sequence that I regretted disposing of it, so I set it aside, then released a shorter version a few months after MoV was published. That one ended after Act III, when the futures of both Padua and the Count himself seem assured.

But after the events of THE PRINCE'S DOOM, this would be a wasted opportunity if I didn't expand the original text to give the tale its own tantalizing arc. So acts IV and V take place between Chapters Twelve and Thirteen in MoV.

Ironically, the name Vinciguerra means "In war I win". That night, he certainly did, though more for guile than martial prowess. An old soldier, the Count understands the value of surprise.

And of public relations. I've often wondered if Marc Antony, in his great (fictional!) funeral oration to the Plebeians, had some trusted voices in the crowd to shout encouragement and guide the mob to the "proper" conclusion.

Of course, in Chapter Two of THE MASTER OF VERONA, we discover the end result of this night's work: the daring and resourceful Katerina della Scala, sister to the Pup, orders the entire suburb of San Pietro set afire, a sacrifice play to gain time for her brother to arrive and rout the Paduan army.

Here, for the very first time, we see the immediate aftermath of that rout from a Paduan perspective. And we see the news that sets the Count scheming again after being foiled on the battlefield.

Yet for all the foreshadowing, the thing I like most is the flashback to Vinciguerra's youth where we glimpse the two brothers, Mastino and Alberto della Scala. This tale allows us to see more into the history of this struggle, and the politics and personalities of those involved in two duels that lasted well over a hundred years—the strife between Verona and Padua, and the even more bitter enmity between the Counts of San Bonifacio and the Scaligeri.

In a wonderfully ironic twist of history, Dante's son Pietro bought land between Verona and Vicenza, and his line eventually merged with another family to become the Serego-Alighieri clan, who were ennobled and made—the Counts of San Bonifacio. A move I have accelerated in this narrative, granting that honour to Pietro in DOOM. What is past is indeed prologue.

As for Fiametta, I am happy to introduce her here, and offer her name for the first time. She is mentioned in DOOM, working behind the scenes, but never seen, never referred to by name. Her background and relationships are spelled out elsewhere, and eagle-eyed readers might have noticed a hint here and there of things to come…

THE DAUGHTERS OF VENICE

FOR FAERIN

"I have done nothing but in care of thee,
Of thee, my dear one, thee, my daughter."

—Prospero
The Tempest
ACT I SCENE II

SER PIETRO ALAGHIERI'S ARRIVAL in Venice felt as though it was heralded with trumpets. For the first time in his life, he was traveling without his father. Nearly eighteen years old, knighted, with money in his purse and a grand task before him, he felt at once both intimidated and proud.

Not that he was alone. No, he traveled with as unlikely a pair of companions a man could imagine, a duo of astrologers.

Ignazzio da Palermo was shorter than Pietro, with the rounded shoulders that bespoke a lifetime of cramped and ink-stained fingers. His thin flaxen hair blew in wisps, uncovering a growing bald spot on the top of his pate. And his monstrous chin was both comical and mesmerizing.

But it was hard to take eyes off his other companion. 'Theodoro of Cadiz' he was called, an ageless Moor with the arms of a soldier and the eyes of a sage. He wore a thick scarf today, not against the biting air but to hide the horrendous scars that ringed his throat, evidence of some terrible torture that had damaged not only his skin but also his voice. The massive curved falchion slung across his back was as formidable and frightening as the man himself.

They drew many gazes as they glided along on the water, but Pietro's eyes were focused outwards, looking everywhere at once. Used to the bustle of Florence, Paris, and Verona, the Serene City was a revelation. Yes, the island city was a hive of activity. But navigating streets made of water made everything seem calmer, more refined, even stately. It was tempting for Pietro to suggest to his father that, when it came time to write about Heaven, he should make the streets of water. But giving the poet Dante advice on how to write never, *ever* went over well. Maybe he'd suggest it to Antonia.

The islands of the Venetian lagoon were first settled during long past barbarian incursions when the people of the Feltro sought refuge in the marshes. The refugees built watery villages on rafts of wooden posts, laying the foundations for the floating palaces that Pietro was sailing past. Thinking of the one important Venetian he had met the previous autumn, he asked, "Are we going to call on Ambassador Dandolo?"

"Perhaps," the Moor replied.

Deploring his servant's taciturn reply, Ignazzio found himself explaining. "We would never escape the palace. Oh, I don't mean we'd be prisoners! No, the reverse—honoured guests. The Doge is rather fond of having his chart reviewed, reinterpreting it in light of recent events. Better to take care of our business first, before they know we're here."

Pietro looked back over his shoulder at the Doge's palace. He couldn't imagine being a prisoner in that edifice. *Especially as there cannot be a basement, can there?*

Once landed, they set a brisk pace. Pietro followed the odd pair into the crowd, which parted for them at once. Ignazzio seemed wary of every stranger, but Theodoro's bulk cut a wide swath through the crowds, careless of the angry stares. There were many negroes in Venice, but most were servants or slaves, and none dared walk with such assurance as the Moor. Pietro, who was himself awed by the man, felt a mixture of fear and pride to be in his company.

Theodoro led the way to the Rivo Alto, known more commonly as the Rialto, the highest point of land in the lagoon and the natural focus of settlement. All around him flew flags bearing the Seal of San Marco. The device was engraved on a dozen walls, and atop a pillar stood the lion holding a shield bearing the Cross. Venice had forever linked its name with San Marco when the apostle's earthly remains were spirited out of Alexandria four hundred years before to rest in the aptly named Basilica da San Marco.

After a series of turns—the streets had no names, which had Pietro wondering how the Moor knew his way so well—they arrived in the small section known as the Yellow Crescent. A curved street only two blocks long, it was so called because it was there that the Jews plied their one and only trade—usury.

Here they were, talking and laughing. To Pietro's surprise, he saw that all the men wore caps with two pointed peaks that resembled horns. Devil's horns. He averted his gaze, though not from fear of the Adversary. He did not want to look, because he had seen such things before.

WHILE LIVING IN PARIS WITH his father Pietro had witnessed all manner of abuse. Peasant debt to the money-lenders having grown to an enormous degree, the late King Philip had thought to wipe it out by exiling those to whom the money was owed, and so had banished all Jews from his realm. He'd been none too particular about their property, either. If Jews were considered unholy, then looting their homes and violating their persons was God's work. Thus while their possessions were ransacked, they were jeered at, kicked and beaten. Most of the victims took the insults and pain stoically. Those who fought back were hanged at once, because Jews were forbidden by law to defend themselves. Not even Moors or Saracens received such treatment.

Pietro's views of Hebrews differed greatly from his father's, whose opinion on the subject had always struck Pietro as a little hypocritical. To the poet, Jews as individuals were perfectly fine—Dante owned several Jewish friends, most notably Manuel, Verona's jester whom the poet had often praised for his fine wit. Dante had never treated individual Jews with anything but the calm dignity he offered everyone.

No, alone each Jew was measured by his own mettle. It was only as a whole that they were damned.

When asked why, the poet's focus was invariably on Caiaphas, the high priest who urged the Pharisees '*nec cogitatis quia expedit nobis ut unus moriatur homo pro populo et non tota gens pereat*': "Nor consider that it is expedient for us, that one man should die for the people, and that the whole nation perish not."

In his inimitable manner, Dante had taken a small revenge in *L'Inferno* by placing Caiaphas firmly in the realm of the hypocrites, crucified upon the ground. The poet cloaked the other hypocrites in lead, but Caiaphas he left naked, feeling the weight of hypocrisy on his own body when one by one every heavy soul around him walked slowly over his outstretched form.

To finish his point, Dante had made Virgil wonder at Caiaphas. The high priest had actually known Christ, the man, in the world, yet he turned against Him. In the poem, Caiaphas masked his own motives for wanting to give over Jesus as a desire for the good of his people, not simple jealousy, thus justifying his presence among the hypocrites.

Pietro never thought to argue that Caiaphas hadn't been the cause of Christ's death—Church doctrine was particularly strict on this point. But to Pietro, the denial of Christ damned Caiaphas alone, not the whole Jewish people.

Only when they were living in Pisa had Pietro had the nerve to challenge his father's assumptions. It had been after the midday supper. Dante, Pietro, and his brother Poco had been taking their ease in the yard behind the house. They were discussing whether the Diaspora, the dispersal of the

Hebrews across the face of the earth, was the ancestor of the current spate of attacks on Jews in France—attacks that Pietro had witnessed, and been sickened by.

Dante was of the opinion that the attacks were barbaric, but justified. "But father," Pietro had protested, "why are we holding modern Jews responsible for acts over a thousand years old. Do we hold the Romans to the same standard?"

"Caiaphas was their priest," Dante had replied. "He spoke for the Jews."

Poco had piped up, looking up at his father slyly from where he lay on the ground. "Does the pope speak for you?"

"Go jump in a well," Dante had said placidly.

"*Pater*," Pietro had said, taking a different tack, "if any modern ruler were to set the life of one man higher than all the other lives in his realm, he would be a fool and a monster—you'd put him even lower in Hell, wouldn't you?"

"Ah," Dante had said, imperiously leaning forward, "you forget Annas. Do you remember Annas, boy?" He'd swatted at Poco's head.

"Caiaphas' father-in-law," Poco had said, ducking.

"Yes. He was the leader over the council of the Pharisees that allowed Jesus to be condemned. It was this action, in my humble opinion, which was punished in the destruction of the second Temple by Titus' forces forty years later, which started the Diaspora."

"You have nothing good to say about our modern priests," Pietro had observed.

"Bah! A pack of fornicating, impious money-grubbers! I tell you, boys, the moment the Church of Rome soiled its hands with gold, the whole world took a giant step towards the Pit. Tithes, indulgences, taxes for Crusades— all to line the pockets of these so-called holy men! There is no creature more loathsome than the seller of indulgences. And don't get me started on the so-called Crusades! Political wars with thin religious relevance, if any. Once, perhaps, they were a noble institution. But they don't even attack the heathens anymore! Now we're declaring Crusades against our fellow Christians!" he added sourly.

"Yes," Pietro had said, having endured this particular diatribe many times before. "But to take a point from my brother—" Poco looked up nervously "—if all the Jews were guilty for the sins of their priests, were not all Christian men damned for the sins of their priests as well? Am I damned for what my priest does?"

"Yes," Dante had said. "If he's corrupt and ungodly and you choose to follow him, you are."

"But the Church preaches that the only way to Heaven is through the priest."

Dante had shrugged. "Life is full of difficult choices."

Even at the time, Pietro had been stuck on this. "Wait—if redemption has to come through the Church, and the Church is, at some level or other, corrupt, how can anyone find redemption?"

"Congratulations. You've discovered one of the real battles of life—fighting to keep the church honest."

Poco had frowned. "That's dumb."

Pietro had expected his father to swat his brother again, but the old poet had nodded instead. "I actually agree. But if we don't get these corrupt men out of the Church, we'll be damned just the way the Jews are." Dante had patted Poco on the head. "But don't worry—Christ is forgiveness. If you accept Christ, you'll get forgiveness for your sins."

Poco had pulled a face. "He didn't forgive the Jews, did he?"

"They didn't accept him, did they?"

"Why would they? He was a troublemaker. Just like you," Poco had added.

That had been a bridge too far. The hand that struck him this time was more forceful, and more deliberate.

And so had ended their debate about the souls of Jews.

NOW, SURROUNDED BY A THRIVING population, forced within the short confines of these two city blocks, Pietro saw their pointed devil-hats and winced. But they seemed to have embraced the imposed custom, making the hats fanciful, or even festive.

But they shouldn't have to endure this, he thought. Here was another reason for which Pietro admired Cangrande—the Capitano was one of the enlightened rulers, and allowed no active prejudice his city.

As they entered the street, the laughter faded from their immediate surroundings. Pietro could feel many eyes upon them, sizing up their strange party with mistrustful sidelong looks. But there was nothing for it. They were here to find one particular Jew, the cousin of Manuel, Cangrande's Master of Revels. Pietro had yet to properly fit the name into his mouth. *Shalakh.*

They approached the house Manuel had described. Theodoro's knock on the solid-looking door produced nothing at first. The Moor knocked again. From inside Pietro could hear the wail of a newborn child. "Manuel did say his wife had just given him a daughter," he observed.

"I should offer to make her chart," Ignazzio replied. The Moor looked dubious. He knocked a third time.

The door opened with a suddenness that surprised them all. Facing the Moor was a small man, a head shorter than Pietro and barely reaching the Moor's breastbone. In his own home the man didn't wear the mandated cap, and his bare head showed a considerable mass of black and grey curls. The face under the moustache and chin-beard was kindly by nature, almost comical. But use had made sagging pouches along the frown lines, and deep depressions around the eyes. Still, there was a twinkle in the eye that struck Pietro as canny as they surveyed the three visitors. "Yes, lords?"

"Shalakh?" said Ignazzio.

The short fellow was wary. "I am he."

The Moor passed him a sealed note, two papers folded into another.

Shalakh glanced at the seal and snorted. "Manuel's friends? Oh very well. Enter my house, but please keep your voices low. My wife is with my daughter." At this his chest doubled in size. "I shouldn't wish her disturbed."

Inside, they introduced themselves *sotto voce*, and he showed them into a small room, very neat, just to the left of the entryway. The only furniture in this room were chairs and a small strongbox. It bore a series of intricate hasps and locks. Waving them to a seat, he perched himself upon this and broke the seal on his cousin's letter. He read it twice, then removed a folded paper that bore a drawing. It was a sketch of the medallion the scarecrow had lost in his attempt to kidnap Cesco. The actual medallion, Pietro knew, was secreted away in Ignazzio's luggage.

Shalakh lifted his gaze from the papers. "I see. Setting aside the secured loan I am to make to Ser Alaghieri," he inclined his head towards Pietro, "there is this other matter. To sum up—you are looking for the name of a tall, thin man who was advanced a large sum this month from an unknown source, who wore a medallion like this one," he held up the drawing, "and who has not received the remainder of his fee."

"His name, and the name of the account holder," corrected Pietro. He was well aware how flimsy their information sounded. Judging by his expression, Shalakh seemed to be aware of it as well. Pietro added, "Money is no object."

Shalakh laughed mirthlessly and snapped his fingers. "Oh, well then, I'll have these names by sundown! Heaven knows, give a Jew enough gold and he can bribe the Pope! You will excuse me, gentlemen, but I have *real* business to attend to." Despite his words he seemed to be enjoying himself. He stared at them, eyes glittering, daring them to speak.

"You won't help?" said Pietro.

"Or he cannot," said Ignazzio.

Shalakh pulled a wry face. "Oh yes, play on my vanity, do! As it happens, I have contacts in all the banking houses, for often men of means require ready monies, theirs being tied up in trade. Since I am forbidden to trade, I have nothing *but* ready money. So, yes, I could make enquiries. If I so chose."

"What could influence your choice?" asked Ignazzio.

Shalakh considered, stroking his trim moustache. Pietro's eye was drawn to a fine turquoise ring on the middle finger of his hand. "I am a fortunate man. I have a new daughter, and she makes me near giddy. I should be providing for her future, so I will accept the Scaliger's gold—oh, don't deny it, please. Manuel is his creature, and it was he who sent you, it's no use denying it. But, to keep his name out of my inquiries, there must be an additional enticement."

Pietro felt himself bristle. Ignazzio, however, was unruffled. "And that would be?"

Shalakh looked up, as if for inspiration. "Oh, anything that would bring a smile to my face."

Pietro almost stood to leave, but the Moor's hand restrained him. Theodoro said, "There is a shipment coming along the Adige this week, a large amount of pine and larch. It will pass safely through Verona, but it will never reach Venice. River pirates shall waylay it."

Pietro looked around in surprise. Ignazzio seemed equally taken aback at the Moor's comment. But Shalakh's face was hawkish with interest, all pretence of airiness vanished. "I suppose if I consent to make these inquiries, I shall be granted the name of the unhappy owner of this wood?" The Moor nodded. "I could find out myself, of course, given this much. But then, I suppose if I do not consent, these mysterious river pirates may decide to take a holiday and let the shipment through."

"A clever man could use this information," said Ignazzio, picking up where the Moor had stopped, "and purchase a great amount of timber."

Shalakh opened his hands wide, his turquoise ring flashing. "But, as I have already stated, I am forbidden to engage in trade."

"Directly. But the timber could be bought through surrogates, which I'm sure you have."

"Perhaps." Shalakh sat, stroking his whiskered chin for a time. Suddenly he made up his mind. "Very well. Because he has been so generous to my cousin, and in the hope that he shall look as favourably upon me, I shall brut about for the great Greyhound. I make no promises, and it may take weeks. If this transaction was made in Venice, no doubt we shall soon learn of it. But it could have happened in Genoa, or Constantinople, or Bruges. Nor can I guarantee results, only effort. Now, the name."

Theodoro's face was expressionless as he said, "Ambassador Dandolo."

One might have thought the Jew would quail at that, but instead his face lightened as if it were a lamp lit by some internal glow. "That's a bargain made," he said, repressing his obvious glee with difficulty. "Now, to more mundane matters. Ser Alaghieri, I learn from this letter that you are traveling to Bologna to pursue your studies. How much money do you require at purse, and how much upon credit?"

Pietro was glad that all the funds originated with Cangrande. Somehow all he could think was how he wouldn't want to be in Shalakh's debt for any reason.

PIETRO PASSED AN UNCOMFORTABLE EVENING in the Doge's Palace that night. Uncomfortable, because seated just beside the Doge was Francesco Dandolo. The Ambassador had spoken of the new house he was building, commenting on the exquisite wood that would be filling the last gaps.

Uncomfortable too for the looks he received from the Doge, a seventy-five year old with a wizened face and eyes made tired by years campaigning. He had been plainly excited to see Ignazzio and Theodoro again, but less so to receive the son of the poet Dante. It may have been a natural distaste for foreigners, but more likely it arose from the slight Dante had given the famous Arsenal in *L'Inferno*.

Yet Pietro learned he was not the sole cause of the Doge's long silences and unusual terseness. As the evening progressed, Soranzo had a pointed question for the astrologer Ignazzio: "Will my daughter ever cross the threshold of this palace again?"

Pietro started in his seat. *What?*

It was Ambassador Dandolo who explained in hushed tones. The Doge's daughter was the widow of Niccolò Querini, a venetian who, like Pietro's father, had been exiled for life from his home. But Querini's crime had been more than mere political opposition. Five years earlier he had been a part of Bajamonte Tiepolo's conspiracy to overthrow the Doge and Council of Venice. The revolt had failed thanks to bad weather and worse planning, but it had resulted in the burning of the Rialto bridge.

"After her husband's death last year," continued Dandolo, "the Doge's daughter was allowed to return to the city—not to live openly, but to remain a prisoner in the convent of Santa Maria delle Vergini. Not even Soranzo can obtain her freedom."

"Then where does the power of Venice reside?"

"In the Council of Ten. We had a string of bad Doges, you see. Soranzo is admired, because his rule has been so very dull. Yet he cannot muster enough political capital to free his daughter. It is sad."

It seemed Soranzo had been to see his daughter just the day before, on a formal yearly visit to the convent. Thus she was much in his mind when he questioned Ignazzio and Theodoro about the stars.

"Alas," said Ignazzio, "unless there are portents and factors unseen, the stars do not predict an alteration from her present fortunes."

The Doge did not rage, nor weep. He merely sagged like a man defeated by life.

THE FOLLOWING DAY, PIETRO WAS given a guided tour of the Serenissima, and saw for himself the boiling pitch made to caulk the ships, just as his father had described it. Though he was careful not to bring his father into conversation. Any mention of his surname brought the same dark looks he had received from the Doge. The Venetians were clearly resentful of being compared to barrators, those who traded gold for high office. It was one step away from simony, and Venetians considered themselves honest merchants, unbought and unsold.

Yet someone had been bought, for it was while he was in the Calle della Bissa being shown the new domicile of a whole colony of silk workers relocated from tumultuous Lucca, that a message found him. Shalakh had already succeeded in his research, but receipt of the information was contingent on the non-receipt of a certain shipment of lumber.

Pietro, Ignazzio, and Theodoro kicked their heels in Venice for a pleasant week, visiting sites of interest and enjoying uncommon leisure. It was Pietro's first time out in the world, his own man, with no duty save his promise to Cangrande—duty enough, but not an hourly pursuit. He thought about Bologna, the destination he had given his family. He was meant to be starting study there. He was surprised to find he was looking forward to it. Idleness did not suit him.

Then, one afternoon, Ignazzio received a note that had him quite excited. He bounced on his heels as he said, "We have been invited to dine."

"At the palace?" asked Pietro a little warily.

"No no. Someplace infinitely more interesting, and infinitely harder to gain entrance." More than that, the astrologer refused to say, just chortling through the grin plastered across his ludicrously wide chin.

It still being March, and a chill and wet one at that, they dressed warmly in cloaks and furs and hats that covered their ears. Their breath misted the air as they rode a gondola to a water door not far from the Rialto bridge. The brick building was unassuming and mostly unadorned, with only one frescoed wall to the right of the water door and, above, high windows in the Eastern style that were so popular these days.

As the gondolier eased them to a halt, the door opened and a servant gave them each an arm to help them into the *casa*. Though Pietro was growing more skilled at this mode of travel, the puckered scar in his leg caused him to be grateful for the assistance. The last thing he wanted in meeting someone important was to fall into the canal.

As the servant took their cloaks, another man arrived. Lit from behind, Pietro only saw a wide frame topped by once-powerful shoulders that were now hunched by age, or life.

"Ignazzio, Theodoro, my friends," said the man, kissing each in familiar greeting. "*Buona sera.*"

"Bless this house," said the Moor.

Ignazzio's eyes danced. "Marco, my friend, allow me to introduce Ser Pietro Alaghieri, son of the poet Dante and newly-minted knight of Verona."

Though they had never met, Pietro recognized this man at once. His face was more lined than in the woodcut pictures stamped inside the pages of the book chronicling his adventures. The beard was whiter. The deep pockets under the eyes were grown to sacks. But the hair was still thick and curling, the nose as strong, and the frown as pronounced.

Pietro bowed and said, "Ser Polo. It is an honour. Thank you for the gracious invitation."

"Please, my friends, this way." Marco Polo swept the heavy folds of gown on his left arm to indicate they should enter the main casa.

Seated in a higher room overlooking a small square, Pietro answered questions put to him, but refrained from pressing his famous host for tales of the travels for which he was so famous. Owning a famous father, Pietro understood that not all celebrities enjoyed their fame.

Yet travel was all that seemed to interest Polo. He asked Theodoro and Ignazzio about their recent journeys, and Pietro learned that before they had come to Verona, they had been on Crete, where they had experienced a small earthquake. Polo seemed disappointed, saying, "I know Crete."

Theodoro smiled thinly. In his terrible rasp of a voice, he said, "Ser Pietro was in Paris the year before this."

"Paris!" Polo leaned forward. "I have never been. Tell me, were you there for the trials?"

They spoke of the Templars. Pietro had departed before the ultimate moment, the cursing of both the French king and the Pope by the order's Grand Master as he burned at the stake. But he had seen other Templar knights trotted out into public view, broken and battered, tortured and tormented. "I saw a man whose bones were hanging from his feet, being forced to walk to his pyre."

Polo clicked his tongue. "Tch. So you were gone before that business with the princesses? I heard he had their heads shaved for dishonouring his sons."

"I heard the same," said Pietro. "But that it was done upon the command of their good sister, the Queen of England. She did not take the cuckolding of her princely brothers well."

"Ah! And one can understand her anger. Like her brothers, she too is cuckolded. That is, if a woman can be a cuckold if her husband intrigues with men." Laughing at Pietro's obvious discomfort, Polo waved this aside. "A philosophical musing only. But what of the king, this Philip the Fair? Did he truly walk among his people each day, measuring their mood?"

Pietro nodded. "In a white hood. I saw him several times."

"Was he as handsome as they say?"

"He was."

"And yet he died, just as Jacques de Molay predicted. The Pope as well. Murder? Or divine retribution?"

Pietro spread his hands. "Who's to say? Though one does not rule out the other." He pointed. "Ignazzio may have a more accurate answer."

But Polo seemed less interested in the magical world, keeping his eye on the temporal one. His questions shifted to more mundane matters— mundane to Pietro, at least. But Polo was quite interested in the customs of the French, their eating habits, their style of building, the kinds of music currently embraced. Pietro quite surprised to find himself vehemently pressed over seeming trifles, and feared his memory was failing to satisfy the old man. Polo was eleven years senior to Pietro's own father, and seemed simultaneously more frail and more vital. A man trapped in a life he did not seem to fully inhabit, shackled by age.

The topic of age seem to be on Polo's mind as well. "You are seventeen?"

"For another month and odd days," replied Pietro.

"A fine age. You find yourself on the cusp of life. That's when I left home, you know, to travel. Are you a sailor?" Pietro shook his head. "A pity. But it's never too late to learn! And you've already done more traveling than I had at your age! You have an added inducement, one I never had—you cannot go home again. Your birthplace is barred to you. So you have the luxury to resist the temptation that lured me back. You are free to wander the world and make it your own. Not get dragged back into petty affairs."

It had been one of those 'petty affairs', Venice's war with Genoa, that had seen him imprisoned for almost a year, during which he had dictated his travels to a fellow prisoner, who had then published those adventures, making Marco Polo the most famous Venetian in the world.

Still, Pietro resisted asking about those travels. Instead he asked after his current affairs, and they passed some minutes discussing the world of publishing. "I see not a ducat from my own work," said Polo with a wry, not bitter, laugh. "Rustichello has it all with the bankers, against the day I die and my heirs have need. No, I did quite well on my travels. And indeed, my name is all the wealth I require these days. I need only voice an interest in an expedition, but it is fully funded, and I reap the profits." He pointed a stubby finger at Pietro. "Though if I were of a mind, I would quite resent your father. Until last year, mine was the greatest book in the vulgar tongue. Perhaps I should suggest Rustichello change publishers."

Pietro couldn't help a chuckle. "You'd have a difficult time wooing her. She is very devoted to our father."

Startled, Polo laughed as Pietro explained about his sister's knack for publishing. "It seems authors are fortunate in their daughters. Would you like to meet mine?"

A few minutes later, Pietro was introduced to Polo's wife Donata and their three daughters. Their eldest was named Fantina. Just twelve years of age, she owned a beauty less from her features than for the twinkle in her eye. Pietro imagined that same twinkle sustaining the girl's father through his months of captivity.

While her sisters Bellela and Moreta were returned to the care of their nurse, Fantina was allowed to remain. Polo stroked her hair with affection. "Heart's Ease, little dove. Sing Heart's Ease."

Fantina obeyed, her voice better than her confidence:

> *Complain my lute, complain on him*
> *That stays so long away;*
> *He promis'd to be here ere this,*
> *But still unkind doth stay;*
> *But now the proverb true I find,*
> *Once out of sight, then out of mind*
> *Hey ho! My heart is full of woe!*
>
> *Peace, liar, peace! It is not so,*
> *He will by and by be here;*
> *But every one that is in love*
> *Thinks every hour a year.*
> *Hark! Hark! Methinks I hear one knock;*
> *Run quickly then, and turn thy lock,*
> *Then farewell all my care and woe.*

Polo's eyes misted. "Forgive me. I was gone for nearly twenty-five years, and have been still for more than fifteen. I am split in two. I envy my younger self, and yet know that same youth longed for the very thing I have—home, family, respect, even a little fame."

"You do not contemplate more voyages?"

Polo again stroked the hair of his daughter, kneeling beside his chair. "To ask for more would be tempting fate. I have all the treasures I require of life."

IT WAS A LATE NIGHT, full of talk of far-flung places. Polo eventually told tales of adventures he had not shared in his book—the foolhardy missteps of a Venetian in an alien culture.

The next morning Pietro woke late to a disturbance as news of the expected robbery broke like the waves over the streets of the city. With the wood vanished and poor Dandolo cracking his palms together in frustration, Shalakh apparently deemed the transaction fulfilled. His intelligence arrived: the account was from a bank in Rouen, and had no name attached to either end. The medallion was the identification of the recipient of funds.

"Well, we have the bank's name at least," sighed Ignazzio. "Ser Pietro, here is where we part ways, I think. We shall travel on to France. We have the medallion now, so this scarecrow of yours will be unable to withdraw his funds anywhere. Perhaps if we draw on the account, we can determine the origin of the funds. He is frustrated for the time-being, hopefully unable to mount another attempt."

So Pietro and his new groom Fazio were ferried back to where their horses were stabled, and set out south for Bologna. As he sat in his saddle under the bright yet chill March sun, Pietro reflected on his experience of Venice.

For all her waters, her unique beauty, he had found the Serenissima a cold city. Not without feeling, no. But full of calculation. The head ruled the heart in Venice. Passion was not rewarded. In so many ways it was admirable—a city run by reason, not emotion. An ideal. But the result left Pietro cold.

The only warmth he had seen had been towards the daughters of Venice. He could not help but compare Shalakh, Soranzo, and Polo. Three men with nothing at all in common save love of their daughters. He thought of the joy and hope of Shalakh, the pride of Polo, the sadness and resignation of Soranzo.

But that is the nature of things. Beginnings are full of possibility, the middle is about appreciation, and the end is full of regret and sorrow.

This was on Pietro Alaghieri's mind as he set out upon his own beginning that day, his own man at last.

Perspicacious as he was, he did not know then where that life would lead, nor could he have predicted the summary of titles he would own at the end of it. Son. Brother. Knight. Uncle. Judge. Count. Husband. Lord. Author.

And, one day, Father. A title spoken with the most love from a little girl's lips.

AUTHOR'S NOTE TO THE DAUGHTERS OF VENICE

This story began with a tiny section cut from THE MASTER OF VERONA. At the end of Chapter 27, Pietro Alaghieri departs Verona after the duel, and we then skip ahead two years to after his studies in Bologna. Pietro's brief journey to Venice with Tharwat and Ignazzio is referred to, but never seen. Which is a shame, because it is the first time Ser Alaghieri spent with these two individuals. In Ignazzio's case, also the last.

This was also to be our introduction to Shalakh, or Shylock as Shakespeare called him. Modeled very much after my friend Mike Nussbaum's portrayal of the character in Barbara Gaines' production at the Chicago Shakespeare Theatre, Shalakh's first appearance was meant to set up much action in the later books. But because it didn't move the central story of MoV along, I sliced him down to a mere hint, a tantalizing mention.

Here is what was lost, expanded a great deal, with added elements of astrology and numerology that also got the axe. It also allows me to give a little tour and history of Venice, from which the title takes inspiration.

The story shifted as I read about Soranzo, a character who is more a device in the other books than a flesh and blood human. But that was also how the Venetians viewed him—he was form, not function. It is amazing that the most remarkable event during his tenure as Doge was the birth of lion cubs in the city, drawing visitors from all over. It was a time of peace after much tumult, and for that, he was adored.

Yet the adoration never reached such heights as to gain his daughter's release. She was still there, locked away in Santa Maria delle Vergini, when he died fourteen years later. He was allowed to visit her once a year. It is enough heartbreak to define a man.

That was when the thought of daughters came to me. I had mentioned in MoV that Shalakh had just had a daughter. That, of course, is Jessica, who will rip her father's heart to tatters one day. Seeing Shalakh's joy over her existence seemed fitting.

Thinking of the rule of three, I started mentally cataloging people in Venice at the time. I considered meeting Dandolo's daughter, who is mentioned in THE PRINCE'S DOOM. But Dandolo was a regular character with much baggage. I wanted someone new, yet known.

I'll never reconstruct the mental chain that led me to Polo, but I am delighted to bring him into the fold. I've already had appearances from Giotto, Petrarch, Bernardo Gui, William of Occam, and so many other famous names. Polo is a natural addition to their ranks.

It also allows me to hint at things to come for Pietro—joyful things, for once. He had many children—five girls and three boys. But his favourite, the one most devoted to him, was his daughter Antonia, who died two years before he did.

Hope, pride, and sorrow.

Varnished Faces

For James Gousseff
King of the Zanies

CAPULET
How long is't now since last yourself and I were in a mask?

OLD MAN
By'r lady, thirty years.

CAPULET
What, man! 'tis not so much, 'tis not so much:
'Tis since the nuptial of Lucentio,
Come Pentecost as quickly as it will,
Some five and twenty years; and then we went mask'd.

—*Romeo & Juliet*
ACT I SCENE V

ACT THE FIRST

WHEREIN THE MASQUED KNIGHT ATTENDS A BALL

PADUA, ITALY
25 MAY 1315

SILK STREAMERS FLOWED IN THE GENTLE wind off the Bacchiglione, and the sweating revelers took it in turns to stand in those places where the breeze cooled the palace yard. Higher up the older folk reclined on the balconies, letting those of hotter blood dance and caper until the purple haze of twilight.

In the center of the throng below was the bride, taking it in turns to dance with each man present. Her groom kept stepping in, and each time he did she would titter and twirl onto another outstretched arm.

Finally, smiling through clenched teeth, he held her firmly by the hand and escorted her, skipping, down the row. "Darling. I *am* the groom."

"Oh, but husband!" cried the bride in mock dismay. "Did you not have enough of me on our actual wedding day? No, my dearest Lucentio, my father has thrown this ball in our honour, and since my sister refuses, I must play the part of hostess."

"Bianca," began Lucentio Ariosto, an unformed chastisement in his mind. But they had reached the end of the line of smiling faces. She drew her hand apart from his and blew him a kiss before latching on to yet another burly arm.

The man attached to it was not dancing, she saw too late, only edging along the side of the courtyard towards a servant bearing a fresh tray of goblets. Still, his face was covered in one of those grotesque Venetian *carnevale* masques—delightful! An uninvited guest!

The rule of hospitality required the household to welcome such creatures, as long as they behaved. And there was always a fee, willingly paid. Most often you could tell by the condition of their clothes if they were laborers or dyers or such, masqued to rub elbows with their betters. But not this fellow! Though he had the body of a laborer, even more muscular than he was tall, he was dressed in the finest of doublets, neatly stitched.

"Come and dance!" she cried, tugging him away from the wine he was reaching for.

"Lady, forgive me." His voice was as rough as his clothes were fair. "I can't."

"What you cannot do," she tittered, "is refuse me—I'm the bride!"

"I would fall on you," he said bluntly. "My leg's not up to dancing."

As she walked another step with him she noticed he was indeed limping. "Oh, poor dear—was that from a battle? Were you at Vicenza?"

He seemed flustered. "I was there, yes."

"Oh, you mustn't be ashamed," she said, interpreting his shyness. "Those awful Veronese only won through a trick. Though I suppose I shouldn't say aught against them, as I'm now related to one." She pointed to a bearded man with long hair, laughing boisterously with his teeth bared. "Signore Bonaventura, married to my sister there, with the red-hair and the scowl." The woman in question didn't seem to be scowling, but that hardly mattered to Bianca. "You think I'm prettier, don't you?"

"You are very lively," said the masqued man by way of reply.

"Am I the prettiest girl you've ever seen?"

That seemed to check the man, but he rallied. "You are as lovely as any girl on her wedding night should be."

"That's a lopsided compliment. O, I see—you have a sweetheart! Does she know, or do you pine from afar?"

But the masqued man had had enough. "Your husband is looking for you."

"Let him whistle," said Bianca. "He's lucky to have me. Now, tell me—who are you really? Do we know each other?"

"No, lady," said the rough fellow. "We've never met. I am a total stranger."

"I don't believe you," she said, leaning close. The flush in her cheeks spoke of more than mere heat and excitement—she had been at the wine. "That is a very frightening masque. Are you hinting at some devilishness in your personality?"

As she batted her eyes at him, he disengaged himself from her arm and turned her back toward the dancing. Too many eyes were turning in their direction for his comfort.

Fortunately the dance was bringing her husband their way. The big man in the masque practically shoved her at the groom. "I believe this lady belongs to you."

"He likes to think so!" cried Bianca as she was led away, back into the throng. "I will not rest until I have divined your name!" she twittered. "I have a penchant for men in disguise—ask my husband!" With a wave over the frowning Lucentio's shoulder, she vanished into the crowd.

Quickly the masqued man moved further off, ending in a corner of the yard that had a little garden with a single lemon tree. Shielded behind its sheltering leaves, he raised the masque and wiped his brow.

Bianca's question repeated itself in his head: "Does she know, or do you pine from afar?"

Both, you little tart. Both.

Antony Capulletto replaced the masque, making sure his fair hair was completely hidden beneath the cowl. It was desperately vital that he not be recognized. He hoped his companion was being discreet. To be found out here, tonight, would be an absolute disaster.

Of course, he was supposed to be here with someone else. This night was one of the many plans he had hatched with his friends—to invade the next great Paduan wedding in masques and show them where they could stuff their beloved *patavinitas*.

But that was before Lent, before the Palio and the duel. Before the Great Betrayal. Both those friends were gone, now. In their stead, Antony's uncle from Capua had accompanied him here, and for a mercenary design. At the moment Uncle Arnaldo was somewhere up above, deep in conversation with some ancient Paduan with scaling skin that flaked and fell from his face with every breath.

Antony's eyes rested once more on the bride. Oddly enough, he'd seen her sister naked a few months back. Most of Verona had witnessed that scene. Antony wasn't gentleman enough now to keep from undressing the dancing younger sister with his eyes to compare them.

But instead another figure swept into her place, dispossessing the bride and all the revels of their luster. In place of Bianca Minola's shimmering red-blonde, there were pure black falls that framed a face so marvelously sad that Antony wanted nothing more in life than to make the world a better place for her. His betrothed. His love. His Giulia.

But another had jumped into his seat. Worse, his best friend, the man he trusted above all others. Mariotto Montecchio. Aided by the girls' cousin, a Paduan knight, Mari had whisked her off and married her before anyone knew aught was amiss. A duel had been fought, with champions instead of their own persons, due to Antony's broken leg. Pietro Alaghieri versus that Paduan bastard Marsilio da Carrara, who had given his Giulia to Mari. Carrara had won, without any honour, so the marriage was allowed to stand. Antony's heart had broken a second time.

Since then it had been awful. Pietro had been packed off to school, and Mari was off to Avignon on an errand for the lord of Verona. They had been his two true friends. Pietro had proved himself to be just that, in the end. While Mari had been the basest of betrayers.

Antony had sat in a blue haze for months, allowing his leg to heal from the break Mari had caused by dropping him out a window. Then, just a week ago, his father had called him into the study and closed the doors.

"Luigi is off fussing over that new brat of his, so we won't be disturbed. First, how is the leg?"

As the question was practical, not paternal, Antony answered in the same vein. "I can't ride yet, but I can get around without the crutches."

"Meaning you're going to miss most of the campaigning season with the Scaliger. Damned shame. With both Montecchio and Alaghieri out of the way, you'd have been able to shine. Well, I've devised a way to make up for the loss. Do you remember your uncle Arnaldo?"

Antony nodded. His father's younger brother.

"Well, he's—acquired a fair assortment of armour, cheap. Not just armour, but pikes, halberds, spears, swords—a veritable arsenal. He's looking for someone to sell it to."

"You want me to talk to the Scaliger? He'll listen to you more than me."

Old Ludo had shaken his head. "No, Verona's not in the market at the moment—well supplied from the Alps. Rumour says Cangrande's even got his own forge up along the Adige River. But there's one city that needs arms, after abandoning so many on the field last fall. Arnaldo figures that they'll pay handsomely for even battered arms." Suddenly Ludo looked flustered, as if he hadn't meant to speak the last part aloud. Antony understood why—the arms his uncle had "acquired" were most likely from some losing *condottiere*, stripped from the dead bodies on the battlefield. There was a huge market in resale arms, but it was deemed both unlucky and ignoble.

Suddenly Antony had realized what city his father meant, and his mouth fell open. "Padua? We can't sell arms to Padua!"

"Of course we can," his father had huffed. "What the Scaliger doesn't know won't hurt us. No, listen. Two weeks after Pentecost, Signore Minola of Padua is throwing a great banquet in honour of his youngest daughter's wedding—though, as I understand it, the marriage took place months ago. Paduans are lunatics, throwing their money away like that. But, as I recall, you had a plan to attend a Paduan ball—in masques."

Antony had stiffened. The plan had originated with Mari, and to even think of his former friend was like a knife to the stomach. Again he merely nodded his answer.

"Well, instead of that execrable bride-thief, you'll take your uncle. This is our chance to break into the Paduan market—"

Unthinkably, Antony had protested. "Father—we're not traders. Not anymore. We need to think like noblemen now."

Ludo had waved him off. "Nonsense! Everyone trades. It's only a difference of commodity, and degree. Business is business."

Antony knew better than to keep protesting. His scruples were less than his father's ambition, and really he'd only argued because he didn't like the idea of going. "Selling arms at a wedding feast."

"Where better? From what I hear, the groom is going to need all the armaments he can muster. Bonaventura was telling me the bride is like an unwalled city."

So Antony and his uncle Arnaldo had ridden into Padua, taken lodgings under assumed names, and donned these ridiculous masques to attend the feast.

All in all, Antony did not like being used. But if Arnaldo could manage to sell his arms, the influx of wealth would have them rivaling the Scaliger himself. Which would, in turn, elevate his family, perhaps in time to impress a single individual, whose marriage was not yet consummate...

Now Antony noticed that he was not the only masqued man watching the dancing. There was another fellow, not part of their little Veronese cabal. His clothes were a little rough, and he wasn't bothering to cover his hair, which was a muddy red and worn rather long.

Just as Antony was reaching up to be certain his sweaty cowl was in place, someone said in his ear, "Capulletto, I know it's you."

Antony jumped and jerked around to see a bearded, barrel-chested man smiling at him through tangles of long curly hair. "Ser Bonaventura," said Antony, completely giving himself away. He realized his mistake and hastily added, "I don't know who you..."

"Oh, come now. The frame, the youth—the Veronese cut to your cloth. With the limp I momentarily mistook you for your friend Ser Alaghieri, but he wouldn't dare enter Padua at the moment. Carrara would eat him whole and spit out the bones. How's the leg?"

"I—it's... I don't—how did you know it was..?"

"Knights aren't supposed to go around in disguise," said Petruchio Bonaventura in mock reproval.

"Nuns aren't supposed to run brothels, but I've heard it happens," came a rich feminine voice. "Ser Antonio, it was I that recognized you." Petruchio's wife Kate, sister to the bride, sidled up beside her husband.

Antony was instantly grateful of the masque, for it hid his flush—the last time he had seen her, she'd been trying to humiliate her husband by appearing publicly in the nude. Astonishingly, she hadn't succeeded.

To divert himself, he bowed low, focusing his eyes beyond the lady to the fresco on the wall behind her. It was of the goddess Diana in her grove, under the watchful gaze of the moon. The trees and animals were all painted with meticulous care. Only, Antony noted, Diana's eyes had been scratched out, and repaired by an inferior hand.

Katerina Minola *in* Bonaventura noted Antony's long gaze at the wall and said, "You admire my handiwork?"

"Yours?" asked Antony.

"Handiwork!" snorted Petruchio mirthfully.

"My father made me repair it. I did rather well, don't you think?"

Antony nodded as her husband said, "For a woman. What made you scratch out poor Dian's eyes in the first place?"

"I forget," said Katerina, yawning.

"Of course," said Antony. "This was your house until recently."

"Until last twelfth night," she supplied, then looked around and added, "My wedding was nothing like this."

"How would you know?" asked her husband. "We weren't there."

She gave him a withering smile and he barked out another laugh. Clearly he was enjoying himself hugely.

"I like your father's yard," said Antony, truthfully. "If I ever own a home, I'd like it to resemble this."

"With better fresco-work, I hope," said Petruchio. His wife surreptitiously flicked his thigh with forefinger and thumb. He ignored her. "Antony, that masque is magnificent. You look like something out of old Alaghieri's poem."

Antony peered into a nearby looking glass, provided to reflect the torchlight, that the festivities might continue past the encroaching dark. The varnished leather face that leered back at him bore a twisting mouth beneath a monstrously hooked nose. Over them both were the holes for the eyes, one molded eyebrow arched, the other squinting. On top of all were the two short horns that made his devilishness complete. "I guess I do at that—though I still haven't read it," he admitted shamefacedly. How could he confess that though he owned a beautifully illustrated copy, he had never opened the cover. It had been a gift for his Giulia.

"It is hideous," said Kate, wrinkling her nose.

Her husband puffed out his chest. "I say, handsome."

Kate bowed her head a little. "Forgive me. It is gorgeous. It must have been the sunlight in my eyes."

Antony looked up. "But, lady—the sun has set."

"Has it?" Kate looked not up, but at Bonaventura, who was laughing. She turned back to Antony. "It is actually a shame that your friend Alaghieri isn't here. He could distract the groom from his plight. They went to school together in Pisa."

"I didn't know that." At that moment Lucentio was dancing with a much older woman, who looked as lustily at him as he was looking after his wife—who paid Lucentio no mind whatsoever. "So, how *did* you recognize me?" said Antony carefully. These two would not betray him—so long as they did not know his errand.

"The way you bowed to my sister. No native Lombard bows that way. You may be a true Veronese in spirit, but occasionally you do betray your Capuan origins."

"Oh." Antony's brow furrowed under his masque. What was wrong with the way he bowed?

Petruchio Bonaventura smacked and rubbed his hands together. "This will be marvelous! The whole evening will be about guessing your identity. I'll win a hundred wagers—mind you, give no sign that you know me."

"Husband. No wagers."

"I was just—"

"O, I know what you were—"

"Wife, do not presume—"

"Oh no! It's the salted horse-hide for me, is it?"

"For the ultimate time, it was a joke! I prefer to kill with kindness."

"Is that what you call it?"

Though growing red in the face, delight gleamed in Bonaventura's eyes. Before he could continue, though, Antony decided to intrude. "There's something I don't understand. Aren't they already married?"

Diverted to gazing at the bride and groom, Petruchio barked out a laugh. "Tell him, Kate. I should die with laughter."

"As bad as a death by mocks. The answer, Ser Antonio, is that there was no official wedding, only a secret affair and a hurried round of drinks after the fact."

Petruchio's eyes twinkled. "There seems to have been a rash of secret weddings lately."

Hot flush rising, it was on the tip of Antony's tongue to tell Bonaventura to take a running leap into the Bacchiglione when the lady said, "I'm glad to see you so well, Ser Antonio. You're recovering from your wounds quicker than poor Mussato."

Antony allowed himself to be diverted. "Oh, is he here?"

"Yes, there." Katerina pointed. "See the man in the lawyer's robes? That's old Bellario, the jurist. Wait for him to move, and—yes, you see? He's wearing his laurel wreath."

"I see him," said Antony with a hidden smile. Six months ago he'd run over the famous Paduan poet with his horse. It was pleasing to see that the old fraud was still suffering for it. Write a play about the Scaliger indeed!

"So, have you found out who he is?" Another man was descended upon them, his accent unmistakably Paduan. A heavy-lidded fellow, he had long puffed-out cheeks and lips set in a pouty moue, so he looked like a somnolent fish stuck in the slats of a fence.

"Ah, Hortensio!" cried Bonaventura. "Come and help us quiz this mystery guest? I've been attempting to divine a name, without luck. Care to make a wager on where he's from?"

"Husband," said Kate warningly—and not just to keep her husband from gambling. She was afraid that, in his enthusiasm to win a bet, Bonaventura would reveal all. A fear that Antony shared.

"Thank you, no," replied the dour-faced man. "Wives, it seems, do not approve of wagers. Especially after that last one," he added, with a significant glance at Kate. "I am forbidden from gambling."

"Speaking of your wife," said Petruchio, looking about, "where is the lovely hearty widow?"

"Why do you insist on calling her that?" demanded the exasperated Hortensio. "She was a widow. She's married now—to me!"

"Making you the widow-er!" laughed Petruchio. "Or the widow-wooer!"

"What my husband means," supplied Kate between the bursts of mirth, "is that you are away from her so often, visiting us, it is as if she were still widowed."

"Lady, if I have intruded—"

"Not at all, you are always welcome. It is only that a lonely wife might invite—trouble. Is that not so, husband?"

"So it is, Kate! That's why I never leave you alone for more than an hour. You might issue Trouble an invitation, and he might accept! Then where would I be?"

"Wearing this fellow's horns!" shouted Hortensio, pointing to Antony and laughing.

Instantly Antony balled up his fists to strike him flat. Then he remembered—his masque had horns on it. He relaxed.

"What's the noise over there?" asked Bonaventura.

The lively bride was being confronted by the groom's servant, marked as such by wearing his master's colours. The mischief in the servant's voice was good-natured as he cried, "I take it much unkindly, lady! You were betrothed to me! Master, should I demand satisfaction?"

"If you demand satisfaction of Lucentio, Tranio," said Lucentio, laughing, "I'll have my second fight my duel for me."

"And who is your second?" demanded Tranio.

"Why, you yourself, of course."

Tranio slapped his own face and pretended to duel with himself, right hand versus left, calling out insults for each one.

Bonaventura was guffawing along with the crowd. "I like that Tranio immensely. Do you think I could steal him away from your brother-in-law?"

"Give it a year, then try," said Kate dryly. "By then he'll have had about as much of my sister as any man not enjoying her could take."

Husband and wife shared a look, while Antony laughed in spite of himself. It was rare to hear a lady be so frank. Rare, and damned refreshing.

There was a sudden commotion at the far end of the yard, and the dancing revelers made way for someone dressed in the finest white doublet Antony had ever seen. Usually the colour of mourning, tonight it made its wearer stand out from all the dazzling rainbow colours of doublets, gonellas, and gowns. Across the chest of the doublet was embroidered the *carro stemma*, four mechanical wheels of the cart that symbolized Fortune, Prudence, Temperance, and Justice.

The crowd applauded for the hero of the hour, the man all Padua was talking about. Inside his masque, Antony swore. "Oh fut!" He knew that symbol, and the man wearing it.

Marsilio da Carrara had arrived.

Act the Second

Wherein the Daring Knight Shows Poor Manners

"I'VE GOT IT ARRANGED," MURMURED Uncle Arnaldo, edging in beside Antony. "The old man's name is Gremio. Turns out he's a jilted suitor for this Bianca trollop, and eager to distract himself by making a nice fat profit." The older man cocked his head, frowning behind the masque. "What's the matter?"

Antony jerked his chin, a significant gesture thanks to the elongated hard leather face over his own. "Carrara."

Uncle Arnaldo traced the gesture to the handsome man so fastidiously and ostentatiously dressed. "So that's the man who gave away your little bride. A shame. If you had been allowed to marry her, you'd be a member of his family, and this whole business would be a snap!"

Business! Unseen, Antony's face set into a glower. It was the kind of statement his father was prone to making. Carrara had stolen his heart's desire, made him a laughing-stock, and all these old men could see was the loss of their precious trade.

The moment Carrara had appeared Antony had excused himself from the others and withdrawn to a corner far from the pretty Paduan knight. If Carrara recognized him, he would be a double-fool, and could never show his face again, here or in Verona. Now he turned to his uncle and said, "So, you're finished? We can leave?" Arnaldo looked wistfully at the magnificent banquet table, but nodded. "Good. Let's be gone."

They began to make their way through the throng towards the arched gates of the Minola house. Their path took them uncomfortably near the knight, but Carrara paid them no heed. He was surrounded by twittering females, recounting for them some heroic deed. It was only as Antony was passing him that he heard a piece of the tale.

"—and he was a trickster. Pretended he'd never fought a duel before. Maybe he hadn't, come to think of it. The skill he showed was more the knife-in-the-back kind of cleverness, not the straight-forwardness a true knight displays. At one point he lured me close and, though no one saw it, tried to stab me with a dagger. I was able to dodge it, barely—oh, he was fast, like a serpent, was Alaghieri. He probably learned his fighting in the stews of France. But I refused to descend to his level. I dismounted and drew my sword, against his spear-shield. He had the longer reach, but I was able to disarm him and make him fight honourably, sword to sword—"

Antony froze in his tracks. *Liar!* It had been Carrara's dishonourable behaviour that had cost him the victory. Pietro Alaghieri, fighting in Antony's stead, had been heroically honourable right to the end!

Nearly Antony turned to make a cutting remark, but Arnaldo shoved him onward towards the gate. Antony kept moving, casting an evil glance over his shoulder.

Not looking at his path, he collided with someone. To Antony's horror, he found himself facing Signore Baptista Minola himself. The fat little man was startled as well, and peered a little drunkenly up at the horrific masque. "Gentlemen of Hades! You're not leaving!"

"I'm afraid we must," said Antony, bowing low. "Thank you for—"

"But you haven't paid!" The father of the bride stepped up onto a stool. It was much too small for his feet, forcing him to stand on tiptoe, his curling shoes close together. He looked like a dancer, and the image was made even more comical by the enormous gut that hung out over his belt, hiding the buckle entirely. Antony found himself facing the gut as their host cried out, "Friends! Our unknown guests, having eaten well of my table and drunk of my cellars, are now trying to escape without payment! It is tradition that each masqued guest pays for his entertainment with a little of his own. Shall we permit them to leave?"

"NO!" chorused the crowd, and Antony felt the dreadful sensation of every eye turning upon him.

"No!" Laughing, Baptista Minola wagged a finger at Antony and Arnaldo. "Come, either sing for your supper, or else we shall have those masques off you and set you to work in the kitchens!" The old fellow looked down at them, beaming in tipsy delight. "Which of you wishes to pay first?"

Antony and Arnaldo exchanged a glance. Arnaldo said gruffly, "I cannot sing, but I will dance for my supper."

Arnaldo had the musicians strike up a sprightly tune and, hairy hands on hips, hopped from aged foot to aged foot, skipping lightly on his heavy feet, to the hilarity of all. Breath heaving and sweat pouring, Arnaldo capered and jogged in and out of time to the music, clapping and making a fool of himself, and winning the crowd entirely with his buffoonery.

When the music ended on a crashing mangle of notes, Arnaldo collapsed to a bench, feted by those around him. "Excellent! Excellent! I crown you

King of the Capers!" Baptista turned to Antony. "Next?"

Before Antony could speak another voice said, "I'll pay next, and gladly!"

Relieved, Antony turned to see the red-haired fellow in his humourously painted masque and shabby clothes pushing his way to the center of the dancers.

Baptista began the applause, and in that moment Antony looked towards the exit, now blocked by half a dozen revelers determined to have their fun. This was but another respite, not an escape.

"Excellent, young man!" cried Baptista in delight, then scolded Antony. "You're next!"

Antony subsided and set himself on a bench. He would tell a joke, maybe. Or sing a bawdy song, and be done with it.

The red-haired masquer crossed his arms and boldly said, "For my entertainment, I offer barbs of wit. Who dares challenge my razor tongue?"

Laughter as Bonaventura shoved his friend Hortensio forward. "Him first! He needs shaving!"

The red-haired fellow looked Hortensio over from top to toe. "More like a fish that needs scaling. Throw him back!"

Long inured to being compared to aquatic creatures, Hortensio shrugged. "Better a fish than a foul fellow."

The crowd groaned and the red-haired jester shook his head. "That's what his wife said when he complained of her on the wedding night!" Hortensio gave a start and looked to his wife, who was laughing lustily and slapping her thighs. The jester snapped his fingers. "Oh, I've hooked him! Away, let's have another!"

Baptista turned and pointed to the aging jurist beside Mussato. "Monsignore Bellario! You are said to have a great legal mind! Surely you can outwit this half-wit."

Smiles creasing his face, Bellario stood. "I have represented many a half-wit, and judge that half a wit is twice the sort of man he is."

"And what sort of man is that?" asked the red-headed masquer.

"A lack-wit."

Laughter and applause that had to die down before the jester could respond, which he did eagerly, pretending to count on his fingers. "Alack! If half is twice the lack, then lack is a quarter of your whole. But if I were to set up as a lawyer, my fees couldn't be one-tenth of yours. Which means I'm a bargain! It's the smart man who will hire an inexpensive lack-wit, and witless the man that pays for your services!"

Laughing, Bellario bowed. "An excellent argument, sir. You should be an advocate."

"And so I am, sir! I advocate wine, women, and song—in roughly that order! Next!"

"To him, Tranio!" cried the groom, nodding his man forward.

Obediently Tranio trotted into the space cleared for the masquers. "Sir, my master has stolen a woman who was betrothed to me—though I wooed her in his name, wearing his clothes. What recourse do I have at law?"

The red-haired jester put his knuckles to his chin in a parody of thought. "An interesting case. Tell me, sir, who gave you his name?"

"My master."

"And who gave you his clothes?"

"He, himself."

"Good, good. Now, when they were wed, what name did he use?"

"His own."

"Had you given it back to him?"

"No, sir."

"Nor the clothes?"

"No, sir! They were on my back."

The masquer clasped his hands behind his back. "Then I believe, as a matter of law, that he was not in possession of his name when he used it to marry the lady, and that she is actually wed to you. Take her, and welcome!"

Bonaventura clapped his hands. "Quite a step up for the son of a Bergamese sail-maker," he quipped.

The masquer cocked his head. "Bergamo is land-locked."

Tranio looked sly. "My father is quite skilled. Come, lady—it seems I am your husband!"

"Fair enough!" Leaving the groom's side, rosy-cheeked Bianca wrapped herself about Tranio in a way that made everyone but her uncomfortable.

Desperately the masquer rallied the moment, crossing to clap the unhappy Lucentio on the shoulder. "Oh, come, Signore Lucentio! You have been given a marvelous reprieve! There are at least a dozen men here who long for their bachelor days once more! I attend weddings in much the same frame of mind as I attend funerals—a dear friend lost in both cases. I understand you were a man of studies, of thoughtful learning, who came to our great city to study at the University. But like a plague or the ague, love crept upon you and unbalanced your humours, upset your mind. Marriage is a bear-trap, and you have been freed of its jaws!"

When Lucentio failed to answer, his sister-in-law came to his defence. "Do you never intend to marry, sir?" asked Kate, sliding free of her husband's arm.

"Never, lady," declared the masquer. "Not for dowry, not for favour, and certainly not for love! I see these married men here as so many lepers—look, your own husband appears particularly diseased!"

"Ha!" cried Petruchio's cousin Ferdinando, pounding Kate's husband on the back. "Diseased!"

"That is only his crabby nature, he caught it not from me," replied Kate. "He came looking for a wife, while I never looked for a husband—as this gentleman will attest," she added, gesturing at the decrepit Gremio.

"No, sir!" agreed old Gremio heartily, stamping his cane on the floor, causing skin to flake from his forehead. "We never thought to see her wed, much less tamed!" The crowd murmured in awed agreement. Petruchio took a bow.

Kate took no notice, instead saying, "I daresay you protest too much against marriage. Does it not appeal to you?"

The masquer did not falter. "Lady, no bachelor longs to be married. But every married man longs to be a bachelor!"

"Spoken like the youth who tugs a girl's hair one year, and is wooing her the next."

"Not I, lady, I assure you. Young as I am, I have lost too many friends to the disease already. I am impervious to female charms."

"Then," said Kate with a sly look of her own, "you have never tasted of them." With a twist and a half-shrug that exuded sultriness, she returned to her husband's side and he kissed her, long and hard.

The crowd erupted. Before the masquer could counter her claim, Baptista clapped his hands, crying, "I call that a debt paid! Don't feel bad, son," he added to the dejected red-headed fellow. "Only one man has ever bested her!" Still in mid-kiss, Petruchio Bonaventura flexed his bicep and pumped it in the air. "That leaves us with one more unknown man to entertain us!"

All eyes turned to Antony, who stood and looked about. His eyes fell on Carrara, who had ignored the whole proceeding, still working to impress the bevy of females clustered about him. Something in Antony fumed at the sight, and his fear of being humiliated evaporated as his natural bombasticity came to the fore.

Antony assumed a voice gruffer even than his own. "I cannot dance. Nor do I have the wit to spar with such great minds as fill this yard." He bowed to Kate, just emerging from the kiss, gasping as she settled herself on her husband's knee. "But I do have one skill that might please—only it requires a partner." He pointed at Carrara. "You sir! You are a famed duelist! Would you oblige me?"

Carrara looked up with a frown. "I am not here to play for the masses," he replied haughtily. "Besides, if we sparred, you would be dead in a moment, which would hardly be entertaining."

"I don't mean to fight you, my lord," said Antony, assuming a tone more humble still. "I only mean that you alone among this assembly have the skill to match me."

Bonaventura's head had a wary tilt, and Kate was visibly apprehensive. Arnaldo was urgently shaking his head. Before either of them could stop him, Antony lifted a lemon from the table in front of him and pitched it lightly towards Carrara, who had no choice but to catch it. Another fruit was already in the air, and another. Lacking a third hand, Carrara pitched the first fruit back at Antony, and all at once they were partners in a juggling display.

Capulletto was a skilled juggler, having progressed so far as to play with knives on horseback. Carrara had seen that skill once, and Antony could only hope that the bastard didn't recall it now. He began to move along the banquet table, setting down each fruit and replacing it with something more entertaining—a spoon, a ladle, a bowl. More and more objects flew over the heads of the guests and they began to applaud. Carrara, not unwilling to show off his prowess, stood and began to circle the table himself, adding to their tally of objects hurtling through the air.

When Antony lifted a torch the crowd gasped, but Carrara caught it in stride and tossed it back, followed by a knife. Antony returned the knife with ease, and the ladies oohed and the men cheered for both performers.

His eye on one particular object on Carrara's side of the table, Antony continued his circuit, building up to a quicker tempo, tossing more objects into the air than they could comfortably manage. Carrara frowned, spending all his concentration now on keeping these things aloft. Antony, too, suffered the strain, but he kept building the momentum.

Then he reached it—a custard dish meant for the bride and groom. He redoubled his pace again, using everything that was close to hand about the dish, throwing more objects than any man could manage. When all else was gone, he sent the dish hurtling not in a gentle arc but directly at Carrara's chest like a discus.

The colourful confection exploded across Carrara's perfect white doublet. Like the sudden stop of a galloping horse, the hilarity around them ended in a collective gasp, followed by a profound silence broken only by the objects falling unheeded to the ground around both men.

Carrara looked down at his ruined clothing. Then up at Antony.

Who turned and ran for his life.

ACT THE THIRD

WHEREIN THE FLEEING KNIGHT FINDS REFUGE IN ART

BURSTING THROUGH A STAND OF PINES growing at the river's mouth, Antony considered making a run across the bridge, but exhaustion made him lie down and watch. He'd been running flat out for five minutes and needed to regain his breath. Besides, the bridge was too obvious. *He ought to double back. I only hope they haven't loosed any hounds...*

The masque was gone, as was the cap, but he'd kept the doublet, dark as it was. However there was the matter of his hair. Sandy blonde, it could betray him in the darkness. He rubbed the dirt from the base of the trees over his face and hair, then had an inspiration. Reaching up, he plucked pines needles down and stuck them into his hair, masquing (he hoped) the light with the dark.

A group with torches came racing out of a side street, Carrara in the lead, still wearing his ruined farsetto. Antony pressed his lips together to keep from laughing. *It was worth it! It was entirely worth it! Oh Pietro, if only you could see it!*

They addressed the guards at the bridge, who declared they had seen no one this last quarter of an hour. "Well, keep watch—a large fellow in dark clothes, wearing a devil masque!"

"Wait!" cried a familiar voice. Petruchio Bonaventura pushed to the fore, squinting towards Antony's hiding place. Antony cursed the man with all the venom he owned. No doubt Bonaventura was having the time of his life! Antony girded himself to run again. His blood was coursing through him, and he grinned in spite of himself. Enjoying life more than he had in months, Antony turned to whisper a comment to Mariotto.

Who, of course, was not there.

Pleasure dying within him, Antony darted a look through the trees. Bonaventura was pointing, and Antony heard him cry, "I think I see him!"

"Where?" demanded Carrara.

"Up there—past those trees, along the wall!"

Carrara was off again, passing mere yards from where Antony lay. Bonaventura was running in the Paduan's wake, and Antony thought he caught the ghost of a wink as he went by.

Antony waited until they were past, and then moved into the shadows away from both bridge and wall, back towards the city's center.

Closer to Padua's Piazza dei Signoria he stepped into the light, keeping his pace even. If he was seen running it would be suspicious. Instead he made a show of chuckling softly and plucking the pine needles from his hair, as if they were a great joke. He greeted the men and women he encountered with a smile and a familiar wave, leaving them wondering if they knew him.

But the pursuers had not given up, and if anyone inspected him closely they would be able to recognize the doublet and hose. He needed a place to hide.

There came a clatter from across the square, originating inside a gigantic basilica that blazed with light—an evening service, perhaps? Whatever, it was the perfect place to hide. He'd lose himself in the pews for a few hours, say a series of prayers for forgiveness and concealment, then go about his business once all the fuss had died down.

As he drew nearer the massive double doors he saw an inscription that heartened him even further—a dedication to San Antonio! *Ha!* He would find refuge in the church of his namesake, who also happened to be Padua's patron saint.

But to Antony's great confusion there was only one man within. He was dressed simply, in a smock and ragged hose. Not such rags as a beggar might wear, but those of a laborer saving his underclothes from the mess of his toil. He was hunkered down near a wall, surrounded by planks of wood with paint spattered across them and a half-dozen bowls.

Entering the huge cathedral, Antony made his way towards the fellow. Whoever he was, he was ugly. Looking at his profile Antony could not help thinking of a skull. Not that the face was thin! No, it was so square and rough as to have been quarried. But something about the set of the mouth, the deep set of the eyes, and the expanse of the forehead made Antony acutely aware of the bones beneath the flesh.

In one paint-covered hand was a brush, and two more of different thicknesses were held between his teeth. His right hand held a bowl that seemed to fascinate him. As Antony approached, the man looked up and held out the bowl. Around the brushes he mumbled, "What does that look like to you?"

Antony leaned over. "Paint."

The artist made an anguished grunt. "What colour!"

"Oh. Blue."

"What kind of blue?"

"Blue—blue, like—" *Like Giulia's eyes.* "Just blue."

The painter shook his head and spat the brushes to the ground. "Terrible thing, when a painter begins to squint. I need more light!" he shouted at a boy just entering the chapel, who scampered off on the double. "If you're here for mass, they'll be at the Duomo. This church is not in service until we're finished."

It was on the tip of Antony's tongue to ask where the Duomo was, but something made him say, "I just need a place to hide for awhile."

The ugly painter studied him with little interest. "Thief?"

"No."

"Murder anyone?"

"No!"

"Then what did you do?"

"I angered an overweening ass."

"Good for you. Put on a smock and keep me company."

Grinning, Antony stripped off his doublet and replaced it with a rough smock hanging over a pew. Instantly he found another bowl and pestle shoved into his hands. "Mix this. And get some on your face and hands. Just not on the floor, if you please."

Hunkering down in the shadow of a pew out of sight of the door, close to the wall the painter was dabbing at with his brush, Antony set to work grinding the ingredients in the bowl. "Thank you."

"No worries," said the painter shortly, his concentration entirely on the fresco. It was a scene from the life of San Antonio, when the Divine Child appeared to the frail holy man known as 'the hammer of heretics.' The haloed child was in the Franciscan's arms as he kissed the monk on the cheek. Out the window there was a choir of peasants, singing the Divine Child to sleep.

Even as Antony studied the painted scene there was a rush of footfalls outside and a hubbub of voices. Carrara's voice called sharply across the apse. "You there! Artist! Have you seen..?"

"Go away!" said the painter peremptorily, not looking up.

Hunching his shoulders, Antony redoubled his work with the pestle. Carrara was coming closer, enraged. "Look here, man! You can't speak to me—"

"Don't want to be speaking to you! It's you what's bothering me!"

Carrara was probably debating drawing his sword and killing the painter, holy ground or no. For a mere artisan to speak so to a knight—it was unheard of, worth at least a week in stocks or a vicious flogging.

Then Antony heard Hortensio's voice whispering in Carrara's ear. Antony couldn't quite hear all of it, but one bit echoed quite loudly through the stone chamber. "…not realize, but that's Maestro Giotto di Bondone. The painter," Hortensio added, in case Carrara didn't know.

But clearly the name was familiar to the knight, for when he spoke again his tone was more deferential. "Maestro, forgive me, but have you seen a big fellow all in black? Someone said they saw him heading this way…"

"Busy!" cried the artist. Then he added, "Leave the torch in the bracket on your way out."

Antony couldn't see Carrara's face, but he could imagine the consternation crossing it. The sound of Carrara's boots made him stiffen, but they were receding, not approaching. He heard an angry *thunk* as the torch was unceremoniously dropped into a sconce. Then Carrara was gone, in high dudgeon. *Poor Marsilio,* thought Antony gleefully. *He's not having a very pleasant evening.*

However, the name of the painter had caught Antony's attention. "You're Giotto."

"So I'm told."

"I know Dante!"

"Do you?" Still focused on the knot of singing faces, Giotto's tone skeptical.

"I'm friends with his son Pietro," explained Antony hastily.

"Ah."

"He talks of you…" Antony hesitated, thinking that perhaps the story Pietro had told was not flattering to the painter.

Giotto finally turned his square head from the fresco and grinned. "Repeating that old line about painting in daylight, I suppose."

Antony laughed in relief. "Yes."

"My one moment of wit." The artist returned to studying the fresco in discontent.

"What are you doing in Padua?"

"Painting."

"Oh," said Antony, subsiding.

The artist seemed to relent—or perhaps he was frustrated, for he threw his brush to the ground. "It's the damn Scrovegni. They've doomed me."

It was a family Antony had heard of—they'd probably been at the ball this evening. "Didn't you decorate a chapel for them? That was, what, five years..?"

"Ten. And this isn't for them. It's because of them. They've been prating about the chapel, showing it off, bragging on my art. Flattering, surely, but ever since I've been hounded by patrons of the arts, city officials, everybody with money. Padua wants something of mine more than the Arena Chapel, if only to shut the Scrovegni up! Ten years of nagging and pleading," Giotto's voice reflected the sneer on his face, "of whining and bribing. I finally accepted. Not for the money, but for them to leave me alone! But do they? No. I agree to paint a scene from the life of San Antonio, and they keep at me. They want something just like—or, to be honest, just a little bit better than I gave the Scrovegni. It's tempting to put three eyes on his face, and move his nose around to his ear. That would be daring! But is that what they want? No. They want something that other buffoons think is beautiful and, ugh, *fashionable*. I have no interest in fashion. I'm interested in painting— the texture, the composition, the story that's told in light and shadow and slight tilts of the head or a roll of the eye."

By this point in the rant, Antony was torn between jaw-dropped awe and tear-streaming laughter. Giotto saw his expression and snorted. "Oh, you may play at shock, young man, but let me tell you! It's quite bedeviling, starting a new fad. They're always expecting me to be coming up with something new. I didn't invent painting. I didn't even invent my style. I just wasn't interested in painting in the same old way as everyone else, so I looked back a thousand years and stole from them."

"Stole?"

"All great artists, son, are thieves. The best ones admit it freely. I'm a great artist. I'm also a great thief. Which makes every artist a little bit of a villain—something we also revel in. Pfah!" Giotto sat in a pew and shook his head. "I tell you, sometimes I curse my so-called innovation. For hundreds of years we painters have worked the exact same way. Oh, there have been refinements in our tools, but the rules have been very precise. We painted this scene, from this perspective, in these colours, with this theme. Done and done. Then I came along and undammed the river."

"So why don't you just go back?"

"There's no going back, even if I wanted to. Which I don't. This new style is the worst—except for all the others." Giotto flashed a grim grin. "I'm a painter, you see? Oh, I do a little architecture, a little sculpting from time to time. And I screw women as often as I can. But all of that is just what I *do*. It's not what I am. I am a painter. I paint."

"Everyone says you're a genius at it."

Giotto laughed until he coughed up a wad of sputum. Wiping his lips, he said, "That's the thing that saves me. Genius is my armour. Because I'm said to be a genius, whatever I paint must be good—even if they don't like it! And being a genius certainly helps with the ladies. But just between us—genius is a fraud. We're all frauds, waiting to be found out. Cimabue, Dante, Occam—we're all terrified of the day that everyone figures out that we're just feeling our way along, making mistakes just like everyone else. But they never do figure it out, so along we geniuses roll on, like runaway wagons behind a frightened mare, pulled along until the mare stops or runs off a cliff."

"Dante seems very certain."

"He has to. He's built a reputation on wit, and wit cannot be seen to falter. But I've seen him at work—he agonizes over every word. He's never certain of the first word until he's come to the last, then he starts again, poking and testing each phrase. Like this," said Giotto, pointing at a singing woman tucked into a crowd of faces. "She's the one I got right. The other faces are wrong, and it's her face that tells me so. We only know what we've done right compared to all the things we've botched. When her face doesn't stand out as anything more than another face in the crowd, that's when I'll be satisfied." Giotto stirred, and took the bowl from Antony's hands. "With that in mind, it's time for you to pay your due."

Antony blinked. "What?"

"You required sanctuary. I provided it. Now you pay. Turn your head into the light. Good. Now, don't move." Giotto picked up a loose piece of planking, as yet unmarred by paint.

"What are you..?"

"Halt! Stop! Move not! Be still!" Settling himself in a place that had the best view of Antony's face, the artist produced a black stick and began to make marks on the plank. "I have an eye for interesting faces. That woman in the choir, she's based on a whore I knew once in Lucca. Most amazing cheekbones on a woman I've ever seen. You, for example, have a tremendously fine jaw."

Feeling a new consciousness of his chin, Antony resisted sticking it out. He watched out of the corner of his eye as the artist made marks on the board. Then, in far less time than Antony would have thought, he was finished. "Here."

Giotto handed across the board and Antony looked at the crude smudges of charcoal that made up his image. "That's not what I look like! I've seen my face."

Giotto's wide flat mouth turned down. "A looking glass is only a reflection. In the right hand, a brush can capture a man's essence. In my hands, even a bit of coal or chalk may do the job." He tossed his tool into the air and caught it again between his grubby fingers.

Antony held the plank up to better light. The hair and the chin he recognized. So too the nose, very like his brother's. But there was something different, something he'd never seen when he had preened and primped himself before the looking glass.

He had sad eyes. Not naturally sad, turned down like a hound-dog's. No, this sadness was in their expression, not their shape. They were the eyes of a slave, or a beaten woman. They were windows into a shattered soul.

It came crashing down on him. *That's the man I now am. Timid. Embarrassed. Shy. Frightened. Less.* It was not something he had understood, not even in the moments when he had hid from Carrara or fretted over exposure. What did it matter if they found me out? Six months ago I wouldn't have cared in the least! Rather he'd have exposed himself and thought it a terrific joke.

I did not realize that this business had changed who I am! I've always prided myself on being a bluff, straight-ahead fellow. But now I see I'm a milksop, a wilting flower in a bull's body.

I will not be that man, thought Antony defiantly. *I will rally—I will win her love or die trying! Only death can end my love for her! And if Mari or Carrara or anyone gets in my way, I'll crush them like so many ants!*

"Now there's a look!" cried Giotto, already making lines on another plank. "I don't know what's in your mind, but it's a fire that matches my lady's there!" He squinted again at Antony, the made some marks with his filthy thumb, jabbing and pulling at the smudges before him. "Ah. You see? All I need is a dozen more faces like that and my choir will be unique— where are you going?"

"Time I was leaving, Maestro," said Antony, rising to his feet.

"You don't want to see?" asked the artist, already turning the plank over.

"No need," said Antony. "But someday I'm going to send you a commission."

Giotto raised an eyebrow. "And how will I know it's you?"

"The commission will have a name. It will be called *Giulia*." With that, Antony left the cathedral of his namesake, suddenly grateful for the wedding and all it had wrought.

A familiar strut returned to his step, Antony ventured fearlessly into the night air. Behind him Giotto called again for more light.

AUTHOR'S NOTE TO VARNISHED FACES

I always knew I'd write this particular story, as I've long been amused by Shakespeare's cross-over between THE TAMING OF THE SHREW and ROMEO & JULIET. In R&J there are two overt references to SHREW—Capulet mentions Lucentio's wedding, and the nurse points out 'young Petruchio' at the party. It would be easy with the latter reference to make the two plays contemporaneous, but with the first we're given a timeframe: it's been between 25 and 30 years since Lucentio's wedding. Capulet mentions crashing Lucentio's wedding while wearing a mask. Which was the whole idea for this story (though the title rightly belongs to a Shylock line in MERCHANT).

For those keeping score, this falls between Chapters 27 and 28 in THE MASTER OF VERONA, at the very beginning of the Fourth Act, entitled THE EXILES.

There are several reasons why this story pleases me. It fills in a few deficiencies in the larger novels. Though he's referenced often enough, we never meet Giotto in either MoV or VOICE OF THE FALCONER. Nor do we spend much time in Padua—the opening scene of MoV, one battle in FALCONER, and little bits in FORTUNE'S FOOL and THE PRINCE'S DOOM. It's nice to have a Paduan tale that is complete in and of itself.

Though the rivalry between Carrara and Pietro has a nice arc, the rancor between Carrara and Antony is left untouched. Rightly, Antony blames Mari for the whole debacle over Gianozza, and that's what plays out in the books. But the Paduan Marsilio played a large part in that drama, and Antony certainly would not have forgotten it.

There are also a few threads here that are important later on. The arms sale comes up in the second novel, as Cangrande's forge does in the third.

But my favourite reason for bringing this story to light is the plethora of Paduan characters. While my novels naturally take place in and around Verona, Padua was one of Shakespeare's favourite places to refer to. Here I'm able to bring all those references together. Characters from MUCH ADO, SHREW, MERCHANT, and R&J all meet here. It was tempting to add Speed from 2GENTS, but according to my own timeline the action of that show happens much later, so I decided against it. Nonetheless, we have Petruchio, Kate, Bianca, Lucentio, Hortensio, Baptista, Gremio, and Tranio from Shrew, as well as Bellario, who is mentioned in MERCHANT, but never seen.

Antony's uncle is a necessity. In R&J there is an 'old Capulet' who once joined Antony in crashing this wedding in a mask. Ludovico is long dead by then, so I invented Arnaldo to fill the void. In fact, I created him for FALCONER, but I'm delighted to retroactively introduce him here.

The red-headed masquer is, of course, Benedick from MUCH ADO, who we know is from Padua. I am literally trying to work him in everywhere—he appears in MoV, VotF, has a miniscule cameo in FOOL before returning to play a major role in DOOM. Here we get to hear young Benedick's views on marriage, which are pretty much the same ones he espouses in his own play.

Historically, Giotto finished painting the Scrovegni chapel in 1305, but there's a blank space between 1314 and 1317 where he was wandering around a bit, and there's evidence that he worked on the Basilica of San Antonio—though I haven't been able to confirm the date of that work. Since that work no longer exists, the date will remain unknown, and thus can fit my story. Also the work he did for Antony, which is a featured part of FALCONER.

Of Giotto's extant work, Scrovegni remains the highest praised and most visited. I first saw it in 1997, when I spent a single day in Padua. That afternoon, knowing I was about to audition for Petruchio when I returned to the States, I sat on a bridge overlooking the Bacchiglione and read through SHREW again.

I landed the part, and it was in that production that I met my wife. So Padua has been very lucky for me. As Petruchio says, 'Padua affords nothing but what is kind.'

Bononia Docet

For Joyce Stewart

"I should do myself wrong if I see not Bologna."

—*Second Fruits*
John Florio

"I can easier teach twenty what were good to be done,
than be one of the twenty to follow my own teaching."

—Portia
The Merchant Of Venice
ACT I SCENE II

IN HIS ROOM NEAR THE LAW STUDIUM of Bologna, Pietro's eyes teared up as he read Jacopo's letter chronicling the events at Calvatone. Such an outpouring of emotion was unusual for his brother. Expecting a battle, he'd instead seen the massacre of a surrendered city. It had clearly scarred him more than any wound. *Poor Poco. He wanted to be grown up for so long. And when he does, this is what he gets? Nico was unfair to dismiss him. Such a scene would have been too much for anyone.*

Yet it was the possibility of someone forging the havoc order that interested Pietro most. Cangrande would never have issued such a barbaric command. No, someone within Verona's walls had already proven himself willing to conspire with Cangrande's enemies to kidnap his heir. Failing that, had they tried to disgrace him?

And here I am, waiting.

In other circumstances, Pietro would have been enthralled by Bologna. The university here was the oldest in the world, dating back nearly 230 years. With as many as three thousand students coming and going among the city's teeming fifty thousand people, the University was the heart of the city's life and reputation.

But Pietro was distracted, restless, unable to settle. Every day he expected a letter from Cangrande or Ignazzio ordering him to leap onto his horse and ride for some secret lair to uncover their enemy. How could lectures on obscure legal arguments compete with the promise of such action?

Distracted, Pietro gazed unseeing at the road that bisected the city. In Roman times it had been called the *via Emilia*, but now it bore several names. Here it was called the *Strada Maggiore*, and from his window he could often make out three of the many towers that dotted Bologna's defensive walls.

Today it was raining, though, and his fellow students joined the citizens that traversed the city under the many arcaded walkways, thus hiding them from his view. It was a phenomenon to which Pietro still had not adjusted, the feeling that one was alone in the midst of this bustling metropolis. As if nothing existed but the city and its books.

Growing up in Florence, Pietro had been trained in the basics of learning: Grammar, Logic, Music, Arithmetic, Geometry, Astronomy, Rhetoric. But one hundred miles north of Florence young men strived to know more. Eschewing the common precepts of learning, they came to *La Cittia Grossa* where the learning was as saw as the sausage invented here. Just as *mortadella* had turned the deadest part of the pig into a delicious meal, so Bologna's faculty explored the darker sides of life to find the unsavoury but longed-for 'Truth'.

Bologna was second only to Paris as a repository for written knowledge. But unlike Paris, where the students ran around creating unchecked chaos, students at the Studium of Bologna made the rules and hired the faculty. Many of the students were already practicing doctors and lawyers. The motto here was *Bononia Docet*—'Bologna Teaches'.

Times had changed from when the students were encouraged to give gifts to their teachers in exchange for knowledge. Back at the founding it had been thought that science, being a gift from God, could not be sold. But the Church had a different attitude towards the monetary value of God's gifts in these modern times, and the teachers were allowed a salary (though gifts were still welcomed, and occasionally encouraged).

Though attracted to the study of law, Pietro had dabbled in other topics during his six months here. He enjoyed finding himself thrust headlong into new ideas, scandalous thoughts having to do with the body as the root for truth. He had not yet attended an autopsy, that new art of opening up the dead for knowledge of anatomy and alchemy, deemed as horrifying as it was enlightening. And the latest argument in the new field of theology was that sex was the path to God. *A path I'd like to tread,* he thought, then crossed himself, a little shocked at his own boldness.

He thought of the stories he'd heard of Bettisia Gozzadini, the first female professor in recorded history. So great a legal mind, so skilled at oratory, she had held a chair here at the university until her death fifty years before. It seemed that one woman had been enough, for no female had yet taken her place. Which was a pity. *Perhaps I should encourage Antonia.* But then, his little sister required no encouragement, ever.

She was by far his most frequent correspondent. His father had written a few times—not the long gossipy missives he'd once sent his daughter, but brief snatches of news. Clearly while under Antonia's hawkish glare, if their father was to do any writing, it would be poetry, not prose.

Take the latest message. Not a letter at all, just a copy of an official proclamation bearing the seal of Florence. Reading it, Pietro had flushed with anger. It was a fresh condemnation Florence had issued against both his father and himself. All true Florentines were commanded to 'apprehend and behead the outlaw Alighieri wherever found, and to offend them in their possessions and their persons freely and with impunity.'

A laconic scrawl at the bottom of the page read:

At least I find myself in good company.—D

Pietro knew his father meant to be amusing. But still his hand trembled with indignation as a dozen legal arguments ran through his head, each half-convincing him to take the whole city of Florence to court.

He had two more letters, and chose to open the one that had traveled the farthest. It was from his friend Mariotto Montecchio, who had rent asunder the promise of a lifetime of friendship by running off with Capulletto's bride. Pietro had sided with Antony as the wronged party, despite the natural inclination which drew him to Mari.

Now settled into the Papal Court in Avignon, Mariotto had written often, pleading forgiveness. Pietro's reply carried the forgiveness, but not a blessing on the union. But it seemed enough, for soon they were writing each other as before.

Today's letter again lamented Antony's refusal to write him, then went on to praise Gianozza to the stars. Pietro skimmed that section, having read it all before. There was a little court news that Pietro thought he'd forward on to Cangrande—the Scaliger might not yet know the leading contenders for the papacy.

The end of the letter returned once more to Mari's undying, unyielding, unfathomable passion:

Gianozza. Even the name fills me, Pietro. It is like music, and I find myself speaking it aloud in the most awkward moments—in company, on the street, even in Church. For she is my religion, my muse, my inspiration. I breathe her, Pietro. I feel as though this separation is one long held breath, a sweet suffocation as I wait to return to Verona to fill my lungs with delicious air.

Pietro frowned out at the rain. *O, the lovely and destructive Gianozza. How I wish she would have never come to Verona. She could easily be dubbed* Padua's Revenge.

Mari was hardly the only one to write of her. The jilted lover penned letters at least twice a week, and those were the mirror to Mari's—both railed at the other, and each were obsessed with the girl. Antony was holding out hope that the marriage would be annulled, while banishment only heightened Mariotto's passion for her.

There was nothing to be done about the feud, so Pietro turned to the last letter. It was from his sister, and Pietro was surprised to see Gianozza's name yet again. Reading it over, he was amazed to discover that she and Antonia had become friends. It seemed their mutual love of poetry had brought them together.

Reading Antonia's comments, Pietro had to smile at her no-nonsense assessment of their bond:

> She has delusions of Romance—too many re-readings of La Roman de la Rose. But she has practical moments. And she has an excellent memory. I have met no lady with a better faculty for memorizing and reciting poetry, and fewer men (Father always excepted). She understands rhyme and meter, and the structure of poetry far better than any of my other acquaintances. She really is remarkable— which is why I can overlook her slight tendency towards the dramatic.

Pietro paused to wonder if Gianozza had similar things to say—*Antonia can be a prig and a fussbudget, but she's the daughter of a great poet and smart as a whip, so I can tolerate her faults.* He chuckled.

Reading on, Pietro learned that Antonia was one for befriending unorthodox people. She described in detail three public meetings in which she argued with Lord Bonaventura's cousin Ferdinando. '*I loathe the ground under which he burrows! How such a charming fellow as Ser Petruchio could have such a brash, uncouth, chuckleheaded relative is beyond understanding!*'

There was something in there that made Pietro wonder. Was there an element in the waters of Verona that drew sane people to unsuitable mates? But no, his sister would never succumb to love. Her burning adoration for their father would eclipse any possible romance.

He returned to the bundle, double-checking it to be sure it was indeed empty. But no, there was no letter from the Capitano this morning. "Damn."

A knock, and the door opened to admit Fazio, Pietro's servant. The boy had proven himself industrious these last months, acting as butler, groom, and page to a studious knight. He arranged all of Pietro's meals, looked after the animals, and had the dubious pleasure of hearing whatever new thoughts Pietro found himself struggling with after a day of lectures.

Now he said, "There is a plate ready, Ser Pietro. It will be cooling even now."

Tucking away his letters, Pietro smiled at him. "Thank you. Bring it here, and I'll eat before I go out."

"So you are going, master?" Pietro had missed the morning lecture.

"Well, if there's no news, there is no reason not to continue my studies. There's a lecture today by Giovanni d'Andrea, on the topic of governance." He saw the lad's expression. "I know. A little dry. But as my studies are already paid for, I should wring every ounce of learning from them. But the standing rule applies," he added. Fazio had orders to collect any post at once and bring it to Pietro, wherever he might be.

After eating, Pietro drew on his boots and left his lodgings for the Basilica of San Stefano. Most often the lectures were given in the professors' houses. But d'Andrea was popular enough that a space was set aside for him in the corner of the square in front of the venerable church. With the rain, Pietro wondered if they would have to move it.

There were generally three lectures each day, the first starting at the morning bell and lasting two hours, ending around nine o'clock, at the bells for Tierce. From then the students were free to nap or eat until after noon, when there would be another two hour lecture, a gap, then a final short lecture of perhaps ninety minutes.

Having missed the first lecture of the day, Pietro had time to amble through the streets, greeting friends and avoiding boors. Having been at the University of Paris during his father's lectures there, he was pleased by the lack of airs the students put on among the locals. Parisians were always battling with students, whereas the Bolognese had embraced the young men who came from all over the world to learn. The University was their pride.

The rain had not slackened. Reaching the churchyard just as the bells rang the end of Sext, Pietro saw that the doors of the church were open and students were actually flowing inside. Clearly there had been no room in a house for such a great number of hearers, and the palaces must have been occupied. Interest kindling, Pietro joined the jostle and passed under the stone archway.

As a knight, he was allowed a seat in the second bench from the front. Only doctors of law were given higher precedence, and today they were present *en force*, which surprised Pietro. True, this was no recitation, but actual oratory—a recitation was where a professor read a pre-written piece, as opposed to the more popular and conversational 'ordinary'. But today must be an extraordinary ordinary.

As the church bells finished tolling around them, the professor took his place in the pulpit. Pietro knew him well, had been attending his ordinaries for months. Pietro's impression of Giovanni d'Andrea was that he was a man of contradictions: bald but bearded, long-legged but stooped shoulders, weak of eye but strong of voice. The kind of man one ignores on the street but not in the courtroom.

After thanking the Bishop of Bologna for graciously giving them shelter from the rain, d'Andrea squinted hard at the crowd. "Today, I wish to speak of government. As we have the best and most detailed example through the history of Rome, we shall use that as our reference point. To begin with, Rome had kings. Beginning with Romulus and ending with the Tarquin, Rome's rule was guided by blood, not merit." He smiled slightly, bowing towards the Bishop. "Given our surroundings, I wish to pass no comment on the religious aspect of kingship—if kings are indeed the appointed of God above, then it is not for me, a mere doctor of law, to meddle or question. I will merely observe that God has ordained no king for us here in Bologna. Perhaps He means it as a compliment." Appreciative chuckles.

"Now, after the expulsion of the kings by the first Brutus—a revolutionary act, in every sense. When before has a man been hailed as king and said, 'No. No more kings. We may rule ourselves.' I find that first Brutus as remarkable as his namesake was despicable. From Brutus to Brutus, I suppose, we have an excellent example of the forms of governance."

He paused, seeming to consider a new thought, though to Pietro's mind it was a trifle theatrical. *Cangrande would have pulled it off better.*

"Rome's first government after the kings was created by Brutus 'for the people'. This is that kind of governance which Aristotle calls 'political'. If run correctly, this government considers the general welfare, dividing both burden and gain equally across the populace. A good government. But if the rulers instead look to their own interests above anyone outside their 'political' class—rich or poor, it does not matter—then this is a bad government. Aristotle describes it with the Greek word *democratia*." D'Andrea gave a fleeting smile. "I call it a perverse populace." More appreciative chuckles.

"The next form of government to rear its head in Rome was the rise of the Senators. Wealthy men, prudent. Again, this has the potential to be either good or bad. If the Senators can work for the common good, it is a government of elders. *Principatus*, I call it.

"But that form of governance too easily slips from good to bad. If the wealthy look to their own interests, then this is an oligarchy. That is a word we hear bruited about often today. And it is apt.

"The last form of governance is single rule. Be it Caesar, emperor, king, duke, or count, call it what you like, but a single man ruling over a collection of people bound by geography," (Pietro admired how neatly d'Andrea excluded the pope from the argument) "this person with 'imperium', as it was called in Rome, can likewise be either good or bad. For the common benefit, good. For himself, bad.

"There is a word for good governance, that which looks to the common good above individual gain. That word is godly."

The collected students hummed in assent. The Bishop nodded sagely.

"There is a word for bad governance," declared d'Andrea, looking suddenly fierce. "That word is tyranny."

There was a murmur in the crowd. *Tyrant* was a much-debated word. Many rulers embraced the title, deeming it a badge of strength. There were many rulers—Cangrande among them—who did not blench when called 'tyrant'.

The slump-shouldered d'Andrea seemed to grow in stature. "Tyranny is self-interest above all. It is not godly, not just. It is when a ruler or group of rulers cannot transcend greed and ambition to do what is right. A godly ruler may fail from time to time, but he is never ousted by his people. So long as the common good is the aim, the common people will never turn upon him."

That seemed a bridge too far. Before he knew what he was doing, Pietro opened his mouth to say, "But it's rarely the common people who choose their leaders."

Heads turned. The doctors on the front bench looked at him disapprovingly. D'Andrea squinted. "Who spoke? Raise your hand." Hesitantly, Pietro obeyed. "Your name?"

Pietro blushed, caught short. He certainly didn't want to use his surname, which would carry all the weight of his father's fame. Nor did he wish to invoke Florence, where tyranny had ordered his exile. "Ser Pietro da Verona."

"Ah! Verona. A shining example of tyranny. Tell me, Ser Pietro, what do you know of Ezzelino da Romano? You are too young to remember him yourself, but your forefathers must have felt his misrule."

Again, Pietro flushed. His forefathers had done nothing of the sort, having been rooted elsewhere. And this was too like his father's trick of quizzing him before strangers, an embarrassment he had never enjoyed.

Still, he had learned of Verona's history to say with confidence, "When his father became a monk, Ezzelino used his inherited lands to fund and aid the strife between factions, ousting Count Ricardo da San Bonifacio. After the Lombard League attempted to remove him from power and restore the Count, Ezzelino changed Verona's allegiance from Ghibelline to Guelph, making an alliance with Frederick II."

"By marrying his thirteen year-old natural daughter," observed d'Andrea.

Pietro had not heard her age before now. Though disgusted, he did not want to be caught out, so he soldiered on. "He conquered Verona by force, Padua by treason, and Treviso by usurping his own brother. He used torture, lies, and murder as his tools. He was excommunicated and attacked from all sides, and captured near Bergamo and torn to pieces."

"I wonder if that was preferable to him than listening to the dialect," mused d'Andrea, to general laughter. The speech of Bergamo was notoriously unintelligible and painful to the ear. "But, in all, as concise a summary of a tyrant as I could have wished. Ezzelino da Romano ruled badly, guided entirely by self-interest. His interest was not the common good. He was the very definition of ungodly. And he was removed."

"Not by his own people," countered Pietro. "By foreign enemies."

"What, is it Lent already?" asked d'Andrea lightly. During Lent, professors suspended their lectures in favour of 'disputations' where they would present a thesis and defend it against all comers.

If Pietro was going to be pilloried for arguing, he would at least make a real effort. "Yes, he was an evil man, and paid the price. But your argument is about the governed within a geographical area, not those outside it. And Ezzelino brought Verona to greater prominence in the world. It could be argued that his evil actions then laid the foundations for the good governance of Cangrande della Scala today."

There were some hisses from the back. *Probably Paduans.* Ignoring them, Pietro stared up at d'Andrea, who was smiling thinly.

"You say his villainy was good for the people of Verona."

"I do not defend his actions. I simply think he is a poor example for your thesis."

"I think he is an excellent example of a tyrant."

"He may have been a villain, but his form of governance remains in Verona. Just as it did for centuries in Rome. You started by invoking the two Brutuses. You said you found the first as remarkable as his namesake was despicable. But you failed to point out that he was overthrowing a good tyrant. Caesar was interested in the common good, far moreso than the Senate of Rome. His laws were fair, and if he warred against his fellow Romans, it was a war waged for the common good."

"I agree," said d'Andrea.

"What you don't see is that—what?"

"I said I agree."

Pietro frowned. "Forgive me, but earlier I thought you said—"

"—that a ruler who has the common good in mind is never ousted by those he rules," finished d'Andrea. "Yes, I said that. But of course he is. *Of course* he is. Because men are susceptible to lies, to rumours, and to envy. Wealth and privilege will always protect itself, as the Senate did against Caesar. A good ruler will be overthrown by bad people. We see it all too often. A kingdom or city can only be as good as the people it encompasses. A godly ruler placed over an idle populace can do only so much. Which begs the question—is it better to have an ineffective godly man, or an effective tyrant? Because, as Ser Pietro points out, Ezzelino da Romano was a monster, but a very effective one, growing Verona's power far beyond its history. We pray such men meet the accounting they deserve. But often a bad man can do more for the common good than a godly one. Bad men have no scruples, are ruthless, and passionate. So I ask again, which is better—a godly man who achieves little, or a tyrant who achieves much?"

"Godliness and achievement are not mutually exclusive," said Pietro.

"But they are rarely found together. Once in a century such a man comes along. He is as rare as Dante's mythical Greyhound. As rare as the man who speaks up against injustice and untruth." Giovanni d'Andrea inclined his head. "My compliments, Ser Pietro, for daring to raise your voice where no other would. How many of you others heard the flaw in my argument and did not speak because I am in authority? If you cannot question authority, why are you at university? How do you hope to learn? I know, I am up here and have the right to the stage. But so will your rulers, your lords, your masters. If you think manners are more important than truth, you must check the weights of your scales, for they are off. If you fear a beating, you had best cease your studies today.

"So many men think of university students as soft, living an idle life of cant and culture. But real thinkers, those who strive to steal the knowledge held in the heads of these great doctors here before me, they know that they must be braver than he who tilts a lance or draws a sword. The men whose names we today admire—Socrates, Seneca, Christ himself—they all spoke truth to power, and were willing to die for it. Are you willing to do any less? To do as you are told is the place of beasts, of serfs, of men without the wit to question. A soldier must do as his lord commands. A man must question those commands. Do you think Ezzelino da Romano could have slaughtered so many without the obedience of those who were too timid to question him? I promise you that if Ser Pietro had been living then, he would have raised his voice. It might have cost him his life. But not his honour. Not his integrity. Think on that!"

For the third time, Pietro was red in the face. As pleasing as the lecturer's words were, he did not think himself at all heroic. He was rude, and somehow incapable of hearing a falsehood and not giving it a challenge. If he was forever bound by the truth, he might make a very poor lawyer.

From the pulpit, Giovanni d'Andrea glared through narrowed eyes at the chastened faces before him. "Now, we will return to the forms of governance. There is a seventh, a monstrous one, where several tyrants vie for rule within a limited space…"

Listening intently and determined to keep his mouth firmly shut, it was some moments before Pietro saw Fazio waving subtly to him from near the baptismal font. *A letter!*

Unfortunately, Pietro was not the only one who had noticed. Pausing as he saw heads turning, d'Andrea peered over through the gloom over his shoulder until he spied the young groom. "Can we help you, lad?"

Fazio blanched, but spoke in a brave voice. "I have a letter for Ser Alaghieri."

That provoked outright conversation. Alaghieri? Did they mean Dante?

Was Dante here? When had he been knighted?

Well aware that every eye would be fixed upon him, Pietro stood and said, "Forgive me, *dottore*. That is the second interruption I have caused. There will not be a third." With that he slid along the bench and gestured Fazio outside, where they sheltered under an alcove.

"A letter from Verona," said Fazio. "Did I do wrong to bring it now?"

"If anyone did wrong, it was me." Pietro's voice caught as he saw the seal. Cangrande! Tearing the wax apart, he opened the missive and started decoding the cypher in the dreary light that filtered through the rain.

It brought the same news as Poco's letter, of peaceful surrender followed by unlawful massacre. Typically, the Scaliger glossed over his personal feelings about Calvatone, mentioning only the order that had disgraced his army by breaking his promise to the citizens.

The closing lines, however, contained a surprise:

> This seems likely to take longer than we expected. As that is the case, I have been thinking about your circumstances. A rented room is impermanent, it suggests mobility. I want your name to be linked to Bologna—or rather, unlinked from Verona. To further this, I have arranged with your father's friend Guido Novello of Polenta for you to be appointed keeper of the Benefice of Ravenna. As a secular post for the Church, your only duty will be to collect tithes and settle minor disputes. It also comes with a fine casa.
>
> Your orders are to move in at once. You will be close enough to Bologna to continue your studies, and it will be more secure if you have visitors.
>
> The job also requires you to train a few men-at-arms. See that they are ready for any eventuality. Contact Manuel's cousin in Venice if you require more funds.
>
> Be well, be studious, be safe, and be ready.
>
> Cg.

Pietro folded the letter and tucked it into his farsetto. "Make sure the horses are ready to travel, then start packing up everything."

Fazio looked excited. "Are we going?"

"Yes, but not far. Ravenna." His smile faded. "Oh, and Fazio. Make sure you're armed."

That made the boy light up. "Are we headed for a fight?"

"No, just being cautious." He thought of his father's note. "You don't want for money, do you? Because it seems you could make a handsome fee for turning me over to a Florentine."

Fazio looked shocked. "I wouldn't do that, sir!"

Pietro stood and patted the boy's shoulder. "I know, I know. I'm teasing. Now go look to the horses. We'll leave in the morning."

A bemused Fazio departed, and Pietro chided himself. *He's young. I shouldn't scare him.*

He was debating heading back into the basilica to hear the final argument when other students started streaming out. He stepped back, not wishing to be seen and pointed at. But he did not leave, either. *I owe Doctor d'Andrea an apology.*

At last Giovanni d'Andrea emerged from San Stefano. Bidding adieu to several of his fellows, he paused to peer out at the rain, then down at the slick steps. For a man so clearly nearsighted, they were treacherous.

Pietro hurried forward. "Dottore," he began, then cursed as he slipped. His bad injured leg was always painful when it rained, but it had seized up at just the wrong moment.

He was humiliated to find himself propped up by the great doctor of law. "Careful there, son!"

"Thank you," said Pietro, flushing for the fourth time this afternoon as he found his footing.

The jurist squinted. "Is that Ser Alaghieri? Also known as Pietro da Verona?"

"Yes," admitted Pietro shamefacedly.

"Also Pietro di Dante? The hero of Vicenza?"

How had he heard about Vicenza? "I don't know about hero. I fought, and was injured." He waved vaguely at his leg.

"That's the mark of a hero," said d'Andrea. "If you had been killed, you would be a martyr."

Pietro laughed. "Are all dead men martyrs?"

"To someone," said d'Andrea wisely. He used his free hand to raise the hem of his gonella. "Come, here are the steps. I must say, it is kind of you to pretend to need my help."

"It's no pretense," said Pietro, feeling the older man's weight now upon his own arm. "But I am happy to return your kindness. And to beg your forgiveness. I did not mean to be rude."

"Ser Pietro, perhaps you did not hear what I said, but I was quite sincere in my praise. There is nothing wrong in questioning authority when it is wrong."

"I think my father would agree. But would add that authority rarely appreciates disagreement."

"True enough! There, we are both stable now. What do you say to some bread and porridge on this wet and chill day?"

Pietro was delighted to agree, and together they retired to d'Andrea's house, where the cook already had pots over the fire. Pietro was introduced to Giovanni's wife and their two little daughters, Bettina and Novella. The two girls curtsied but spared hardly a glance for him after that, well-used to their father bringing students home. But his wife joined them as Giovanni quizzed Pietro about his famous father for nearly half an hour.

"And what of your patron, the Greyhound?" asked the legal scholar as his wife took the girls upstairs to nap. "Is he a godly man?"

"I think so," said Pietro. "He is clever, and ambitious. Energetic."

"The good tyrant," mused d'Andrea. "Like Caesar. Like Charlemagne. Perhaps it has to be men whose names begin with C." He squinted harder at Pietro. "And what of that other C name—Calvatone?"

Pietro grew instantly defensive. "It was not his fault! His orders were not obeyed."

"And I hope that is so. But a wily ruler might see the advantages of such a slaughter. As you yourself argued this afternoon, a skilled villain may be a better prince than an unskilled saint."

"Was that my argument?" asked Pietro. "I seem to have been steered into defending a position I do not hold."

"Then you will make an excellent lawyer, because you defended it well."

"I would never support an evil man," said Pietro firmly. "One who acts out of self-interest. But Cangrande is not such a man. I know you oppose single rule—"

"Do I? Perhaps it was I who was maneuvered into defending something I do not believe. You did not have a chance to hear me out, but after you stepped away I posited that single rule is the best form of government. In a crowd, villainy can hide. But in an individual, it will out in time. The massacre at Calvatone, for example."

"It was not his villainy," insisted Pietro. "My brother was there. He described the Scaliger's fury."

"Excellent," said d'Andrea. "Then perhaps it was happenstance. Certainly in war, mistakes are made. He is young, and has decades ahead of him. As I say, time will out."

Departing with a promise to return, and to attend more observatories in the future, Pietro wended the wet streets of Bologna with an ill feeling somewhere around his sternum. It was true, the massacre at Calvatone had quelled much of the resistance to Verona's army to the west of the city. And none of the odium had clung to Cangrande, since the order hadn't been his. *'A wily ruler might see the advantages of such a slaughter...'*

No, thought Pietro with ferocious certainty. *If I know one thing, it is that Cangrande is an honest man. That rarest of creatures. The honest tyrant.*

Years later, Pietro would recall the lesson Bologna had tried to teach him that night. Yes, *Bononia docet.* But that did not mean men learned.

AUTHOR'S NOTE TO BONONIA DOCET

This story takes place in the midst of Chapter Twenty-Eight of THE MASTER OF VERONA—after Calvatone, before Ignazzio's death.

First off, I must confess to filching an argument from Bartolo of Sassoferrato, a later professor of law at the University of Bologna, and attributing it to one of his mentors, Giovanni d'Andrea, about fifteen years too early. And I did not use the complete argument, which is an interesting whirligig of knot-tying to reach the conclusion that single rule is best. It comes rather near a discussion of the concept of 'consent of the governed', yet cannot entirely reach it due to either political or conceptual restraints of the time. If you wish to read it in full, you can find it under the title "Tractatus de Regimine civitatis".

There's also a cameo from Bologna's second female lecturer. Giovanni's daughter Novella grows up studying at her father's knee, and eventually took over his lectures in his occasional absences. After her untimely death, her father dedicated one of his works to her memory. Her sister Bettina likewise was a legal scholar and professor, only her post was at the University of Padua. Should the opportunity arise, I hope to see these ladies again someday.

Pietro's time in Bologna is often mentioned—he spends a great deal of time there between MoV and FALCONER. But readers have never experienced the university there, nor even the one in Padua, 'nursery of arts' as Lucentio calls it. I did not want to go too greatly into depth describing Pietro's collegiate experience—though imagining medieval keggers would be fun. But it seemed the perfect setting to explore the quality in him that he views as a flaw, but that actually makes him the best character in my books—and by best, I mean most godly, as d'Andrea would say. A person always concerned with truth, with justice, with honour. It was also a fine place to discuss Pietro's idolatry of Cangrande, and what it says about his coming disillusionment.

And it was a place to pose the argument I've been having with my friends a lot of late—which is preferable to elect, an effective villain, or an ineffective saint? Not that the terms are ever so clear. One man's villain is another man's pragmatist. But competency does not always reflect quality of outcome. Neither does godliness. So where is the balance? It's a question they were debating at the start of human society, and the only answer seems to be "those who work for the common good". You'd think we'd have gotten further in four or five thousand years...

ILLYRIA

FOR VICKI KONDELIK

"And what should I do in Illyria?"

—Viola
Twelfth Night
ACT I SCENE II

S O RED THEY MIGHT HAVE been made of actual flame, the banners snaked out, unfurling with hearty cracks before whipping back under the fury of the mighty wind called the Mistral. Oarsmen swept back and heaved in rhythm with the choir that sang holy songs in both Latin and French—but not Italian. The gentlest hint of things to come.

The banks of the Rhône were teeming with onlookers. It was almost a holiday, an impromptu festival along the river's edge. Some hapless souls plunged in, pushed by those eagerly seeking a better view. When again in their lifetimes could they lay eyes upon Saint Piere's heir? Especially as there was so much pressure to return the papacy to Rome, making Clement's transplanting of the Holy See a temporary aberration, a Gallic hiccough in the history of the Church. So French citizens between Lyon and Avignon now flocked to the riverbank to watch the new pope pass, that when they prayed they could attach a face to their pleas.

Not that anyone could see his face. Aboard ship, the throned figure was practically swallowed by his hat and gown, despite their being tailored to him. A gnome of a man, delicate and diminutive. Even the throne itself, high on its pedestal, was cleverly designed to hide the fact that his feet couldn't reach the deck. A step pretended to be a footrest for the most mighty man in all of Christendom.

His might was more frightening because as yet no one knew how he planned to wield it. Pope for less than two months, as yet there was no sign of his nature. Would he be benevolent or tyrannical? Waiting for some sign, his fellow cardinals were growing uneasy. In the absence of a pope these last two long years, they'd grown used to life without an overlord. Added to that was the unimpressive stature of the new Holy Father, more suited to a foole than a prince.

Disappointed by the dwarf on the papal throne, several young ladies on the shore cast their eyes about the massive barge for a sight more pleasing to their eyes. Almost at once they found a most deserving figure tucked away on the lower level, far from His Holiness. The young man's naturally fair complexion was tanned but not burned, his fashionably long black hair whipping in the wind from beneath his square, feathered cap. Dressed to perfection in demi-cape, high boots, and hose cinched so tight it showed the muscles of his thigh, he was the very ideal of the modern knight. More, his slight air of suffering made him all the more attractive. And the cut of his doublet was so high as to be almost scandalous—just below the richly embroidered hem, girls could see the faintest curve of his firm buttock. How daring! How delightful! How *French*!

Had he known he passed for French, he would have been deeply gratified. Nineteen years old now, married for over a year and still yet a virgin (a status which many French maids had attempted to correct), Ser Mariotto Montecchio was the epitome of chivalry. And true chivalry, as everyone knew, began in France.

A youth stood near him, just twelve years old last July. He was rather plain, with drooping eyes and a face that was still sorting itself out. Dressed in a drab second-hand gonella and a floppy cap that was woefully out of style, the lad gazed at Mariotto as if he were a god.

Summoning his courage, the boy pointed to the girls on the shore. "They're staring at you."

Mari was pleasantly startled. The lad had an Italian accent! Was it Florentine? Too honest to pretend he had not noticed the girls, Mariotto chose to be generous. "Perhaps they're staring at you."

The boy looked ruefully at his poor clothes. "No. You're like the sun. I'm just a cloud blocking their view."

Mariotto felt a curious pity rising in him. "Very poetic. What is your name, my friend?"

"Francesco. Though I suppose it should be François. We live here, now."

"Me too," said Mari, hiding his sadness behind a smile. He had no inkling how long this noble exile would last.

Young François surprised Mari by nodding. "I heard the story." He pointed at the girls on the Rhône's bank opposite them. "If they heard it, they'd drown themselves like the Donna di Scarlotta did for Lancelot du Lac."

Mariotto winced. The reference to Lancelot was apt. As Lancelot had betrayed Arthur with Guinevere, so Mariotto had betrayed his closest friend by stealing his betrothed.

Aloud he said, "That would be a shame, as I'm married." *Though not yet a husband,* he reminded himself.

The boy continued to nod wisely. "Some men say you did wrong.

I don't think so."

"No?"

"No! If chivalry is all about the wishes of women, great deeds in their names, hardships for their sakes, you did the right thing. You made her happy by marrying her."

To Mari that argument rang false. "Alas, François, chivalry is about pining from afar, the idea of an unattainable woman. Dante never wed his Beatrice."

"Dante is an idiot."

The youth pronounced the words with such certainty that Mariotto had to laugh. "Be careful! I'm a friend to his son."

"And my father is friends with Dante himself." The twelve-year-old shrugged. "I don't mean to smear his poetry. Just his notion of love as an idea. Love is real, and real love makes you act. That's why you married your friend's betrothed."

Mari didn't want to answer that, so he argued for love. "It's the relationship between Beatrice and Dante that's legendary, a love that transcended the physical. Ideally, love and marriage are not meant to be joined. Marriage soils love's perfection."

"So why did you marry her then?" asked the young man with direct simplicity.

Gazing out at the cheering folk on the shore, Mari was silent. His unspoken answer was equally simple, and eternally shaming. *I wanted her. I couldn't bear to be a great lover, to love from afar. O, Gianozza...*

Yet Fortune had conspired to make theirs a great tale of love after all. Fate, in the guise of the Lord of Verona, had separated them, sending Mari here to the papal court on the very day of his wedding. His exile from his bride made him pine, and long, and dream. From her letters, Gianozza felt the same. Theirs was indeed destined to be a great love, like Dante and Beatrice, Antony and Cleopatra, Odysseus and Penelope.

"My son isn't troubling you, is he?" asked a grave man, dressed exactly as young François.

Mariotto recognized the exiled Florentine as a notary to one of the cardinals. "Not at all, Ser Petracco," said Mari with a winning smile. "We were debating the nature of chivalry and the love of poets."

The notary's chin lifted as if to remove from his nose a foul smell. At the same moment his son shot a reproachful glance to Mari. With apologies for troubling the Veronese knight, Ser Petracco took his son off, a firm grip on his shoulder. *Not an admirer of poetry,* mused Mariotto.

A burly cardinal approached, a smile bursting through his beard. "I know that look. Has little Francesco been reciting verses again?"

Mari bowed. "Cardinal Orsini. My fault, I'm afraid. We were discussing courtly love."

"Ah, *l'amour*." With that polite acknowledgement, Cardinal Orsini took up station beside Mariotto to stare out over the water slipping by.

Mari knew that most men on this ship thought him a damned romantic fool. During the past year, as he grew more and more worldly at the leaderless papal court, he'd been forced to rebuff—sometimes physically— the attentions of dozens of girls. This drew laughter from many prelates, and earned him a few equally unwelcome advances from his own sex.

The only man who had never mocked him was Cardinal Napoleone Orsini. In spirit both the lion and the bear his name indicated, he was a generous, gregarious, and bluntly gracious man. Upon arriving in the summer of 1315, Mariotto had attached himself to Orsini's party. Back then the cardinal had been rumoured as a favourite for the papacy, and as they spoke nearly the same language (Veronese Italian differed from Roman Italian, but only in dialect), it seemed a natural move. Mariotto had orders to lobby the new pope in Verona's favour, and if he had a friendship with that new pope before the office was granted, so much the better.

The election of Jacques d'Euse had come as quite a shock, and not only to Mari. After two years without a Holy Father, the latest French king had bullied and bribed all the cardinals together and forced them into a castle to do their duty and choose a pontiff. It gave new meaning to the term conclave—*con clave*, literally, 'with key'. While they held the key to God's heir on Earth, Philip V held the key to their freedom.

Mariotto recalled waiting with so many others outside the castle, watching for the telltale smoke that would signify Orsini's election. But when the white smoke had come and the doors had opened, it was instead a cordwainer's son who had mounted Saint Peter's throne. The little man had taken them all by surprise, doing the unthinkable and nominating himself. Trained in both law and medicine, his career in the clergy had been mostly spent presiding over the seaside See of Frejus, a pleasurable duty, and in Avignon, providing advice more legal than spiritual. How he had swung them around to vote for him, no one quite said. Certainly Orsini had been mute on the subject. But rather than look displeased, Orsini appeared quite content.

Now looking out over the water, Orsini softly murmured, "Illyria, I am coming."

"Pardon?" said Mariotto.

Abashed, the cardinal rubbed his whiskered chin with the back of his hand. "I have a cousin, prince of a city on the coast of Anatolia. It's called Dubrovnik, but he has renamed it *Illyria*."

"Illyria? After—?"

"—Ilium, yes, the fabled city of Helen and Paris." Orsini smiled smugly. "He's a fanciful fellow, for all that he's a good prince. In fact, he's rather like you! He pines. O, how he pines! He writes of a young maiden for whom he would eat every apple in the world. Her father is a great man of the city and her brother is one of the handsomest men in the land—by report, he would even rival you," added the cardinal with a cheerful wink. "Certain that with such men in her life already he would pale in comparison, my cousin has talked himself into loving the lady from afar."

Mariotto pulled a face. "That's falling off the horse before you get to the rail."

"I told you, fanciful. Come to think of it, he's not at all like you. You abandoned convention and seized your moment. That's the difference between true love and this airy popular nonsense. True love demands *action*. Only in false love can a man wallow, peak, and pine."

"You and young Petracco see eye to eye. But it's contrary to what the poets—"

"Pfah! Poets love words, not women. It's like the Church. There are men of the cloth who mouth the words of Christ, and those who live them. Love of Christ demands action. Misguided as many of the crusades have been, one cannot fault the passion with which the crusaders spurred off to fight. Christ himself was a man of action—his love of his Father made him perform miracles, and he beat the craven moneylenders. I tell you, if I have been tempted to any violence in my life, it has been to emulate him in that act. For I swear to you, Ser Montecchio, I detest even the smell of money!" The steel in Orsini's voice underscored his vehemence.

Mariotto paused, then returned to his original query. "So why do you say you are coming to Illyria?"

Again the cardinal looked abashed. "Your fault! I was thinking about courtly love—desire as the be all and end all. To me, my cousin's Illyria is all about desire. An ideal, a mythical state, a place where one pines for the thing one wants most in the world. And therefore that thing is most often denied." Orsini chucked Mari on the shoulder. "We all know what your Illyria is—your Gianozza."

Mariotto grinned. "And yours?"

"Rome," said the cardinal simply. "As Rome has been denied us these many years, Rome is my Illyria." Orsini released a huge, happy breath. "But at last we are returning."

Mariotto perked up at once. This was news! "His Eminence is returning the Holy See to Rome?"

Orsini nodded. "There is no harm I think in speaking of it, now the election is past and he is enthroned. Our new Holy Father has sworn an oath to me, upon the consecrated Host and before all the entire conclave, that he will never again mount a horse or mule except in the direction of Rome."

Mariotto lacked a lawyer's mind, but this seemed a convoluted oath to take. "Is that why—?"

"—we float instead of ride? Yes," answered the cardinal. "He is keeping his word. Rightly, he points out that Avignon is the current site of his authority, and he must attend to matters there before he makes such a drastic change."

"No disrespect, but he is very old, and quite frail," observed Mariotto. "What if, God forbid, he does not live to see his promise carried out?"

"Then we shall elect another who will. But that won't be necessary. Jacques d'Euse is famous for being a man of his word, else he would not have been elected."

They sailed on for hours, the cardinals and bishops and knights waving and smiling to the throngs along the Rhône. There was great cheer, particularly among the Italian clerics—they were at last to return to San Pietro's true throne. They were going home.

The sun was low in the autumnal sky when Avignon came into view. With great decorum the little pope lifted himself from his throne and crossed to the rail where Orsini and Montecchio, along with many others of their nation, had congregated.

"*Mon frère!*" cried the wizened pope to Orsini. "See how vibrant the heavens are above my beloved France."

"Indeed!" agreed the cardinal warmly. "I am certain it seems all the more lovely, as you contemplate leaving it behind. If death is indeed the mother of beauty, then exile is the father of patriotism."

"What you say is both profound and true," said the pontiff in his curious style of speech, both headlong and monotonous. "I find in me no inch that is not filled with love for France. And it is for that reason I have decided that I must delay preparations for a return to Rome."

Orsini's generous spirit was devoid of the suspicion that Mariotto, listening intently, felt all too keenly. "For how long?"

"Indefinitely," said the little pope, his sorrowful expression not reaching his eyes.

For a suspended moment Cardinal Orsini wrestled with the meaning of this word. Then like a thunderclap the pontiff's purpose was made clear. Orsini looked as though his ribs had been levered open and his heart removed before the gaze of all the world. "You do not intend to return the Holy See to Rome?"

The little man in the grand hat and gown blinked several times. "You wish me to leave my own country for all eternity, to lock myself away in that ruined country you call Love? No. I fear Roma is not *Amor* for me."

"But—it has been the home of the papacy since the first pope, the blessed Peter himself. He chose Rome as the finest and grandest city in all the world!"

"But is that true today? The world has shifted away from Rome, *mon frère*, and we must follow the world's lead."

"Holy Father, you are charged to lead, not to follow."

"And so I am, by leading us away from blind adherence to tradition. But in one way you are mistaken. I must lead my flock, true. But I must follow God. God has led the papacy to Avignon. Where He leads, I must follow."

Orsini kept his voice level by sheer force of will. "Your Eminence, one of your titles is Bishop of Rome."

"I have so many titles, I can do without that one. My dear Orsini, the same Lord that gave the blessed apostle Peter the power to bind and loose— he is everywhere, is he not? Certainly he is as present in this lush and vibrant land as he is in the decayed maw of the seven hills. I am afraid this journey has quite determined me to stay in Avignon. No, I pray you, do not protest! Your Italy smiles to you, but for me it would only be a land of exile and despair."

Struggling, Orsini's obedience lost to his need to protest. "Your Grace, Rome is the capital of the Christian world."

"The Christian world needs no capital, *mon frère*. The Lord our God is everywhere, ever present. He will forgive the whims of an old man too tired to travel so very far."

"But your Holiness, your promise! You vowed upon the sacred Host—"

Jacques d'Euse held up a hand. "My dear friend, I promise you I will not be forsworn."

Mariotto spied a litter awaiting the pontiff on the quay. A litter that had already been arranged, did not have to be sent for. He had sworn never to ride again, unless it was towards Rome. And as Cardinal Orsini had said, Jacques d'Euse was a man of his word.

Jacques d'Euse, now Pope Jean XXII, possessor of immense—and irrevocable—power.

As Mariotto Montecchio joined the procession that followed the dwarfish Pontiff back onto French soil, the bear-like cardinal lingered behind, as bereft of words as of recourse. Like his cousin and namesake in distant Illyria, all that remained in Orsini was his longing.

AUTHOR'S NOTE TO ILLYRIA

For those who've read FORTUNE'S FOOL, this will be easily familiar—I used it as the Prologue to that novel. But I had written it to stand alone, and it fits neatly into the chronology here.

This story also falls somewhere in the midst of Chapter Twenty-Eight of THE MASTER OF VERONA, in the fourth 'Act' entitled THE EXILES. That appellation certainly applies to Mari, who was banished to France on his wedding night. Little did Cangrande know that in the eyes of Mariotto's bride, this would render him irresistible—he was now a Tragic figure, and theirs a Great Love Story, like the Arthurian legends that were so very popular at the time.

But the pretext Cangrande used to separate the lovers was rooted in a very real concern for Verona, as it was for Dante, and indeed for all the world—the election of a new pope.

The removal of the papacy to Avignon is fascinating and horrifying. As corrupt as the Church in Rome often was, the Church in Avignon was infinitely worse, at least through the papacy of Jacques d'Euse. His sole goal, it seemed, was to fill the papal coffers, and he succeeded beyond anyone's dreams. When he became pope, the treasury held seventy thousand gold florins. Hardly an insignificant sum. When he died, he had swelled the coffers to seventeen million florins. That figure does not include the gold and silver plate, miter, crowns, and jewels, valued at an additional seven million florins.

While the so-called Babylonian Captivity of the Church is a horrible chapter in its history, it's a great one for an author. I visit Avignon for a while in FORTUNE'S FOOL, but we'll be back. The great thing about this pope is that he's a man of his word—and he chooses each word with such care.

Clearly this is my nod to Shakespeare's *Twelfth Night*. I have a vague suspicion that I will touch on the characters of that play in the briefest way in the planned 6th book of the STAR-CROSS'D series, but only because we'll be in that part of the world. Orsino and Viola play no part in the greater tale I'm telling. But when I encountered Cardinal Orsini, it was far too much to resist the reference.

A Poet's Nightmare
Part Two

"I LIKE IT."

"I'm utterly gratified."

"'*Osanna, sanctus Deus sabaòth…*' What does it mean?"

"What good is a cypher if I give away the key?"

"Can I help?"

"I don't know, can you?"

"I helped once."

"I don't recall."

"DXV! I gave you that!"

"You give me gas, too. Should I be grateful?"

"You're a mean old man."

"And you're a mannerless brat."

"Bad manners are still manners."

"Feh."

"You've mixed Latin with what?"

"Hebrew."

"You speak Hebrew?"

"I know Hebrews. They speak it."

"That's cheating."

"I'm a cheater."

"Speaking of, shall we play a game of chess?"

"I thought you were going to let me work."

"I'm a puzzle. Chess?"

"No."

"Why not?"

"You've begun to win too often."

"Then let's play something else."

"Absolutely. Let's play 'stick your head in a bucket of water for an hour.'"

You begin."

"Age before beauty."

"Ha! You tempt me, I confess. It's the only way to escape."

"Death is the ultimate escape."

"And you make it seem inviting."

Paradiso

For Sharon Kay Penman

WHOSE BOOKS ARE PARADISE

"The weariest and most loathèd worldly life
That age, ache, penury, and imprisonment
Can lay on nature is a paradise
To what we fear of death."

—Claudio
Measure For Measure
ACT III SCENE I

THE HOUSE WAS ALL IN WHITE. The servants worked chalk into every hanging at the windows, every stitch that would be worn. It was the old style, the classic style. To honour the classical nature of a man out of time.

He had once remarked as much. "I was born in the wrong era. I should have lived among the great thinkers, great doers. Instead I am left to nibble at their leavings, regurgitating their thoughts like birds to feed their young. Pabulum. That's all my work amounts to—pabulum."

So spoke the greatest writer living. Who was living no more. The man out of time had at last run out of time.

His eldest son was surprised by how empty the death left him. For Pietro Alaghieri, his father's presence had invaded every fibre of his being. First as his traveling companion during those early years in Paris, then Pisa and Verona. They had been apart for two years, while Pietro set up a life and a house here in Ravenna. Then father, brother, and sister had come to live with him, and life had seemed very full indeed.

The famous names had all come to pay homage, to request inclusion in the final volume for their ancestors—who didn't want their beloved dead to appear in Heaven? Aspiring poets had sat without the doors, hoping to gain greatness through proximity. And the important had come, seeking aid and wisdom, hoping to add the luster of his name to their causes. Quite a change from those years when he'd been spat upon, shunned, turned away.

His past suffering made his achievement all the more heroic. It had also made him aware how fragile a thing his notoriety was. If Pietro's father had feared anything, it was returning to that state of exile. Of being nobody. So he had, all unwilling, forced himself leave his writing to receive the famous, greet the aspiring, and oblige the important.

And it had killed him.

Such a stupid way to die. Contracting a sickness due to the mala aria while returning from an embassy to Venice. Antonia blamed the Venetians for refusing their father passage along a safer route. But their guest astrologer, Tharwat al-Dhaamin, had said it had been in the stars. *And how does one fight that?*

Dante Alighieri had been granted a magnificently-carved stone tomb inside the Frati Minori, just a mile from Pietro's own home. The funeral had been held nearly two months past, and Pietro had found himself walking to the site every day since. He ran his hands over the slab, feeling the smoothness of the marble under his fingertips, pausing over any imperfection.

It is not the death that hurts, thought Pietro. *In the shock of the moment, there's so much to do, there's almost no time to grieve, to accept the loss.*

No, it's the punch each day when you turn to talk to them, and find that they still insist upon remaining dead.

But Pietro was not concerned for himself. He had struck upon a home truth. His best way to forget his loss was to focus on helping others cope with theirs.

If they would only let him.

Jacopo had departed just after the funeral, heading to Verona to drown his sorrows in wine with his friend, Alberto della Scala. And Antonia—Pietro had expected his sister to fall to tears, to be entirely smote by their father's loss. He had been such a fixture in her life, a beacon, a calling—to have that removed must be an unfathomable shock.

Yet Antonia had very calmly announced that she had decided to enter a nunnery. "I have always wanted to be a nun, to devote myself to study and quiet."

"And Christ?" Pietro had asked.

"Of course." She'd blinked at him, entirely clear of eye. After the initial shock, there had been no tears from Antonia.

A deficiency made up from another quarter.

CROSSING HIS THRESHOLD AFTER VISITING his father's tomb at midday, Pietro could hear a familiar refrain ringing through the house. "It has no ending! How can it not have an ending?!?"

Seven years old, his foster son Cesco was inconsolable. For four years he had watched as *Purgatorio* was finished and *Paradiso* begun. But it would never finish. The poet had died with four cantos incomplete. These were not a mere dénouement, a close to the action and a summary. These were ultimate cantos, as the poet who had traversed Hell and Purgatory before ascending to the Heavens finally reached the heart of the Divine. Just shy of six hundred short lines of verse stood between the poem and completion. Verses that would now never be inked.

The great *Commedia* had no ending. And Cesco was in mourning.

The original plan for the summer had been that Cesco's friend Detto would come to Ravenna to stay. The theory was that one day Detto would be Pietro's squire, learning the craft of knighthood and honour.

All of that was, of course, a ruse. Detto was in fact Cesco's cousin. But Cesco's true identity was a closely-held secret. In Ravenna, it was given out that the boy was Pietro's nephew, the son of his later elder brother Giovanni.

Even Cesco believed this, remembered nothing of his old life in Vicenza. So to him the death of Dante was the loss of a grandfather, one he had revered and feared in equal measure. And in his grief, they had told Detto to remain in Vicenza—this was not the time to reunite the duo. While it might have done Cesco a world of good, it promised nothing but misery for his cousin.

The loss had been violent for Cesco, and he had turned violent, throwing objects and gnashing his teeth like a parody of grief. Only his was quite real. Cesco felt the loss as a cosmic injustice, and he had wailed in protest, howling at the·stars and the sky and Pietro and anyone within earshot. For two months, there had been just one refrain: "It has no ending!"

This thought kept them all up nights. A man's life's work, unfinished. With other artists—sculptors, painters, architects—a skilled apprentice might come in to finish the statue, the painting, the building. There would be sketches, drawings, models, something to guide those left behind towards completion.

But Dante's medium was words, those most ephemeral of edifices. The consummate craftsman, only one who had lived inside his mind could have crafted the proper conclusion to the epic of his journey through the heavens. And no such person existed. Not even Antonia, so well versed in every word and thought that appeared upon the page knew what he had planned for the end. He had confided in no one. Which meant there was no one left to carry on. The *Commedia* would instead be a Tragedia, the final words ever unwritten.

At seven, Cesco was unable to comprehend that there might be beauty in this. There might be pathos and a very human sense of loss and mortality in the great work that is never finished. Instead he howled at the walls, unable to let go of the idea of a great work incomplete.

"Why did he ever talk to me? Why did he sleep? How can such a thing be started, and left unfinished?"

"It is finished," replied Pietro. "When you die, your work is finished."

The look he received was scathing. "Do you think *he* deems it so?"

"There is something poetic in it, don't you think? Hell is known, Heaven is not?"

Cesco just shook his head.

"To my mind, there is something beautifully tragic in it. My father ascended to Heaven just as he reached it in his poem. Perhaps Heaven is meant to be unfinished. Perhaps it is beyond human comprehending."

Cesco slammed his hands together in frustration. "Then it should never have been started!"

"What if men never started, for fear of never finishing? What would be done?"

Having no answer for that, Cesco looked mulish.

"You miss him. Cesco, that's what this is. You miss him. It is a crime your time together was so short. 'There is no greater sorrow than to recall our time of joy in wretchedness.'"

Cesco loosed a snort like an angry bull calf. "He was a cantankerous old man with a mean tongue and a belly full of snakes."

"Cesco!"

"Am I wrong?"

That was hard to answer truthfully. "It is unkind to speak ill of the dead."

"You didn't let me finish. He was also a genius who died before he was done geniusing!"

"That's not a word."

"You say it's not. Because only a genius invents words."

"Meaning you're a genius?"

Cesco brushed that off with a wave of his little hand. It was a familiar gesture, one Pietro's father used to make it often when annoyed.

That was the real loss. Having genius in the house to ape, to study, to use as a sculptor does a handsome model. Ever since Cesco and Dante had come to live under the same roof, they had bonded over words, over wit, over will. Of every person living within Cesco's world, he saw himself most in his grandfather. To have his Lighthouse of Alexandria snuffed before the last ship had come in threatened all of Cesco's future. What if *he* died untimely as well? What if *his* work was left undone?

"Cesco—listen." Pietro sat, clasping his hands before him and looking directly at the boy. "Nothing man creates is permanent. Not even art. Think of all the plays lost when Alexandria's library burned. Think of the invasion of Visigoths, of barbarians who destroyed statues, defaced buildings, tore down monuments. All of those were someone's life's work as well. Of the Seven Wonders of the World, how many are still standing?"

"One," said Cesco.

"One," repeated Pietro. "The rest are lost. But that does not mean *art* has been lost. Only the physical manifestation. As long as men emulate God by creating works dedicated to beauty, the idea of art persists. Nothing can be lost, except the shell."

"But this piece is unfinished! It was never completed!"

"Perhaps it was not meant to be. Perhaps it was left for someone else to finish."

That thought made the little brow furrow. As well as he knew the boy, Pietro did not at once see the meaning.

"Have you been in there?" asked Cesco.

"No." A pause. "Would you like to go in?"

A shake of the head.

"Do you want me to go in with you?"

A pause. Then a small nod.

THEY ASKED ANTONIA TO JOIN them. She had ever been the most devoted to the poet, and she viewed the fact that *Paradiso* was not complete as a personal failure.

Pausing at the door as if to knock, Pietro pushed it open and walked through.

Though the study had been cleaned regularly since Dante's death, such was the awe that the household staff had for the poet that not one of the quills had been moved, none of the papers shifted. It felt as though Dante had just stepped out for some apples and cheese, and would return in a moment to shout at them for entering without permission.

Enter they did, the lack of shouting an unwelcome void in their ears. They saw his preferred goblet, clean and awaiting the wine that should be decanting in the sun from the open window. He had liked full-bodied wine, well aired.

"Not that vinegary stuff," murmured Pietro. The others looked at him, then smiled, recalling. That was the beginning of the healing.

They roamed the room, touching nothing, but pointing, chuckling. Their eyes might occasionally mist, but mostly they smiled.

Then came the opening of a drawer, a cabinet. They found a gonella, stained with food and hidden away, as might a naughty child. They laughed aloud at that.

Inside a barrel table, Pietro discovered a heavy wooden box with a domed lid and brass hinges. It was light-weight, and might have been empty. But it was locked.

"No jewels," joked Pietro, shaking it. "No hidden treasure. Do you see a key?"

The box became their mystery. They speculated as they searched the desk for the key. "Perhaps it's full of angel feathers plucked during his journey."

"Or all the broken quills he used to write the Commedia," suggested Antonia.

"He *was* hopelessly cruel to his quills," agreed Pietro.

"Perhaps it's a copy of *De Monarchia*," said Cesco, who had never been allowed to read it. Hell was a suitable topic for a boy, but not a challenge to papal authority. They all agreed he challenged authority enough on his own, and needed no fresh example for ammunition.

At last they found the key. Cesco discovered it wedged in the desk's underside, where it joined the right front leg.

Setting the box atop the desk, Pietro inserted the key and turned it over, then lifted the lid.

Scraps. Little bits of paper, torn from larger sheets. The occasional bit of plaster peeled from a wall with an image or a word. There were small wax tablets with minuscule scrawls upon them, and two twigs with words carved rudely into them.

Curious, Pietro turned the box over, meaning to dump the contents upon the desk, the better to sort through them.

"No!" shouted Cesco, throwing out his hands. Pietro desisted, and Cesco plucked up a piece of plaster from the box. "It might disintegrate."

Antonia lifted another scrap from the box, this one on paper. There were written on it twelve names—Albert, Philip, Edward, Ferdinand, Wenceslaus, Charles, Frederick, James, Dionysius, Haakon, Stephen—and the letters *l-v-e*, with dots in between each. Though capitalized, these were not Roman numbers, but a terrible word. *Lue* meant 'plague'.

"I know this," she murmured. "This was his acrostic in Canto Nineteen."

"Paradiso?" asked Pietro. He did not know the unfinished work nearly so well.

"Yes." It was not Antonia, but Cesco who replied. "*Lì si vedrà, tra l'opere d'Alberto...* You were wrong, Nuncle. These are jewels. Dante's hidden treasure."

"These were his notes!" said Antonia with a gasp.

"I didn't know he kept these," marveled Pietro. His father's mind had always seemed a metal trap, containing all the effluvium of his creativity.

"Nor I," answered Antonia, running her fingers carefully through the piles of words, phrases, thoughts that had tickled the poet over the years.

"I did," remarked Cesco. "He was afraid, he said, of losing his memory, as old men do."

With a sudden energy, Cesco lifted the box as gingerly as he would an infant and carried it to the center of the tiled floor. Without more words, he set to work, spreading out the notes one by one.

Antonia knelt down to raise one and read it, but he waved her off, his hand fluttering madly. "It's a puzzle. A word puzzle."

Sharing a long glance with his sister, Pietro and she both retired from their father's study.

FROM THAT DAY FORWARD, NO ONE dared enter the study. The windows were sealed against the slightest breeze, and candles were covered, lest a stray drop of wax obscure a precious word. Night and day Cesco laboured, his little brow furrowed as he untangled the jumbled poetic genius they had discovered. He copied sections, called out for words. Four separate times he had visited the local priest, and he kept both a Bible and a copy of the Aeneid close to hand. One day, Pietro found him across the road, questioning a gardener. Pietro lingered until Cesco returned to the house, then quizzed the man about their conversation.

"He was asking me about roses," said the man. "And bees."

"Roses?" repeated Pietro.

"And bees," confirmed the fellow.

Then, on an August day where the very air seemed to press down in silence and it was too hot to move, he emerged with a sheaf of papers.

"Have you solved the puzzle?" asked Pietro.

"Some," said Cesco tentatively. "I need some help."

Pietro felt a swelling in his chest. Cesco never asked for help. He held out his hand. "May I?"

"No," replied Cesco, clutching the pages close to his chest. "Antonia. She'll know if I've got it right." Off he scampered, leaving Pietro bemused, equal parts injured and amused.

Cesco returned two hours later with Antonia's corrections and suggestions scribbled in the margins. Entering the study without a word, he shut himself away again.

Antonia appeared, looking dazed.

"Well?" said Pietro. "How was it?"

"I don't know," she said.

"Was it bad?"

"No! No, not at all. It—"

"What?" said Pietro, started to be concerned.

Antonia shook her head once, as though dismissing a gnat. "The trouble is that I don't know if I felt this way because I wanted to, or because it really is. But it felt like father's work."

Pietro frowned. "Antonia. He's seven."

"I *know*," she insisted. "I *know* it. But still—it felt right. It felt complete. I had suggestions, of course. There were better words for certain phrases, and a few inelegant constructions. But I think—I think he might have done it."

Pietro's jaw was slack. He had viewed this as a project that might do Cesco some good—allow him a path through the dark wood of grief. Never had Pietro dreamed it might be something more.

I T WAS AT BREAKFAST THE NEXT morning, as Cesco mentioned publishing to Antonia, that Pietro decided to say something.

"Cesco. I know you've been working very hard."

The boy just gazed at him.

"And I know you're quite clever for a boy your age."

That brought a slight frown.

"But—you know you're not a poet. Not yet."

The frown became mulish.

"You might be someday. But your grandfather, he worked all his life learning to put words together as he did. You're seven."

"Pietro," said Antonia uneasily. "I think you should read—"

Little Cesco cut across her. "You never figured out the 515 prophecy, did you? He meant you to."

Now it was Pietro's turn to frown. "What?"

"The five-fifteen. At the end of *Purgatorio*. He meant that for you."

Pietro looked at Antonia, who appeared as puzzled as he. He remembered the five-fifteen passage clearly enough. It was a mysterious throwaway line at the very end of *Purgatorio*, added at the last moment. Two years earlier, he had asked his father about it. He recalled holding up a page and saying, "What's this?"

Dante had squinted, creating several creases across his brow. "Writing."

A breath. There were times his father was as trying as his foster son. "What is the writing meant to be?"

"Is that the prophecy?"

"Yes. *Cinquecento diece e cinque.* 'Five hundred, ten, and five.' What is it supposed to be?"

Leaning back, Dante had steepled his fingers. "A variation on Virgil's three-thirty-three prophecy. You know what that is?"

"Yes, father, I know what that is." As if he had not heard it half-a-hundred times. In the Aeneid, in a passage just preceding a prophecy of Roman hegemony, Virgil's Jupiter predicts the period of time between Aeneas' first military foray in Latium and the founding of Rome proper, divided into three parts—Aeneas waging war, Ascanius founding Alba Longa, and Romulus' birth. The first, according to Jupiter, would last three summers and winters. The second would take thirty years. The last would take three hundred years. Thus Virgil 'predicted' a three hundred thirty-three year span between Aeneas' landfall in Italy from the birth of Rome.

Dante had lifted some drying pages. "I'm referencing it in Canto Six of *Paradiso*, so I thought I'd sneak this into the end of *Purgatorio*."

Pietro's mouth had offered his crooked smile. "Missing Virgil, are you? Sad to leave him behind?"

Dante had looked grave. "Sadder than I'd be to leave you."

"So why five-fifteen? Three-thirty-three is Trinitarian, and the opposite of the number of the beast. Why not nine hundred ninety-nine, then?"

Dante shrugged. "Honestly? I failed to find an event that happened a thousand years ago that would work for a prophecy."

"Why not pick an event nine hundred ninety-nine years after the birth of Christ?"

"I want it to reference recent events, as I did with *Il Veltro*. That seemed to work out, no?"

Not wishing to discuss that particular prophecy, Pietro had continued his questioning. "So, why five hundred fifteen? It's not Trinitarian. What does that signify?"

Dante had shrugged. "It was someone's suggestion."

"Whose?"

"I forget."

A bald-faced lie, but one Pietro had forgotten about until this moment. He gazed at Cesco, who was looking smug, leaned back with his fingers steepled in imitation of the poet. "You. He got five-fifteen from you."

Cesco smiled in a way that meant the boy was feeling clever. "Maybe."

"Must be. So? What does it mean? When do the five hundred fifteen years start?"

"Charlemagne was crowned Emperor in 800."

"Yes. And…"

"Eight hundred and five-fifteen equals…"

"1315?" Pietro frowned. "You don't mean to say it's about you. You were born the year before."

Cesco's eyes lit up. "What day?"

"I forget," said Pietro roughly. "So, if not yourself, what does it reference?"

Cesco broke his poet's pose to perch at the edge of his chair. "Well, really it should be five-fifty-five. That's if we wanted to hold the mirror up to Virgil. But we don't know what's going to be happening thirty-four years from now. Personally, I really wanted it to be five hundred five and ten, but that's not how Roman numerals work."

Roman numerals. Pietro quickly converted the numbers.

Five hundred—D.

Ten—X.

Five—V.

DXV? What had Cesco just said? He'd wanted it to read *DVX.* Also known as *Dux,* or *Duke.* A lord of war. "You got father to predict a lord of war born in 1315?"

"Not quite." Cesco's smile grew wider as he felt appreciated. "You became a knight that year."

The blood rushed into Pietro's cheeks. "What?"

"Your father quite liked making you a part of his epic. That's why he added it at the very end." The little eyes became sharp. "It was my suggestion."

Pietro flushed a second time. "Cesco, I'm—that's very—"

Suddenly Cesco waved his hand. "Don't thank me. I meant it as a joke. It was a present for Detto was born in 1315. But I didn't think grandfather would put Detto in, so I made him think it was about you."

Pietro laughed, trying not to show his bruised feelings. *But father had thought it was true. He put in a prophecy for me.*

"Still think I'm not a poet?"

It was clever. Clever enough? "Very well. Let me see the pages."

Antonia gave a silent sigh as Cesco hopped up and dashed off to fetch them.

It was as the boy was leaving the room that Pietro was struck by a sudden thought. Yes, Cesco had been born in 1314. But he had been baptized as Cangrande's heir in 1315.

Had Cesco unwittingly made a prophecy about himself?

PIETRO STARTED BY READING THE LAST Canto his father had completed, which had been about angels. Then he started reading the words written in Cesco's inexpert hand:

Forse semilia miglia di lontano	About six thousand miles away from here
ci ferve l'ora sesta, e questo mondo	the sixth hour burns and even now the world
china già l'ombra quasi al letto piano,	inclines its shadow almost to a level bed.
quando 'l mezzo del cielo, a noi profondo,	when, deep in the intervening air, above us
comincia a farsi tal, ch'alcuna stella	begins such change that here and there,
perde il parere infino a questo fondo;	at our depth, a star is lost to sight.

e come vien la chiarissima ancella	And, as that brightest handmaid of the sun
del sol più oltre, così 'l ciel si chiude	advances, the sky extinguishes its lights,
di vista in vista infino a la più bella.	even the most beautiful, one by one.

Looking for flaws, Pietro found himself drawn in by a speech by Beatrice as she announces their entrance into Heaven's purest light.

Con atto e voce di spedito duce	With the voice and bearing of a guide who has
ricominciò: 'Noi siamo usciti fore	discharged his duty, she began: 'We have issued
del maggior corpo al ciel ch'è pura luce:	from the largest body to the Heaven of pure light,

luce intellettüal, piena d'amore;	'light intellectual, full of love,
amor di vero ben, pien di letizia;	love of true good, full of joy,
letizia che trascende ogne dolzore.'	joy that surpasses every sweetness.'

Pietro marveled. Beatrice's words were an extraordinary example of interwoven language, a perfectly distilled version of the Occitan technique of *coblas capfinidas*. Here the final word of a verse became the first word of the next verse: *luce—luce, amore—amore, letizia—letizia*, creating resonant beauty as appealing on the page as to the ear. *Cesco wrote this?*

"How much of this was you?"

Cesco was inclined to look innocent. Then he shook his head. "It's all there, in the notes. It was just about finding the links."

But that couldn't be entirely true, as Pietro soon realized. The conversation with the gardener was explained as God's Divine Love appeared as a massive rose, with the blessed seated on petals. Angels swarmed like bees pollinating the thousands of saints, preparing for those to come. How much of the rose had come from Dante, and how much from Cesco?

It was like reading a dream, where the landscape shifts and time moves in all directions. But this was a technique Dante had used before, and perfectly suited the experience of reaching the center of Heaven. The character of the poet is left by Beatrice, who took her place upon the rose. In her stead comes an old man suffused with joy, who leads Dante on a tour of the divine rose—not a physical tour, but using only his eyes, now able to perceive everything at once. They both gaze upon the Virgin, who becomes the object of their devotion even as other female saints were introduced, including Eve, whose original sin has been healed by Maria.

The old man, revealed to be San Bernardo, explains the division of the blessed, who are placed based upon grace rather than merit. The angel Gabriel opens his wings, and the whole court of Heaven sings with him. Bernardo prays to Maria, a prayer that spread into the final canto. As Maria accepts the prayer, they all look up, and Dante's divinely-endowed sight allows his to stare into the radiance. Words fail him:

Qual è 'l geomètra che tutto s'affige	Like the geometer who fully applies himself
per misurar lo cerchio, e non ritrova,	to square the circle and, for all his thought,
pensando, quel principio ond'elli indige,	cannot discover the principle he lacks,
tal era io a quella vista nova:	such was I at that strange new sight.
veder voleva come si convenne	I tried to see how the image fit the circle
l'imago al cerchio e come vi s'indova;	and how it found its where in it.
ma non eran da ciò le proprie penne:	But my wings had not sufficed for that
se non che la mia mente fu percossa	had not my mind be struck by a bolt
da un fulgore in che sua voglia venne.	of lightning that granted what I asked.
cA l'alta fantasia qui mancò possa;	Here my exalted vision lost its power.
ma già volgeva il mio disio e 'l velle,	But not my will and my desire, like wheels revolving
sì come rota ch'igualmente è mossa,	with an even motion, were turning with
l'amor che move il sole e l'altre stelle.	the Love that moves the sun and all the other stars.

Pietro sat for quite some time, looking that the words, gauging his feelings. At last he admitted the truth. Unthinkable as it was, Cesco had achieved the impossible, crafting a close to the epic that had seemed so horribly unfinished. And Pietro would never know how much of it was Cesco's puzzling of Dante's scattered musings and how much a child's innocent invention.

Some verses were far from perfect. There were references Cesco did not understand, as well a couple understood only by himself. But now, in tandem with Pietro and Antonia—the scholar-knight and the *de facto* publisher who knew her father's work better than anyone—he worked to hone these words. Pietro focused on meaning, Cesco on the poetics, and Antonia the final arbiter of what sounded Dantesque.

"You refer here to Bernardo as old," Antonia pointed out. "That violates the rule that no one in Paradise is older than Christ was at his death."

"I know, but Dante wrote it particularly," replied Cesco, hunting up the note. "See? 'Bernardo—Old Man'."

Antonia studied the note with a puzzled expression. "Why?"

Pietro attempted an answer. "Perhaps he's meant as God's substitute in that moment. He's the last of the father figures, and as he's acting for God, can he be more aged than the others?"

At another point, the objection was Pietro's. "Beatrice is Moses, and Dante is the Hebrews? Isn't that heretical?" Again a note was produced, and the issue was, if not resolved, set aside. It was ever their guiding principle— the poet's will.

Two weeks more of work. It consumed them, frustrated them, delighted them. They had never been more united in purpose and spirit. A time all three would look back upon with wonder and a profound sense of longing.

At last it was done. And, as they cast sand across the final page to dry the ink, they realized they, if they had not discovered Paradise themselves, they had at least emerged from their grief.

THE QUESTION AROSE, WHAT TO DO next? It was already known that the great epic was unfinished. To appear after months with a completed manuscript would be suspect.

As per usual, it was Cesco who hit upon the perfect answer. "Auntie Imperia—how skilled are you at forgery?"

The use of the hated 'Imperia' was deliberate. It was the title given her by Pietro's younger brother, Jacopo. Pietro smiled. "I think I'll send Poco an invitation to call."

"WHAT A FOOLE YOU ARE, BROTHER!" cried Poco. "You had the missing pages all along, and never even bothered to look!?!"

"We couldn't bear to go in there." Though the words were a lie, Pietro's annoyance was unfeigned. His slothful and debauched brother got under his skin quicker than a sliver, and was just as irritating.

"Can you imagine the uproar this will cause? The Scaliger will be delighted! Father always meant to dedicate this canticle to him. Perhaps you can even mend this false feud of yours—"

"That seems unlikely for some time yet," said Pietro pointedly. Cesco was within earshot.

Poco held up his hands. "I know, I know. But Verona is the place to be! I lament to think of you stuck here, in this sleepy backwater where nothing ever happens. What diversions could you ever possibly find here?"

"I agree with Uncle Jacopo," said little Cesco, grinning as he skipped towards the door. "What could we ever find to divert us here?"

AUTHOR'S NOTE TO PARADISO

A tale alluded to, both in FALCONER and DOOM. It takes place in 1321, between MoV and FALCONER.

This story was my original concept for this volume. It was originally entitled DXV. Those numbers in PURGATORIO were already significant, being one of Dante's cryptic prophecies. But I had to go and include it in Maria's message to Cesco at the end of FALCONER. A mother who saw her son's love of puzzles and, as her last earthly act, gave him one. One that has yet to be fully unraveled.

I know, it's hard to think of a seven year-old penning the end of the greatest epic since the AENEID. That's why I decided to use a trait that was in Cesco from the very beginning—his love of puzzles. Clearly he talked with Dante for years, and the great poet shaped his thoughts.

This is something that interests me about Cesco—what he adopts from those around him. We all imitate those who raise us, it's natural. But in Cesco, he has the imprint from Cangrande's sister, from Dante, Pietro, Antonia, and Tharwat. Then Cangrande. All before he's reached his teens. If his nature wasn't already mercurial…

Still, genius is genius. Poor Cesco really is more clever than those around him. Which is perhaps why the stars put such obstacles in his path. Otherwise he might dwindle, peak, and pine. He needs to strive to show himself to best effect.

In DOOM Cesco rejects the idea that suffering ennobles. To him, it just reveals the nature already within. This was the first time Cesco truly suffered. I think his reaction says a great deal about his character. Turning pain into art is, I think, one of the greatest things a human can do.

And in case anyone is wondering, no, there are no notes for what comes next in this series.

SERENISSIMA

FOR ROBERTA PEDEN

"Make not your thoughts your prisons."

—Octavius Caesar
Antony & Cleopatra
Act V Scene II

DARKNESS. IT WAS LIKE A WEIGHT, a burden, sitting on his chest, squeezing the air from Pietro's lungs like an invisible fist.

Those are Sunday bells. But which Sunday? He thought he had been here three weeks. Had he missed one? He thought not. But he was beginning to cease caring if he did—a worrying sign.

I am going mad. It was not a fearful thought. More an interesting one. *I am going mad. I wonder, will that make me a poet, like my father? Or a raving, spittle-flecked villain like Pathino?*

Perhaps this is my trial. Like Job. Only why would God bother, when I am out of His sight? Especially in darkness, excommunication hung heavily on him. For what excommunication, but to be outside of God's light?

Light. He wished they would allow light. Light, and perhaps paper. Marco Polo had dictated his travels while imprisoned. It would be a shame to have all this time, and nothing to show for it save madness.

Polo. His casa was not far from here. If he could pry free the metal grate on the floor and drop into the water below, he could swim there in about ten minutes. Unless he drowned.

"At this point, any escape would be welcome."

He was startled to hear a voice. It took him a moment to recognize it as his own. He did that, sometimes—spoke aloud without meaning to. It was a comfort to hear a voice, even if it came from his own throat. And it echoed so around the small chamber that it could be coming from anywhere, really.

Sometimes he provided dialogue for the rats that swarmed up from the grate to harass him. He wondered how long it would be before he ceased caring if they bit his toes and fingers. Part of him—a larger part than he cared to admit—was looking forward to that day. There was a kind of serenity in apathy.

"Serenity." The word echoed off the stone walls. "Serene." Again, the echo. "The most serene city."

Perhaps that was the secret of Venice. Apathy. A profound state of *lassiz-faire*, of fatalism, of ambivalence. Was that the source of the Serenissima's title? Was the root of serenity indifference?

Perhaps that was why Polo never left again, he thought. Perhaps while he'd seen the world he had cared too much, and returned home to cease caring. *I should ask him.* Again, he imagined swimming to the house, climbing up to knock upon the water door. Then he remembered that Polo was dead, had died nearly two years past. Another kind of escape.

"He is exploring Paradise now. I wonder if he will bring back any silks."

That made him laugh as he whittled away some moments imagining the colours of the silks of Heaven. Then, thoughts returning to Polo, he recalled ten years earlier, and the daughter who had sung. She would be twenty-two now, and married, most like. What was her name? Fantasia? Fatale?

Though he could not recall her name, he remembered the song's title. *Heart's Ease.* It had grown popular, and though he couldn't recall her name, he knew the words well. *Perhaps it will give me that gift. Heart's Ease.*

With that in mind, he began to sing, his voice bouncing back off the walls so that it sounded like a round, or a call and response song. Through the first two verses, he found the perfect timing and volume to avoid getting lost in the reverberation, and so he was able to embrace the story of the next verses:

Come, gallant, now! Come loiterer!
For I must chide with thee;
Bet yet I will forgive thee once:
Come sit thee down by me.
Fair lady, rest yourself content;
I will endure your punishment,
And then we shall be friends again.

For every hour that I have stay'd
So long from thee away,
A thousand kisses will I give;
Receive them, ready pay.
And if we chance to count amiss,
Again we'll reckon every kiss;
For he is blest that's punish'd so.

Unlike the song's first singer, Pietro did not raise his voice to a woman. He instead sang to light. The idea of it, the memory of it, the hope to have it again, feel its warmth on his face, have it again in his eyes so that he could appreciate colour, shape, movement...

Life. Light. "Let there be light," said God. Amazing how God's voice boomed.

Was that the nature of God? Was that what he was denied? His father had depicted God's love as a rose. Which was lovely. But to Pietro, God's love was light.

Blinded by darkness, the memory of light was cold comfort. But it was all the comfort he was allowed.

If God is light, then this must be Hell. Not torment, not torture. It is simply the lack of God. Which is darkness.

"Hell is darkness," Pietro heard a voice say.

"Darkness is ignorance." He didn't remember his mouth moving.

"Ignorance is bliss," the voice answered. "Therefore, Hell is bliss."

"But what is bliss, but peace?"

"Just so. And what is peace, but serenity?"

"So, at last, we discover a truth. *The* truth. Venice is Hell."

"Really? Then I am jilted. I thought I was your personal Lucifer."

And then Pietro recognized the voice. "How the hell did you get here?"

Cangrande chuckled. "Pietro, Pietro. Wherever you go, I am there. Whatever would you do without me?"

Pietro struggled to his feet. "Live. Really live. And happily, too." *How did Cangrande enter? Not through the door…*

"O no. You would dwindle, peak, and pine. You, my knight valiant, are the kind of man who shines best when faced with opposition. You require a foe, an intellectual nemesis. You need something to fight against—or at least resist, because you never do fight, do you?"

"Pathino might disagree," said Pietro harshly into the darkness. *He came up with the rats.*

"Oh, you'll fight someone else's battles, in someone else's cause. You fight for Cesco, as once you fought for me. You are defined by those to whom you pledge allegiance, not by yourself."

Through gritted teeth Pietro said, "I am my own man."

"Hardly. You don't fight me, just as you didn't fight your father. Isn't that true, poet?"

"Absolutely true," replied Dante from the shadows. "At least Jacopo I could respect. A drunken lecher, yes. A blot on my name. But he became that in order to counter my wishes, become his own man."

"An interesting phrase," said Cangrande. "I recall using it once to manipulate this young idiot. What, five years my junior, and ever in reverence? He should have been my peer, not my tool."

"Authority is his weakness," snarled Dante. "The wound at Vicenza is a perfect metaphor. He's weak in the hams for those in power. If he had been exiled, as I was, he would have begged forgiveness, pleaded for pardon. Look at him now. Excommunicated, and forever apologizing. I'm surprised he hasn't gone to Avignon to lick the dirt from the pope's crimson slippers."

"You are so right," echoed Cangrande. "He doesn't have the stomach for an open revolt. Instead he tries to keep me in check, trick me into doing the 'right thing', in spite of my nature. Who is he to say what is right? Who is he to be the arbiter of justice and holiness?"

"I'll tell you who he is," replied Dante. "He's an arrogant momma's boy."

Cangrande clucked his tongue. "Tch! That explains his puppy-eyed besottment with my sister. Even her perfidy couldn't sever those ties. Just as mine cannot make him cleave himself from me."

"Stop it!" shouted Pietro.

"You see?" snapped Dante. "Weak. A real man would fight back."

"But then a real man wouldn't be talking to himself," laughed Cangrande. "I see now I was correct in my latest posting. You are well-suited to being a judge. You are the most judgmental person in the world."

"And he judges no one more harshly than himself," said Dante.

"You are not here," said Pietro as he screwed up his eyes, creating lights behind them to counter the darkness.

"Of course we are," said Dante. "You let us in."

"Invited us, in fact," laughed Cangrande. "Because we define you."

"You do not!" shouted Pietro.

"No? Tell me, why are you a lawyer? Why the devoted foster-father? Knight. Bannerman. Judge. Everything you are, you are because of me."

"That's not true!"

"Oh, but it is! Where once you craved my praise, today you will become anything you must in order to foil me. For good or ill, you owe your being, your life, your self to me."

"Without you, lord, I am still myself."

Even in the dark, Pietro could see Cangrande's grin. "Here's hoping we never have cause to know."

Pietro was silent for a time. Dante whispered to Cangrande, "I think we've broken him." Cangrande laughed.

Perhaps it was that which caused Pietro to stand on his cut and bitten feet. "Thank you."

"What?" asked both older men.

"Thank you," said Pietro in a soft voice. "I'm grateful."

Cangrande snorted. "Gratitude is foxglove. It's Dog's Mercury. A fig for gratitude."

Straightening his back, Pietro took up a formal stance. "Father, I thank you for the gift of criticism. It made the moments when your pride shone through acutely real. My early life was defined by your absence. Now it is again. I miss you every day."

Dante did not answer. Perhaps he hadn't heard.

"You needn't act so formally, boy," snarled Cangrande's voice. "We're in the dark. No one knows if you're upright or no."

"I do," said Pietro. "I know. And that's what matters. Father was right. I am most judgmental where I myself am concerned. I hold myself to an exacting standard. I don't remember my successes. Only my failures. I'm not sure who taught me that, but it is who I am. I would not wish to change it."

"Even if it ties you into knots?" mocked Cangrande. "Even if it sometimes freezes you in a block of ice, keeping you from moving? Even if it spoils your every happy moment?"

"It is who I am."

"I see. And for what am I to be thanked?"

"For showing me the best and the worst of what a man can be. You're correct. We define ourselves both by what we are, and what we are not. For so long I've tried to counter you, I stopped listening to that inner voice of right and wrong. I've just tried to not be you. And in so doing, I became more like you than I am comfortable admitting. When Cesco was poisoned, I considered murdering a man. I was ready to do so. Tharwat stopped me by shaming me, reminding me of who I am supposed to be. Perhaps that's the definition of shame, a reminder of our better selves when we fail."

Limping, Pietro began to pace the small cell. He knew it so well by now he could sense where the domed roof began. "Who am I? A knight who vowed to live a life worth of respect and honour, to protect the innocent. Those words were my choice. That's the positive. Yes, you made me a knight. But I am the one who accepted. Would I be a different man without you in my life? Of course. Because through you I have experienced the trials that show me who I am. Who I can be. Who I could be. Who I may be. And who I must be.

"I must be better than I have been. I must live that life, and protect those I can. If I try my utmost, then I can live without shame. Can you say the same?"

Silence.

It was the first time he had won an argument with the Scaliger. Laughing, Pietro wished Cesco were here. He needed someone to share the jest with. And soon, or else he might not recognize the voices in his ears as his own…

No. I will not go mad. I will escape. I will gain my freedom, and then I will prove myself the knight I always claimed to be. I may die out of God's sight, but I will not die unable to look my reflection in the eye. I am the arbiter of my behaviour. No one else. No excuses. No madness. No pity.

And with that thought, Pietro found a calm inside himself. A certainty.

Serenity, discovered in the Most Serene City.

"Almost poetic," said his father from the darkness.

AUTHOR'S NOTE TO SERENISSIMA

This is clearly set during Pietro's imprisonment in the Doge's palace in 1325—between Chapters Forty-One and Forty-Two of FALCONER.

On a trip to Venice in 2005, my wife and I explored parts of that palace, and there is a photo of us together in a small chamber with an arched ceiling, lifting a plank and looking at the water below. That photo was the inspiration for Pietro's imprisonment. I liked the idea of isolation, of giving Pietro room and time to think. Because he is a thinker. Not in Cesco's way, or Cangrande's. He isn't given to hatching plots. No, Pietro is a philosopher. He considers the morality of every action, every thought. In many ways, he reminds me of my own father, whose own moral compass has a very strong north. As opposed to my own, which took a great deal of time finding the true direction to point...

I am often asked if I am my characters. Certainly there are bits of me in all of them—how else could I write them? I recognize each and every trait, for good or ill. But ever since my first attempt at a novel (which has still not seen the light of day), I have never been tempted to put myself into my stories. I am not as good as Pietro, nor as brilliant as Cesco, nor as charismatic as Cangrande.

This scene, however, hits close to home. When alone with my thoughts, I sometimes converse in my head, judging myself far more harshly than anyone in my life ever has. I don't relive past conversations, as I know some others do. I hold imaginary ones with people I know, whom I have wronged, or who have wronged me. I know I've given some of this to Cesco, and I think it's a very common—and human—practice. Certainly I see it in my own son. I hope for him these become fewer, grow farther between. They have for me. Perhaps that is a measure of assurance, that I can allow myself to be less judgmental.

That I might find a speck of serenity.

THE SUN, THE MOON

FOR RANIA MELHEM

PETRUCHIO
I say it is the moon.

KATHARINA
I know it is the moon.

PETRUCHIO
Nay, then you lie: it is the blessed sun.

KATHARINA
Then, God be bless'd, it is the blessed sun:
But sun it is not, when you say it is not;
And the moon changes even as your mind.

—*The Taming Of The Shrew*
Act IV Scene v

"IF WE HAVE TO HOUSE YOU, we may as well use you," growled Berthold von Neifen, Count of Marstetten.

A grim pronouncement, not received in the spirit it was intended. "Oh excellent! Shall I start with the soldiers and work my way up? Or is it like bathwater, nobles first?"

It took the one-eyed count a few moments to parse the lad's meaning. When he did, he scowled at the implication. If the imp hadn't been both princeling and hostage, he would have used the back of his hand. Instead he chose to ignore the words entirely. "You have proven yourself able to speak in public, and to recite from memory. If we wrote you a speech, could you speak it?"

"Of course," said Franz der Hund, making a curtsey. "I am a skillful parrot. But I should perform better *extempore*, from my own pure brain."

"I've seen," grunted Berthold. "But in this case, we may wish to be certain your words reflect our intents."

Clasping his hands behind his back, the thirteen year old stood blinking repeatedly in a mockery of attention. "And what are your intentions, my lord?"

In spite of himself, Berthold von Neifen laughed. "*Herrgott*, your marrow must be insolence."

"On the contrary, I am sure it's composed of good Germanic butter, adding flavour."

"You are too thin to be made of butter."

"I have been starved all my life," said Franz unseriously. "Of good food, good company, and good manners. Now that I am surrounded by manna, I feast upon joy like those in Paradise."

"You certainly are making a meal of us," said the Germanic nobleman, often called the Emperor's right hand.

It was true. In the seven months the heir to Verona had resided at the imperial court, he had become the darling of the intellectuals and artists who were always kept by great rulers, as if their thoughtfulness would rub off on their patron.

At this court, these elite thinkers served a very particular purpose. Since his recent excommunication, Emperor Ludwig felt more than ever he needed a long list of prominent names at his command. He would counter his infamy before God with a glowing wreath of famous faces, their earthly reputations bolstering his own.

This young fellow, not yet a man yet with a mind both too mature and eternally infantile, had stature on two separate tiers. The first was worldly— he was the heir to Cangrande della Scala, arguably the most formidable lord in Italy, whom the Emperor had dubbed *Der Hund*, to mock his self-aggrandizing title of Greyhound. Hence the lad Cesco was known at court as Franz der Hund.

The second tier was artistic—the boy had been raised at the knee of the poet Dante. It was this Berthold had decided to use. "Odd that you should mention Paradise. Heaven is in fact the argument we wish you to make."

"You want me to expand upon grandfather Dante's epic conclusion?" asked Franz, his eyes twinkling. "No one better."

"That, and a little more. We wish you to attend a symposium on *De Monarchia*. It will be led by Marsilius of Padua."

"I am ornamental?"

"More or less. When you speak, you will speak in support of Marsilius' statements."

"How could I not support them?" asked Franz innocently. "He stole them wholesale from grandfather Dante."

Berthold drew a long breath. "Remarks such as that prove me correct in scripting your remarks. You must at least understand the reason for this symposium. In four months the Emperor will enter Rome and be crowned, in defiance of papal authority. So we must refute this notion that the Emperor's power is derived from the Pope. You understand the argument?"

The gaze he received was frosty in the extreme. But Berthold was a man who had lost an eye because he had failed to flinch before worse threats than a child's pique. "Do you understand?"

Franz shrugged. "The sun, the moon."

"Just so. You have an interview with Marsilius tomorrow. The symposium will take place in the court the following day. Your behaviour at the former will determine your role in the latter." He paused. "I should note, your foster-father is reported to have his hearing before the Inquisition soon. If you are allowed to take part in this, it may cause him some discomfort."

Franz pulled a careless face. "He should be used to it by now."

MARSILIUS OF PADUA WAS OVER FIFTY, owning a kindly, paunchy face and tufts of hair on either side of his head, with a weak tuft perched atop it. It was the face of a kindly grandfather, not a great thinker.

Upon entering the doctor's chamber after morning prayers, Cesco had to bite back several cutting remarks. *You are no Dante.*

Neither are you a Morsicato. Hanging from the Paduan's neck was a *jourdan*, the urine glass worn by physicians. But the man had spent more time writing than healing. Cesco wouldn't let him lance a boil.

They had met several times in passing. Marsilius had been an imperial pet for over a year, ever since his anti-papal tract had earned him the Pope's enmity. A fixture of the court, very sensitive to Ludwig's moods, Marsilius had often complimented Cesco on his recitations from the great *Commedia*. But the pair had never conversed in any depth.

Welcoming him in, Marsilius now remarked as much, offering his apologies. "I don't want you to think it is due to your tender years. Clearly you are an uncommon young man."

"Clearly," said Cesco with a roll of his eyes. "I promise, it never entered my mind. I assumed it was because I am a hated Veronese, and any self-respecting Paduan would never be caught chin-chuntering with such vermin."

Marsilius laughed. "I am a man who believes in the unifying power of the prince. It is my opinion, as I think it was Dante's, that all cities should be ruled from a central location."

"So you'll state publicly that Padua should submit to Cangrande, the emperor's chosen vicar?"

"Of course," said the Paduan with a smile. "We must all acknowledge authority. It is the only path to peace. Now, before we go further, I must ask—do you prefer Franz, or Cesco? I have heard both."

"At court, I am Franz. In private, you may call me whatever you please."

"Thank you, Cesco."

"You're welcome, Marsilio."

"Marsilius," corrected the Paduan.

Cesco clapped his forehead in feigned stupidity. "Ah, of course! Forgive me. I have no Latin pretensions, myself. But I understand your need to distance yourself from the other Marsilio da Padua, he of the family Carrara. In truth, I don't think you've gone halfway far enough. If you want to distinguish yourself as Silius, make yourself grand! Be Super Silius!"

Marsilius was not affronted. Quite the reverse, he laughed aloud. "That would be silly of me, indeed, to describe my character so keenly. A writer should deal in truth through metaphor, not be so obvious. And besides, I have published under Marsilius. Imagine calling back all those copies, just to cross out Mar and inscribe Super in its stead. That would indeed mar my work."

Just like Berthold the day before, Cesco found himself laughing in spite of himself. "I like you, Marred-Silius. And that is a miracle."

Marsilius smiled beatifically. "Then let us perform another one and change the mind of the Church. Now please, you knew him in life, and surely know his work better than I ever will. What passage of De Monarchia sums up Dante's thoughts? Where do we begin?"

"Peace be with you," said Cesco simply.

At once Marsilius lifted pages from a copy of De Monarchia, found the passage in question, and began to read:

"'Since it is true that whatever modifies a part modifies the whole, and that the individual man seated in quiet grows perfect in knowledge and wisdom—'"

"That is not my experience," remarked Cesco.

"'—it is plain that amid the calm and tranquility of peace the human race accomplishes most freely and easily its given work.'"

"I do my best work when things are least peaceful."

"'How nearly divine this function is revealed in the words, 'Thou hast made him a little lower than the angels.''"

"Only a little?"

"'Whence it is manifest that universal peace is the best of those things which are ordained for our beatitude.'" Marsilius paused for Cesco to scoff, but was greeted only with a polite expression. "'And hence to the shepherds sounded from on high the message not of riches, nor pleasures, nor honours, nor length of life, nor health, nor beauty; but the message of peace. For the heavenly host said, 'Glory to God in the highest, and on earth peace among men in whom he is well pleased.''"

Cesco finished the passage from memory. "'Likewise, 'Peace be unto you' was the salutation of the Saviour of men. It befitted the supreme Saviour to utter the supreme salutation.'"

"Yes. Peace. And the best argument for a single temporal authority is the example of the Pax Romana. It is the closest we have ever come. But how can we make the case for contemporary power to be invested in the Emperor rather than the Pope?"

"I have an answer for that. One that the Church can hardly denounce." He explained, and Marsilius was well pleased.

"Oh, that is excellent! Yes, by all means, say that. But I am also wondering how best to refute the argument of the Sun and the Moon."

The view from the Holy See was that God's power on earth flowed through the Pope, who was the sun, and that imperial power only came through the grace of the Pope, making the Emperor the moon—his light was reflected, not intrinsic. This was the view that needed to be challenged. Dante and done it in his piece *De Monarchia*, and Marsilius had followed suit recently with his tract *Defensor Pacis*.

Cesco began to laugh. Marsilius blinked with open question on his face. "What did I miss?"

"Only an ongoing argument between husband and wife. In fact, a Veronese husband and his Paduan wife. You have been gone so long, perhaps you have not heard of Katerina Minola."

"I have!" cried Marsilius. "Eldest daughter of Baptista. I knew him as a boy. What was it she was called?"

"*La Megera*," replied Cesco. "A title she has now embraced, in jest. Once upon a time, the story goes, Petruchio and Katerina were to visit her father's house for the wedding of her sister. At noontime along their way, Petruchio remarked how bright the moon was shining. His wife corrected him, and he threatened to turn back home unless she said it was the moon. After several minutes of squabbling, she decided it cost her nothing to call the sun the moon. Whereupon he called her a liar, and said it was the sun. She expressed amazement and said he was right, she had been blind not to see it. From that day she has mocked him by asking what the thing in the sky is upon any given day."

Marsilius was smiling in a thoughtful way. "Did they finish the journey?"

"They did."

"So they found peace."

"Yes."

"Through submission," said Marsilius. "I am not sure if that aids our cause."

"Ah, it only appeared to be submission to the untutored eye. It was mockery. Her sons have told me the couple that day established the rules for the game they will play the rest of their lives. There is today no more loving couple on earth."

"Peace through mockery, you say."

"Yes," said Cesco, his eyes twinkling.

"It is novel," said Marsilius thoughtfully.

"And you can hardly be more excommunicated than you already are." With that observation, it quickly became a lively morning as they settled in to plan the following day.

BERTHOLD ORDERED THE DOORS OPENED early, the better for men to take their places before the imperial family's entrance. Ludwig and his close kin would be seated upon a long stage, with a low chair at the far end for the Veronese prince. The Paduan doctor-philosopher had a lectern behind which he would stand. Regality was the desired effect. It was the purpose of their entrance into this divided and divisive land—seeing the Emperor crowned.

Everyone was in place when the trumpets blared and Ludwig strode in, looking bland. Berthold knew that expression, and who had caused it. The emperor's two nephews, here to make peace and hopefully regain their father's lost rights. The elder of them was docile enough. But the younger, just eighteen years of age, was as outspoken as he was irreverent. *Much like the Scaligeri heir.*

Berthold's eyes fell upon that particular lad, standing until the Emperor was settled upon his throne. He looked placid. Too placid. *If you embarrass the Emperor as you did your sire, I will have your toenails torn out and then have you walk to Rome.*

It began formally, with Marsilius thanking the Emperor upon his throne, greeting the courtiers and nobility with measured tones and deep sweeping bows. Not a natural performer, the Paduan did well enough, keeping men's attention if not commanding it.

Through those opening minutes Franz der Hund was uncommonly still, looking almost bored as he waited to recite his dutiful piece. Berthold von Neifen watched in grim satisfaction. *Good. He means to behave.*

Marsilius reading from his own tract defending peace was followed by Franz standing to recite a Dantean piece on monarchs, and the value of peace. Finished, he sat again without any trouble.

Thinking the lad's portion was complete, Berthold made the mistake of relaxing.

As soon as Marsilius switched to challenge the papal argument of reflected light, the Veronese prince showed the feared independence. Rising, he interrupted Marsilius. "My lords, some things are better seen than heard. Allow me to illustrate." He leapt upon his chair at the end of the platform, arms held wide. "I am the sun! Behold!" He pointed at the Emperor. "You take your light from me, as the moon does the sun!"

Before anyone else could object or intervene, Marsilius demanded, "Do you mean to say you are papal?"

"I do. I am the source of God's light on earth, the sole authority. Like the sun, I shine on you all constantly."

"Then why does the moon wane?" asked Marsilius.

"Because sometimes I turn my back on the imperial throne." Franz did this in dramatic fashion. The Emperor's nephew, seated just behind the 'sun', chortled in his sleeve. In the center of the platform, Ludwig looked unamused.

Zum Donnerwetter! thought Berthold, bracing himself to end the symposium there and then.

Marsilius pressed on. "So you are changeable."

"As my mood dictates," agreed Franz.

"Like a woman."

"What?" said Cesco in mock dismay.

Marsilius ticked off points on his fingers. "You have fits of pique, just like a woman. What's more, if you are the sun to the imperial moon, your light changes just as a woman's cycle, monthly! And you go down at night—just like a good woman. So the papacy is the feminine to the imperial masculine!"

Laughter now, as everyone began to see this show had been staged. Even Emperor Ludwig was no longer frowning. His lugubrious lips began to twitch with mirth.

"I am no woman," insisted Franz der Hund in a huff. "For women are the originators of sin, and I am the redemption. I am the stuff of Paradise!"

"Just like a woman," said Marsilius with a very-staged wink. A roar of laughter.

"I am a man!" cried Franz.

"Who forswears women and keeps the company of other men," observed Marsilius dryly.

In answer, Franz made a series of exasperated gestures that had the imperial court laughing aloud. But Marsilius pressed on. "If the earth is the house of the Lord our God, then the papacy is not the sun to the imperial moon. It is the wife, the caretaker, who mends and sews and cooks. Only its chore is to mend men's souls, sew their spirits, and cook their sins.

"Thus is the Emperor the husband, the man, both provider and protector. It is he who must defend the house, see to its prosperity, and—most important of all—keep the peace. Peace is essential. Man will only prosper through peace. If the house is calm, the wife may do her duties unmolested. But if the house should burn, the wife has no home at all.

Franz now stepped down, abandoning his role as papal wife to exclaim, "It is the duty of the Emperor to keep this earthly realm under his protection. His strength does not come from the papacy. Rather, it is the imperial strength that allows the papacy to continue its work."

"And what of the sun and the moon?" asked Marsilius.

"At night, when things are black, the sky is littered with unnumbered sparks," replied Franz. "There is only one moon, hanging there, changeable, cold and distant. Does that sound like the Emperor, whose matter is here on earth? No, to me that sounds more like the Pope. Visible at night when all is black, his light may be reflected, but it comes from God."

"Which makes God Himself is the sun," agreed Marsilius. "What is the Emperor, then?"

"The third part of our trinity," said Franz.

"Yes!" cried Marsilius, pretending to understand for the first time. "God, the sun. The Holy Spirit, the moon. Both focus their light upon us—the earth. The son. Christ, divinity made flesh. It is through Christ we are saved. Christ came to earth, therefore the earth is the third part of this trinity."

"Yes," declared Franz. "The Emperor is the land beneath us, the mountains above us. He is the world, and his domain is worldly. God's light shines upon us during the day, and Satan has power at night. It is up to the Emperor to defend us, while the Pope raises our eyes to that long night, that eternal sleep, when our souls ascend to the heavens, to those million million sparks of light above, the pinholes in night's curtain through which Heaven peeps."

Now the murmurs were not amused but impressed. The lad had clearly been raised at a poet's knee. But the counterpoint to the papal argument was sound, it felt firm. Moreover, he had painted the pope as womanish, while at the same time portraying the Emperor as both masculine and Christ-like.

Berthold was grudgingly pleased. Standing beside the imperial throne, he squinted his one eye at the pair, wondering whose idea this had been. He thought he knew.

As the rustles and murmurs subsided, Marsilius cross to the far end of the raised platform and turned to face Franz. "From the mouth of babes. And what do you say to the notion that the Emperor's realm is connected to the Pope's? That the earth owes homage to the moon?"

"I say that Christ himself refuted this. Did he not say, 'Render to Caesar the things that are Caesar's, and to God the things that are God's.' How should we know which belonged to which, unless they are indeed separate? The temporal realm, this earth, is the authority of the Emperor, while the realm of the spirit belongs to the Pope. Christ himself spoke this. Who are we to—"

"Christ speaks through me!!!" cried a man standing in the crowd at Cesco's end of the platform. Throwing off his cloak, he leapt onto the low dais even as he hurled a silver knife end over end at Marsilius, while at the same moment stabbing at Franz, nearer at hand, still perched atop his chair.

It was a close thing, all later agreed. The blade would have pierced the boy's breast had not one of the imperial family leapt forward to drag the arm down. So much force it had that it pierced the imperial scion's thigh above the knee.

Berthold was in motion even before the first knife was loosed. He saw it narrowly miss Marsilius, who had dived with alacrity for the ground. Berthold's sword cleared its scabbard and was swinging downwards in the flash of an eye. He used the flat of the blade, shattering the assassin's arm rather than severing it. He looked first to see that the Emperor was guarded, then scanned the roiling crowd for new threats.

There were none. As the man was dragged away and the injured fellow was helped from the hall, the Emperor strode forward to take command. "Well! An exciting conclusion to a lively debate. I feel that we might have hit a little close to the heart," he added, grinning through his beard. "You always know you're speaking truth when someone tries to cut out your tongue. Marsilius, Franz—I thank you both."

As the Emperor departed, Marsilius made straight for the young heir of Verona. "Thank Heaven! Tell me you're not hurt!"

The young man's eyes twinkled. "Not even scratched. Which is more than I can say for the fellow who rescued me. Who is he?"

"The Emperor's nephew," said Marsilius, wiping his brow. "He's called Rupert."

THE IMPERIAL NEPHEW WAS STANDING with his blood-stained hose around his ankles as a doctor applied a poultice to the cut, both under the single eye of Berthold von Neifen. "You are fortunate, my lord," said the imperial physician, "it is not deep."

"Oh, nevermind then," said a voice from the door. "I thought he had done a heroic thing. But if it is only a scratch, I'll keep my apology for one who needs it."

Both Berthold and Rupert saw the languid figure who, despite his words, did not leave his doorframe. Rupert pressed his lips together and whistled. "Not the gratitude I would expect from a hound's puppy."

"O, forgive me!" cried Franz, striding nearer. "Should I lick you all over your face?"

"Franz der Hund!" snapped Berthold even as Rupert laughed. "Watch your tone! You address a scion of imperial blood. This is Rupert, younger son to the Duke of Bavaria, nephew to the Emperor and grandson of King Adolf of Nassau-Weilburg."

"Estranged nephew," corrected Rupert.

"Eh? Strange?" asked Franz quizzically. "What, are you touched?"

"I must be," said Rupert, "to have saved the son of Cangrande."

"Estranged son," said Franz.

"Eh? Strange?" asked Rupert quizzically. "What, are you touched?"

"I must be," said Franz. "To let myself be saved by Rupert the Red."

"The Red?" asked Rupert, flushing even as he spoke. His cheeks were famously quick to crimson.

"For your temper," said Franz with a laugh.

"Tempt her?" retorted Rupert. "What, am I the serpent Satan?"

"The serpent's taint," replied Franz.

Rupert grinned. "Where does one find the serpent's taint?"

"Between hissss legs, of course."

Though there was a gulf of years between them, they were perfectly matched in temperament. As both laughed, and Berthold von Neifen groaned. "Oh dear lord! Just what this court requires, vying jesters. If you'll excuse me, my young masters, I have an assassin to interrogate and some fooles to dismiss—we clearly won't be needing them."

"You won't need to interrogate the assassin either," said Franz lightly.

That halted Berthold. "No? Do you know him? Is he one of your sire's foes?"

"No, I've never seen him before. But I think you'll find him claiming to have come straight from Avignon."

"To murder Marsilius of Padua," said Berthold, stating the obvious.

"I think that's what he'll claim, at any rate."

Berthold scoffed. "What—do you believe he was here for *you*?"

"I think he'll say not."

"Then what are you gabbling about?"

When Franz made no reply, Rupert filled the gap. "I think he means that you're going to be told a plausible tale that is far from the truth. But that the truth will be impossible to prove."

"And what truth is that?" demanded Berthold.

Franz and Rupert exchanged a look, then both stared at the doctor, who had just wrapped Rupert's wound. The man was dismissed, the door was shut, and Berthold repeated, "What truth is that?"

Rather than answer, Franz tossed a careless question to Rupert. "What is a hero?"

Rupert looked puzzled. "A foole? Or—no, a victor."

Franz nodded. "And who is victorious?"

"The righteous, naturally."

"And who is naturally righteous?"

"He who does right."

"Who determines what's right?"

"God."

"Where does one find God?"

"In Paradise."

"And, as we noted a few minutes ago, what is a man's earthly paradise?"

"A woman," said Rupert with such an over-eager leer.

"And where do a man and woman live?"

"In a home."

"And if a man lives in a home and wishes to seek Paradise when he dies, whom must he serve?"

"Two masters," said Rupert with dawning comprehending.

"The sun, and the moon," agreed Franz.

Berthold had followed this exchange with mounting frustration. "What are you two on about?"

Rupert turned to his estranged uncle's favoured councilor. "I think a little mining would reveal the assassin was hired by Marsilius himself to murder my strange young friend here."

Berthold opened his lips to object, then recalled Marsilius' quick fall to the earth when the dagger was thrown. Almost as though he had known it was coming. Marsilius? That meek, clear, inoffensive scribbler? Damn.

Rather than protest an idea he felt was true, Berthold attempted to digest it. Such things were always more palatable with reasons. "Why?"

Again it was Rupert who answered—he seemed to be showing off for the Veronese. "While the doctor-philosopher is very much the Emperor's man, he is also a Paduan. The death of the Greyhound's heir at the hands of a papal assassin serves two objectives—first, drives Cangrande further into Uncle Ludwig's camp, with the added benefit of a vengeful spirit. Second, it removes the next in line in Verona, always to Padua's good. Marsilius is beholden to both the Emperor and Padua, and meant to serve both."

"By serving my head upon a platter," added Franz with a smile.

Rupert snorted. "If that were the case, he must needs trade his gonella for a gown."

"A sight that might indeed murder me with laughter," answered Franz.

Berthold scowled at both guffawing princes. "I fail to see amusement in accusing one of the Emperor's favourites of attempted murder. This will cause great embarrassment, and more complications."

"Yes," agreed Franz. "It would."

"If," added Rupert.

"Yes," repeated Franz. "If."

"If?" echoed Berthold.

"*If* that was what I were accusing him of doing," said Franz.

"Which he is not," said Rupert.

"Which I most definitely am not," agreed Franz, his smile a trifle fixed as his eyes grew more intent upon the single eye that gazed back.

Berthold was never given to extraneous movement. Yet he seemed to grow entirely still under that glare. He doubted his heart was even beating. "I do not understand. A man attempts to take your life and you wish to leave him be?"

Franz and Rupert exchanged a knowing look.

"First," said the younger one, "what you said before is paramount.

The Emperor must not be embarrassed."

"Second," said the elder, "if you know an enemy is an enemy, and he does not know you know—well, there is advantage to be had."

"Yes," said Franz brightly. He, too, seemed to be preening for the other, like a bird does its feathers when in competition. "I like knowing my enemies are close. Feels like home."

Berthold scowled. "I cannot allow a man to make a false confession."

"How like Ser Alaghieri you are!" cried Franz. "Honest to a fault. And trust me, it is a fault. Besides, what's false? He attacked when I spoke against the papacy. Surely that is enough to damn him without you condoning perjury."

"Indeed, Berthold," said Rupert, restoring his bloodied hose to cover his legs and standing. "Tell my uncle the truth, if you must. He will not thank you. He is a man for whom the truth must be palatable, or far from his ears." The imperial prince held out his arm to Franz. "Come. Shall we see if this arm will sustain a tankard or two? Or are you still on your mother's milk?"

Rising, Franz's laugh disguised a slight flutter of anger. Was it because of one dig too many at his age? Or was it the mention of his mother? Regardless, it was gone so swiftly it might have never been. "Mother's milk, of course! But she was a small-breasted women. Not proper melons, mere grapes, and old ones at that."

"So you suckle upon the vine," snorted Rupert. "I'm certain we can find you some. Come, shall we go?"

Watching the pair saunter off, cocks of the walk, Berthold feared what havoc had been unleashed. Two disgruntled heirs to secondary empires, both of them full of their own wit and daring, both of them eager to impress the world, both of them ready to burn that world down rather than be proven wrong, or weak, or wanting.

But one was imperial, the other provincial. The sun, and the moon. What would happen when the moon began to resent sunlight, and decided to rebel?

"God help us all."

AUTHOR'S NOTE TO THE SUN, THE MOON

This occurs during Cesco's time as both guest and hostage at the imperial court of Ludwig IV of Bavaria, in between Chapters Twenty-One and Twenty-Two of FORTUNE'S FOOL.

In DOOM Cesco remarks that Rupert once saved his life. I wanted to show that moment, as it will come to matter more in years to come.

Obviously the sun and moon argument comes from Kate and Petruchio in *The Taming Of The Shrew*. But it was also a very real theological debate about the role of the Holy Roman Emperor, and from where he got his power. Dante, who had been exiled by a party that supported the papacy, naturally took the opinion that imperial power was separate from the Church. DE MONARCHIA caused a stir, but nothing like the acclaim of L'INFERNO. And, unlike his great epic, Dante wrote his seditious anti-papal piece in Latin, intending it for scholars, not the public.

In 1324, Marsilius of Padua followed Dante's lead, writing his work IN DEFENCE OF PEACE. It caused more of a stir than Dante's had, and certainly endeared Marsilius to Ludwig. The Paduan journeyed with the Emperor for the coronation, and continued to be a part of his court until 1342. There is nothing marking him a villain, and indeed his portraits are placid and cheerful. He is the most innocent-looking fellow. Which in my world makes him capable of even greater perfidies. But never without cause.

I imagine we'll see him again. Much as ILLYRIA became the introduction to another book, look for this story to reappear in a future volume. We are not done with the imperial court, Marsilius, or Rupert.

THE HYBLA BEES

FOR FARRELL FREUND

"But for your words, they rob the Hybla bees,
and leave them honeyless."

—Cassius
Julius Caesar
ACT V SCENE I

VERONA, ITALY
THURSDAY, 4 SEPTEMBER 1328

THOUGH SUMMER WAS PAST, THE LIGHT still lingered into evening. A frustration, as it meant the lovers could not meet until very late—they had to take care not be seen together until their wedding.

Fortunately, they only wanted to be seen by each other.

They met at street-level for once—Cesco's broken fingers made climbing awkward, and Lia said she did not want to inhibit his recovery.

"I'm grateful," he said, his nose against hers, his chest against hers, his legs against hers. "Surprised, but grateful."

She moved her mouth to his ear. "Why surprised?"

"You have never been one to give up an advantage."

"True," she murmured. "But I have other uses for that hand."

Which left him cursing his injury once again.

This had not been their plan. They had agreed not to meet again until their wedding day. But being in the same city, with nothing to do at night but pine, had proven too much. Cesco had sent a teasing note:

> Death, cruel mistress, relent,
> Let Lia out to play,
> That I might die in her lap,
> Forever there to stay.

She had responded in kind:

> The Foole who courts Death
> Shall find it his too soon
> And of Man's many failings
> Quick dying makes no maid swoon.

His answer was pointed:

> Then No Maid should the Foole find
> Out of hope, of breath, of mind
> Where first they spoke without disguise
> Where Romans fought under the skies.

Thus, in the shadowed arches of Verona's famous Arena, Lia found Cesco, loitering in the darkness, composing a sonnet to his mistress' eyebrow.

"My eyebrow?"

"I want to leave no part of you unremarked." He pulled her close. "Or untouched."

He had a room nearby, ready for them, and as she undressed him, he recited the ode to her brows, kissing them in turn between each verse. "My plucked Rose, could I love you any lessly?"

"Lessly?"

"Shh. Language that is static is dead. It's a truth my grandfather knew."

"It's funny."

"Sad, I think."

"No. Whenever you refer to Dante, you call him grandfather, even when it isn't true."

"It isn't fact," said Cesco. "But it is true. Now hush, the poem is growing cold."

"If it doesn't, I will. And I can think of better things your mouth could be doing."

The broken hand made some things difficult. But they were young, eager, and inventive. They made do.

Afterwards, as they lay in the tangled sheets, sweating in the warm stillness of the night, Lia nestled into the crook of his wiry arm, Cesco recited:

> *Now my will and my desire, like wheels revolving*
> *with an even motion, were turning with*
> *the Love that moves the sun and all the other stars.*

Lia recognized the quote, as he'd known she would. "Paradiso."

He kissed the top of her head. "My point exactly."

"Is that where we shall live?"

"Yes," he sighed, drawing her close, reveling in the feel of her skin against his. "In the rose of paradise, filled with God's love. Like the blessed, we shall be seated on the petals for all eternity, with angels flitting about like the Hybla bees."

"Not the Hybla bees!" she protested, slapping his chest.

"Whyever not? Their honey is said to be the sweetest."

She made a rude noise. "That may be. I've never tasted it. But you're forgetting the legend of Glaucus."

"The idiot son of King Minos who fell in a vat of honey?" Cesco certainly had not forgotten the story. It just seemed irrelevant. His good hand found employment. "What of him? Are you saying I will drown in too much sweet?"

Lia moved his wandering hand. "Hardly. Remember, a wise man finds the boy's body when he spies an owl keeping the bees away from the vat. Just as the soul was kept from his body."

"So we'll infuriate Athena and keep no owls," said Cesco, nuzzling her neck.

She turned her head. "The bees symbolize a soul kept from its body."

"Ah, but like Glaucus himself, you forget," said Cesco, pressing her insistently, "it's a flower that brings him back to life. And who is it that brings fruitfulness to the flower? The lowly Hybla bee." Pressing his lips to her ear, he made a low buzzing noise that made her want to laugh. But what his hand was doing was more pressing, invading her senses, making her arch, shiver, and coil all at once. Then she laughed aloud as he rolled atop her and began, ridiculously, to sing a child's song about bees in time with the movement of his body.

Mid-laugh, Lia snorted in a most unladylike manner that left her horrified. "What are you doing?"

"Don't you know?" he asked innocently. Then he grinned. "I'm trying not to die too soon. I hear that no maid likes it."

"And I am no maid," she answered, pulling his shoulders closer with both hands.

After that, talking ended—though Cesco did buzz from time to time, which set them both to laughing.

He awoke to sunlight, which sent him into a panic. But the bed was empty. She was gone, returned to the convent where she was staying until the wedding could be announced.

In her place, she had left him a scrap of paper, folded corner to corner, and again, until it formed a flower. A rose.

Opening the first petal revealed a joyful note:

> This is a note of Celebration,
> Of Love, and of Poetry.
> It takes so little to make me smile now,
> Because of thoughts of you, my love.

> Let us celebrate every hour, on the hour,
> The celebration of the anniversary
> Of the hour just past.

Another petal turned back revealed something more earthy:

> I am your Rose, my wicked bee,
> And however oft you sting,
> You may buzz my petals,
> Deflowering me again and again.

A third petal brought prose to light, the words cramped together:

> It will never leave, the stranglehold you have wrapped around my heart. I imagine any aspect of you, and I am cheerfilled. It is a new way to experience time, and light, and breath, to miss you the way I do. I am missing you already, here beside you, in anticipation of the gaping maw I will feel when you are gone from me.

The final petal revealed her ultimate thought:

> My love for Mercutio
> Is never-changing.
> Mercutio's love for me
> Is never-ending.
> Is not that strange?

Cesco did not know why his eyes were full of water. Never in his life had he been so joyful. So content. So unmercurial. She was correct. It was strange. And wonderful.

Looking at the paper flower, he realized he'd been wrong. They would not reside in Dante's rose, for he was there already. He would play the Hybla bee, and bring nothing but sweetness into the life of his beloved Rose.

Rosalia. Cesco's rose of Paradise.

AUTHOR'S NOTE TO THE HYBLA BEES

This takes place somewhere in the middle of Chapter Forty-One of Fool, before Cesco sets out for Venice for the signing of the Pax Verona.

It is too easy to write Cesco and Lia. I don't know why—perhaps because they are so well matched. I find myself smiling whenever I put them together. So when I realized I'd foolishly ignored the symbol of God's love from Paradiso in all their interactions (what on earth was I thinking?), I leapt at the chance to include it here.

The story of Glaucus is a strange one, and absurdly complex. From Mary A. Grant's translation of Apollodorus:

> One day Glaucus, while playing with a ball or chasing a mouse, fell into a jar of honey and thus he died.
>
> Unable to find their son, his parents went to the Oracle at Delphi who told them "A marvelous creature has been born amongst you: whoever finds the true likeness for this creature will also find the child." They interpreted this to refer to a newborn calf in Minos' herd. Three times a day, the calf changed color from white to red to black. Polyidus observed the similarity to the ripening of the fruit of the mulberry (or possibly the blackberry) plant, and Minos sent him to find Glaucus.
>
> Searching for the boy, Polyidus saw an owl driving bees away from a wine-cellar in Minos' palace. Inside the wine-cellar was a cask of honey, with Glaucus dead inside. Minos demanded Glaucus be brought back to life, though Polyidus objected. Minos was justified in his insistence, as the Delphic Oracle had said that the seer would restore the child alive. Minos shut Polyidus up in the wine-cellar with a sword. When a snake appeared nearby, Polyidus killed it with the sword. Another snake came for the first, and after seeing its mate dead, the second serpent left and brought back a herb which then brought the first snake back to life. Following this example, Polyidus used the same herb to resurrect Glaucus.
>
> Minos refused to let Polyidus leave Crete until he taught Glaucus the art of divination. Polyidus did so, but then, at the last second before leaving, he asked Glaucus to spit in his mouth. Glaucus did so and forgot everything he had been taught.

The story of Polyidus and Glaucus was the subject of a lost play attributed to Euripides. Glaucus later led an army that attacked Italy, introducing to them the military girdle and shield, which was the source of his Latin name, Labicus, meaning "girdled".

Like Glaucus, Cesco forgot to divine how this relationship would end. But for this one stolen moment, their life is sweeter than the honey of the Hybla bees.

They have not yet felt the sting.

LADY IN WAITING

FOR NANCY TYRREL THEODORE

"Their aunt I am in law, in love their mother.
Then bring me to their sights. I'll bear thy blame
And take thy office from thee, on my peril."

—Lady Anne
Richard III
ACT IV, SCENE I

"Would'st thou have that
Which thou esteem'st the ornament of life,
And live a coward in thine own esteem,
Letting 'I dare not' wait upon 'I would,'
Like the poor cat i' the adage?"

—Lady Macbeth
The Tragedy Of Macbeth
ACT I, SCENE VII

IN THE NOGAROLA PALACE, THE LADIES were gathered in the Great Hall around Katerina della Scala. The first lady of Vicenza was seated beside a fire, her loom in her lap. It was clearly not easy, working a loom with only one useful hand. But she had devised a system that kept her occupied. Her ladies-in-waiting had once made every effort to work as slowly as she, but she had no patience for such nonsense. So now they sat on the benches in the early evening air and worked industriously.

To entertain them as they wove, Katerina had asked son, ten year-old Valentino, to read to them from a collection of poetry. His youthful voice high and uncertain, he squinted in the torchlight as he struggled with the rhythm of a stanza by Guido Cavalcanti:

We sad, despondent quills,
sorrowing scissors and knife
have written in anguish
these words you've heard.

Now we speak to you leaving
and coming to your presence:
the hand moving us feels
doubtful things appear in the heart—

So destroying him,
so taking him near death,
so but to sigh...

We ask you how much stronger we must be
that you don't disdain us—
until you look with a little pity.

Valentino looked up from the pages. "I don't understand. What's it about?"

Katerina smiled at him, making sure she did not lift her mouth on its right side higher than her stroke-felled left. "Love."

"That again," sighed Valentino, earning sly smiles from the ladies-in-waiting. "Can't I read from *L'Inferno* instead?"

"No horror-shows tonight," chided Katerina. "Even Maestro Dante started with love poetry." Valentino looked skeptical, but turned to another page. The ladies continued to work their fabric. Idle hands, after all.

Among them was a new young lady, ward to a wealthy Vicenzian trader who had bought nobility just before his untimely expiration. Just two months earlier he had married well, to a wealthy Paduan widow with a teenaged daughter. Suddenly widowed a second time, the lady was reportedly too busy managing the traders estates to present herself properly. In her stead she had sent her child to introduce the family to Vicenza's nobility and pay homage to the chatelaine of their new home.

Katerina studied the young lady with mild interest. She was still growing into her features, which could go either direction—she might be a beauty, she might be a horse. With that wicked widow's peak and reddish hair around her slightly chubby face, she would always catch the eye.

The girl's name continued to amuse Katerina. "Tell me, Vincenza, how do you find Vicenza?"

Vincenza smiled politely. "I found it on a map."

Katerina laughed, knowing she had already been measured by the young woman. Another lady might have taken the answer as insolence. But not Katerina, who prized wit. "And are you at home here?"

Vincenza blinked her long lashes. "How could I be at home? This palace does not belong to me."

"It could," said Katerina airily, waving her gloved hand towards her son. "All you need do is convince Valentino that there is merit in love poetry."

"Is that all?" asked Vincenza.

"That, and make him compose some for you. For I swear, the woman who convinces him to grow poetic is destined to be his bride."

Val scowled in the face of such a doubtful concept. "I'm never going to be *poetic*."

Several years his elder, Vincenza was not insulted. She lowered her eyes. "Even if I had the ability, I could never make such a match, my lady. I have done nothing to deserve it."

"Oh!" exclaimed Katerina. "If we got only what we deserved, this would be an intolerably boring world indeed."

She was about to continue her teasing of the latest member of her retinue when a noise caught her attention. Hearing the approaching footstep, Valentino looked hopefully for an interruption and was rewarded as Katerina's steward stepped beyond the pillars and into the atrium. "Madonna?"

"Yes? Has one of the dogs given birth?" There were always pregnant bitches in a Scaligeri household.

"No, Donna. Master Bailardetto has arrived."

"Detto!" cried Val, joyfully abandoning Cavalcanti and leaping up.

At once the ladies set aside their labours and rose as Valentino's brother strode into the Great Hall. Only Katerina remained seated—if infirmity was an excuse, it was not the reason. She did not care to rise to greet any but her superiors. Of which she had few.

Bailardetto Nogarola was a strapping young man of thirteen, but his size made him look older. With a broad-shouldered father and an uncommonly tall mother, Detto was likely to be both. Unlike Val, who was bird-boned, Detto appeared already to be a pillar of strength. Combined with his dark hair, he might have been a forbidding figure, were it not for his open and ingenuous face. Here was plainly writ his delights and his sorrows, his dreams and his torments. Years of company with his wild cousin may have taught him how to dissemble upon occasion. But it was not in his nature to be false.

"What an unexpected pleasure," said Katerina from her seat. She held out her hand, and he approached to kiss it before bowing to his mother and her ladies. "What brings you to us this night?"

"On my way from Padua my horse threw a shoe." Rising out of his bow, Detto stepped back, unconsciously lifting his toes to stretch muscles that ached from riding. A dog appeared, then another, and soon all the palace hounds were around them, snuffling at their favourite master. Detto always had a way with animals.

"I am saddened to hear it took a lame steed to bring you home." Katerina snapped her fingers and gestured for the servants to remove the dogs. "But I will take whatever occasion I can. Come, sit. Tell us the news from Padua and Verona. I hope there is no evil meaning in your journey to Padua. Is the peace holding? Will the double wedding proceed as planned?"

"The peace is holding," said Detto. "The wedding is happening." He did not sound pleased, but resigned.

"You relieve my mind. Then what was the purpose of your visit?"

"To exchange tokens between Cesco and his bride. He is staying in Padua, but–" Detto shook his head. "I couldn't. I just couldn't."

The lady was cool in her comfort. "I hope you mean no insult to Padua. After all, we are all now united. In fact, you have not met the newest member of my retinue. This is Vincenza. She and her mother are both from Padua."

Detto bowed, Vicenza curtsied. Neither made eye contact.

"Her mother married Boco Pigafetta, who made so much money speculating in spices. Unhappily, theirs was the briefest of unions. Pigafetta died just a few weeks after the wedding. Which leaves Vincenza's mother—forgive me, my girl, I have forgotten her name."

"Fiametta, lady."

"Lady Fiametta twice a widow, and twice as wealthy. I have been attempting to foist Vincenza upon Val here, but he is of an age where her prefers the sword in his hand to the one in his codpiece. But you are older. Perhaps you have learned the pleasures of both."

Katerina watched with amusement the scandalized looks on her ladies' faces. Val was crimson-cheeked. But Vincenza wasn't blushing. Neither was Detto. Instead his face was pale as he turned to the young woman and said, "I'm sorry to hear of your loss. Please give my regards and best wishes to your lady mother."

"I shall," said Vincenza. "If you will do the same to your cousin—Cesco, he is called, yes?"

Detto blinked. "You know Cesco?'"

"No," said the young lady at once. This time she did blush. "I only know his reputation in Padua. And thought I have only been here a short while, your mother speaks of your cousin often."

"He has always fascinated her," said Detto, his face a contradiction of emotion.

As interesting as Katerina found her new lady-in-waiting's questions, she had more important matters to discuss. "My dears, please sit, continue your work. Val, be a darling and continue to entertain them. You may speak with your brother when I am through. Bailardetto—a word." Leading the way, Katerina exited the Great Hall by a side staircase. She drew him far from the ladies, into a long gallery rife with shadows, well out of earshot. "How is he?"

Detto's face continued its contortions. "As well as could be expected."

"Is he reconciled?"

"To the marriage? It was his idea."

"Will he go through with it, do you think?"

Her answer was a frown. "I don't know. He seems to mean to."

"And what of the girl? Not his bride, the other one."

"She has gone back to her father. Cesco has not heard from her."

"You're certain?"

"No," he said, again demonstrating that he offered truth before he ever thought to lie. "But I think I'd know," he added. "He's just—empty. Like there's no point in trying to do anything."

"Perhaps he is waiting," said Katerina.

Detto's shrug was lost in the darkness. "If he is, I don't know what for."

"I can tell you. He is waiting for me." Katerina seemed to swell, suffusing her presence and voice with a majesty that always added luster to her beauty, even despite her fallen face. "I have a message for him. One I insist you convey. Tell him I still possess the weapon he requires."

"Weapon?" echoed Detto, suspicion in his voice.

Katerina gazed at him imperiously. "He will know precisely what I mean. Tell him I am waiting."

To her dismay, her son laughed softly. "He told me you'd say that."

"Say what?" demanded Katerina.

"He said you would make an offer. That you're waiting for him to come to you."

Katerina did not like having her moves predicted. "And what did he say?"

Her elder son took a slight step back, as if readying himself to be struck. "He said, 'Let her wait. I have seen my Fate already.' What did he mean, see his Fate?"

"You know what he meant. The girl. The incest. All of it."

"Then what weapon do you have?"

"That is no concern of yours."

Detto answered his mother's insult with silence.

"He refused it before. But he will want it now. Tell him he is correct. I am waiting."

Detto shook his head. "I won't."

"And why not?"

"Because he might give in. He's not himself."

"That's certainly true." Turning, Katerina crossed the shadowed gallery and strode down the stairs, gripping the handhold carved into the stone. "Tell him I am waiting for him to shed this cowardly self-indulgence, grow up, and become who he's meant to be."

After she had gone, Detto said softly, to no one, "I just want my friend back."

But someone did hear. Excusing herself from the ladies below, Vincenza had followed her mistress up the stairs. Hiding behind a tapestry in the long shadowed hall, she had listened with care to every word. For a terrible moment she had feared discovery. But Katerina had passed her by without noticing.

What to do now? Vincenza considered going now to comfort Bailardetto, heir to Vicenza. Her mother would surely approve. And not just because of the symmetry of names.

Vincenza, however, saw now was not the time for her. Nor this the place. Slowly, softly, she slipped from behind the tapestry and retreated down the stairs, away from the life of Detto and his infamous cousin.

For now.

AUTHOR'S NOTE TO LADY IN WAITING

Set between FOOL and DOOM, this is a brief visit to a character who dominates whatever scene she is in—Katerina della Scala in Nogarola.

Planning THE MASTER OF VERONA, I saw from the first that I had a real dearth of excellent female characters. I knew about Gianozza from the start, though not entirely that I would grow to hate her so deeply as I do. Likewise, I knew about Lia, someday. And there was Antonia, Dante's daughter. But other than those three, I had little inkling about the nature of the women in the world I was creating—who they were, what they wanted.

I found help from both history and Shakespeare. In the end, Cangrande's wife became a villain of sorts. And introducing Kate from *Shrew* was a nice side-character. But I still needed someone with teeth, someone to be the central pivot of all the actions, interactions, and relationships.

In the research I read a brief mention that Cangrande had been raised by his older sister, at the court of her husband, lord of Vicenza. At once I was fascinated. If Cangrande was a genius, how much more demanding and brilliant did the woman who raised him have to be? What a dynamic, the push and pull of sibling and parent/child, all in one place! It was too obviously important, and at once worked into the narrative.

The book was published, and I was deep into research for FALCONER when I discovered her death-date: 1305, or thereabouts. Nine years before my story even started.

Of course by then, MoV had been published and she was so firmly a part of my story that I couldn't imagine losing her.

Yet, in a way, I did. But for an entirely different reason. She's just too damn over-whelming. She is always and forever the central focus of whatever scene she is in. Oh, I can throw strokes at her, I can make her suffer a blow and a second stroke, I can make her family revile and resent her. All this will do is make her more determined, and more powerful. She is perhaps the most formidable character I have ever created.

And yet she's trapped.

Her brother would say she's trapped by gender. But more than that, she's trapped by her own expectations. She is so determined to prove herself important by upholding her role in the Greyhound prophecy, she keeps herself from actually achieving what she's capable of. For, let's be honest, there is nothing she could not achieve were she not shackled to her own twisted concept of 'mother' to *Il Veltro*.

This causes her to be in a perpetual state of waiting. A shame, both personally and narratively. On the personal front, she misses so much. She entirely misses being a mother to her firstborn son—her only interactions with Detto are about Cesco. On a narrative level, waiting is not exciting. In the first couple of books, she was plotting and seeding future events. But for FOOL and DOOM, her part was reduced to watching the harvest of all her work.

This story, then, is that in its purest form. She may have ladies who attend her, but Katerina is the real lady in waiting. She is waiting for Cesco to embrace his star-told destiny, and thus define her as something more than mere mortal woman. She expects to become a figure of myth. Igraine, perhaps. Or Rhea Silvia, mother to Romulus and Remus.

Sad, then, that she will never learn who it was she gave metaphorical birth to. Neither king nor emperor, she raised a scoundrel, a rogue, mercurial to the extreme. Whereas her actual son is a good man, an excellent knight, and the perfect friend.

Katerina is the most tragic of figures. Combined with her brother, theirs is an epic tale of expectation, dissatisfaction, insecurity, ambition, and loss. Both forever in a perpetual state of anticipation, waiting to become who they long to be.

I Dodici Apostoli

For Anna Lerario

"What's become of the wenching rogues? I think they have swallowed one another. I would laugh at that miracle—yet, in a sort, lechery eats itself. I'll seek them."

—Thersites
Troilus & Cressida
ACT V, SCENE IV

"Do you think because you are virtuous, that there shall be no more cakes and ale?"

—Sir Toby Belch
Twelfth Night
ACT II, SCENE III

ONE OF THE FAVOURITE HAUNTS of the Rakehells was a tavern with exquisite fare known as *La Pentola*—'The Cookpot'. Through its narrow half-door and large interior portal were wide rooms with long polished tables that would quickly be heaped with delicious foods.

The story of its founding was made to amuse Cesco. One of the palace's former cooks had departed in a fit of pique during that week when Cangrande had played at being dead and Mastino had the running of the palace. Insults to his person, the cook could have endured. But insults to his food, never. So, leaving his son to continue in the palace, Antonio Gioco departed in a fit of temper.

He did not travel far, just a few streets away, around the corner of the Piazza delle Erbe, to an inn with an invidious reputation that happened to be run by his wife's cousin. And here Antonio began cooking furiously. Within weeks the place's reputation had changed. It now drew monied but common folk, those who had never dined at the palace and wanted to taste creations invented for the Scaligeri.

No foole, the cousin-in-law, Mondadori, quickly altered the nature of his establishment. *La Pentola* was no longer a mere trader's post and feeding trough for traveling merchants. The Cookpot was now a destination for both travelers and locals wishing to eat noble foods.

Mondadori was afeared, after Cangrande's miraculous resurrection, that his cousin's husband would return to the palace. Certainly Cangrande asked. But it seemed the elder Gioco enjoyed being his own man, not tied to the vagaries of a lord's whims.

Business got an even more impressive boost some months later. There was a dish Cangrande particularly favoured, based on Hebrew cuisine, a baked onion salad. Though the younger Gioco did his best, he could not recreate the dish as it had been made at the hands of his father. So one day, to the astonishment of those within and without, the Scaliger had strode into the inn, sat himself at a trestle table, and commanded a bowl of it.

From that moment onwards, *La Pentola* had to turn business away. Gioco introduced the people to Golden Morsels, those sugared bread delights that so fascinated the nobility. He offered lamb, duck, and boar in sauces that lingered in the memory, making the mouth water. He taught the trick of reversing a fish so the fat was rendered, leaving only the flavour. The costs of the spices and meats were huge, yes. But Mondadori was able to command magnificent sums—there was no price too high for someone wishing to eat as well as the Prince.

In three years, the place had undergone a transformation. It was now well-lit and clean (the latter allowing the former), and decorated with magnificently carved tables and stools of the darkest hue, so brown they were almost black. They had been able to pay for a new façade, the banded red brick and cream marble that was so much the Veronese style.

It was still an inn, attracting all types. This last month it had been filled to bursting for the wedding of Verona's heir, and the ongoing revelry had hardly slackened their demand. When the heir himself appeared this evening, carting a sack and looking for food for himself and his companions, Mondadori was hard-pressed to find space for them.

To his relief, Cesco grinned at him. "While we wait, I'll just pop into the kitchens and say hello to Antonio." And, his satchel over his shoulder, he vanished around the corner and down the stairs, into the kitchens built into the ancient Roman ruins beneath the building.

The rest of the young men (some of them not so young), stamped their feet free of snow and clapped their arms. It was an unusually cold winter, and the snow had come early and lay heavily over the ground. Most of the time you could just sweep the light dusting away. But not this year, when the Adige had a thin skein of ice across it and little children were able to fashion snowballs for the first time in their lives.

Clearly the Rakehells, as they were coming to be known, had spent the day in some active sport out-of-doors. They were covered in snow, blue of nose and red of cheek. Some Mondadori knew well—the Bonaventura twins, Petruchio and Hortensio; the Nogarola brothers Detto and Valentino; Cangrande's bastard sons Bartolomeo and Ziliberto; and Prince Rupert, nephew of the Holy Roman Emperor, some of whose party were still lodged here.

Others he knew only by their reputations. Fabio Scolari and Yuri Castorani, the hawk and the bear, adult mercenaries in Verona's employ, whiling away their winter cavorting and sporting with Verona's heir. The little sour-faced blond lad was obviously the young Capulletto boy, Thibault, who so often sparred with his uncle. And the last pair were Paduan by their accents, and possibly the eldest after Yuri and Fabio. The red-haired one had to be Signor Benedick. Which made the other one with the calm voice, happy face, and liquid eyes Salvatore.

Cesco returned just as a table was cleared, the previous occupants chivvied to their rooms with an extra helping of wine. Still carrying his satchel, Cesco plopped himself down in the midst of the party and made idle talk until the wine, bread, and cheese had been served. "Don't be gluttons with the bread," he warned. "I've seen what Gioco's cooking tonight, and we may never move again."

"This," barked Yuri, "from a lad thin as a whippet."

"That would be a fine name for him," agreed Fabio. "Isn't whippet a smallish breed of greyhound?"

"A bastardized breed," agreed Yuri.

"The bastard of a bastard," chortled Thibault.

Cesco snorted. "That jest is so old, I wonder it hasn't turned to vinegar."

"Or piss," said Petruchio sourly.

"What's that?"

"Oh, my dear brother was quite inventive. He discovered that if you take a platter outside in this weather and urinate into it, you will soon have a sheet of frozen urine."

"That can be slid under locked doors," added Hortensio, chortling. His twin smacked him across the back of his head. There were gravely amused looks all around, as everyone eyed the fellows they lived with suspiciously.

"Speaking of terrible ideas," said Salvatore, pointing, "Ser Francesco, you should send that back to the kitchens. It's gone bad."

The loaf of bread he was indicating was dark and hard, less inviting than the flaky warm bread along the rest of the table. Cesco glanced at it, then drew it closer. "It is dark as my heart, and somehow I will choke it down." He clapped his hands. "Well, I'm certain you're all desperate to know why I've asked you here. The fact of the matter is this—I have need of you all, my friends! The Capitano has deputed me to oversee the Christmas revels!"

"That's like asking Lucifer to oversee a Christening," laughed Cesco's half-brother Barto.

"Or a tart to run a nunnery," opined his other half-brother Berto.

"Two sides of a coin, those two," muttered young Petruchio.

"Obverse and Reverse," chortled his twin, Hortensio.

"Quiet, dunce, or they'll use those names on us!"

"Speaking of coins, Obverse," said Cesco (Petruchio rolled his eyes heavenward), "I'm to be given the dies for the minting of new coins. I've decided to have my own made. Any suggestions?"

They all bandied about ideas, roaring more loudly with each progressively foul suggestion. It was only when the image of a greyhound killing a hare while tupping a goat was floated that they had to rein in their creativity—because the food had arrived.

There was Apple Muse, boiled apples in almond milk and honey; there was a delicious platter of fawn-meat in a light applesauce; and a favourite of every true Veronese, boiled meats in *Pearà* sauce. A thick winter dish combining day-old bread, butter, marrow from the *osso buco* bone, meat broth, cheese, nutmeg, and a heavy dose of black pepper.

In a season of feasts and revels, this was perhaps not the most lavish table set. But it was sumptuous, and the intimacy and simplicity of the place combined with the lack of ceremony to make it a thoroughly enjoyable meal.

"Better than anything you'd get at *La Rosa Colta*," said Detto softly.

Cesco arched an eyebrow his cousin's way. "Not *anything*."

It would have been perfect left there, but several men had to add their wit, and there were many jokes about fish. Blushing, Detto deflected the jests by turning to Cesco. "So, cos, what are these Christmas chores you need our help with?"

"Well first, I was thinking of decorating the Advent Sunday trees with these apples," said Cesco, dumping the contents of his satchel onto the long table. They were deeply red, hard and crisp to look at, and had the table not been replete with apple dishes already, they would have been devoured at once.

"What's special about these apples?" demanded Yuri suspiciously, lifting one.

"They're magic apples," said Cesco. Everyone laughed, knowing the old joke. Detto blushed again. "No, truly they're from the Garden of Eden. One bite and you will have the knowledge of good and evil."

Yuri stared at his, then slowly put it down. "I do not trust you, I."

"Aye?"

"Aye."

Cesco grinned. "With good cause."

The moment the apple was still, it rattled and fell over. "Jesus!" cried Yuri, jumping backwards. The laughter was stifled by rattles coming from the rest of the apples, which were twitching and quivering on the table. One apple started to roll towards Prince Rupert, who speared it to the table with his knife. That stopped its approach, but not the rattle within. Noting the butt of the apple was not quite flush, he tugged at it. A beetle shot forth, darting off the edge of the table towards the shadowy back stairs.

"See?" said Cesco lightly. "The knowledge of Good and Evil. Good without, evil within."

"Ser Francesco!" cried Mondadori, blanching in dismay as he ran over to collect the other rattling apples. "We cannot have beetles in the kitchen!"

"Oh come!" retorted Cesco. "Where do you think I got him?"

Several people in the inn eyed their dishes askance, unsure if he was joking. Mondadori rushed from one to the next, assuring them he was.

"Obverse! Reverse!" Cesco snapped his fingers at the Bonaventura twins, who winced, realizing the names had stuck. "I have a task that can only be performed by you." Their eyes became warily eager. "I need you to sit down and recount, word for word, you parents' best fights. I have a mind to pen a Nativity play, but with the Virgin and her husband as Kate and Petruchio."

The table might have shattered into pieces, so loud was the roar of laughter that shook it. Embracing the task, the twins rose at once to portray the Saviour's parents as their famously combative parents. Petruchio played his namesake, Hortensio their shrewish mother.

"If you don't like the ass, woman, dismount, and I'll take my ease! These boots are murdering me!"

"Good! I had them made just for that purpose. And I never said I didn't like my mount."

"You complained of the ass!"

"I was speaking of you!"

"You adore my ass."

"Yes yes, the ass that launched a thousand ships. But though the ass is admirable, the ass that wears it is abominable. How much longer must I bear it?"

"'Tis I that bears it."

"My swollen belly proves you a liar."

"Look, he said we may refuge in that manger."

"I may refuse my refuge. A mangier manger there never was."

"You'll manage that manger, then, to make it less mangy."

"Oh, I'm to clean, am I? What, is the divine child supposed to wait until I'm done tidying up?"

"Hardly! If he's divine, he can pop out and help with the sweeping!"

"You mock his divinity?"

"Not at all. I mock myself for falling prey to such a tale. 'O, I love you, Guiseppe, I truly do. Don't mind I'm pregnant. The baby belongs to the Lord.' Which lord, I ask. Because if it's that nobleman with the fancy camel up the road—"

"I'd never fancy his camel as much as I fancy your ass, dear."

Howls, tears, fists pounding the table. They carried on through the birth, responding as much to the heckling Rakehells as to each other. At last the Saviour was born, portrayed by Cesco crawling out from between Hortensio's legs and proclaiming, "Here I am! Where are my gifts?"

Yuri, Fabio, and Salvatore played the three wise men, offering gifts of lint, dust, and spit. They sang scandalous versions of Jacopone da Todi's Christmas rounds, shocking the ears of some other guests but gaining the approval of even more. They danced and cavorted, flapping their arms and clapping their hands, singing until their voices creaked and croaked.

"Bring me some water," cried Cesco, coughing from too much mirth. "And in that fine glass vessel!"

Mondadori looked stricken. The Cookpot's glass pitcher, made in the Holy Land, was a truly treasured piece. Yet he could not deny Verona's heir.

He was relieved to see when he returned that the table was more ordered, with Cesco returned to his seat and the others gathered around.

"So, here I am, the Saviour at table surrounded by my twelve closest friends. I seemed to have aged prematurely, leaping from birth to Last Supper in a single night. And I haven't even performed any miracles!"

"Loaves and fishes!" shouted Barto and Berto, still hungry.

"Not if we're starting with that loaf," sneered Thibault, pointing at the untouched dark loaf beside Cesco.

"And wait until we're at *La Rosa Colta* to multiply the fishes!" added Yuri loudly.

"Are you planning to raise the dead?" asked Salvatore.

"Or walk on water?" snorted Rupert.

"No no. For my first miracle, I shall turn water to wine!"

"You mean wine to urine!" shouted Benedick.

"We needn't see you do it, though," added Thibault wryly.

Cesco plucked up a chunk of unbroken bread that had been sitting by him, untouched through the meal. He tore it in half over the clear pitcher, so that chunks of it fell to disturb the water. "Take. Eat. This is my body—"

"Then your body's a corpse," mused Fabio, staring at the bread.

Cesco frowned. "Fine." He dropped the butt of bread he was holding into the pitcher.

"If that's your body," laughed young Petruchio, "then you're planning to walk on water after all!"

They were chortling and teasing when suddenly Berto shouted, "Look!"

Amazed, the watching Rakehells saw the water turn cloudy, growing darker and darker until the liquid was unmistakably the colour of wine.

"Cesco, what did you—?"

"*How* did you—?"

"What in Heaven's name—?"

Cesco waited for their amazed gasps and questions to end. Then he poured from the pitcher into each other their cups. "This is my wine. You are my apostles." He gazed around at them. "I wonder which of you will betray me." He let that linger for a time, then grinned. "But until we find out, bottoms up!"

Some time later, after Cesco had made Benedick pay for the meal from a borrowed purse and everyone prepared to depart for their next bit of sport, Detto drew near his cousin. "How *did* you do it?"

He would not answer anyone else. But for his childhood playmate, Cesco could not resist a teasing answer. "How do you think?"

"It was the bread. But how?"

"Simplicity itself. Yesterday I soaked the bread in wine, then let it dry. When we arrived, I went downstairs and asked Gioco to help me set up my 'miracle'."

Detto grinned. "Well done. For a moment they were convinced. I think Thibault still is."

Cesco laughed. "He thinks I'm divine now, does he?"

"Infernal, more like."

"Either will do." Shrugging, Cesco wrapped an arm about his cousin's shoulders as the pair of them headed for the door. "Thank Gioco, will you, Mondadori? And thanks for the use of your pitcher. It was—miraculous!"

Thinking the real miracle was that the glass vessel had survived, Mondadori waved them out. "Glad to be of service, my lord. You and your twelve apostles are welcome any time."

There was an unforeseen effect. The story spread swiftly that night—of the playacting, the singing, and the 'miracle'. Some recognized it for what it was, others scoffed or crossed themselves. But some believed. People began to come to the inn, hoping to find the twelve new apostles there.

Mondadori was a businessman. As with Gioco, he knew a good thing when he saw it. Within two days, he'd commissioned a new sign to hang above his door, effectively renaming his inn: *I Dodici Apostoli*.

The Twelve Apostles.

AUTHOR'S NOTE TO I DODICI APOSTOLI

This occurs in the middle of Chapter Eleven of THE PRINCE'S DOOM, the night after Cangrande's big feast at the palace. And I confess I am absolutely butchering a piece of Veronese history here. But I couldn't resist.

The Twelve Apostles is a real restaurant, and a marvelous place to dine. I was taken there by film-maker Anna Lerario, her husband Antonio Bulbarelli, and their friend Joyce Stewart, an American journalist living in Verona. It was a fantastic experience, and the basement houses an excavation of Roman ruins that, once again, I imagined long before I ever saw beneath Verona.

However, this was no early-Renaissance establishment. The restaurant was founded just after WWI, not in the 14th century. And it was named for the dozen merchants who regularly gathered there to eat and discuss their trade. These men were jokingly called the Twelve Apostles, and the lighthearted title attached to the place where they met.

The names, too, I've repurposed. Giorgio Gioco is the name of Cangrande's cook. It is also the name of the famous cook at The Twelve Apostles, whose father took over the place, and whose son runs it today. I like to think that these men would not mind me weaving the tale of their restaurant even more deeply into Verona's lore. But with the food they serve and the friendship they show, they hardly need my help.

As for my Rakehells, I know there are several untapped stories in their antics. For a brief winter and a briefer spring, they were the devils of Verona, reflecting all that was both good and evil in Cangrande's time. Having hinted in the novel about the Nativity play with a warring Mary and Joseph, it was fun to dabble in what that might sound like. And I discovered the apple prank too late for DOOM, but was delighted to put it to work here.

Just as I was unable to resist putting I Dodici Apostoli into my Verona, felt compelled to put the band back together, if only for one more night of Cesco's impiety.

It will do him harm one day. But not today.

Illyria Lost

For Patrice Batyski

"You cannot love her;
You tell her so; must she not then be answer'd?"

—Viola
Twelfth Night
ACT II, SCENE II

"My love is as a fever longing still,
For that which longer nurseth the disease;
Feeding on that which doth preserve the ill,
The uncertain sickly appetite to please."

—Sonnet 147

AFTER THE EASTER MASS, a dozen riders departed Verona by the road leading east. Eleven men and a boy.

"Father?" asked a young voice.

"Yes, son?"

"Will we be at the castle long?"

"Long enough," said Mariotto Montecchio, leader of band of men, all of whom bore his crest. "We are tasked with raising our muster to add to Verona's army for the coming attack on Treviso." He leaned sideways in his saddle to ruffle his son's dark hair. "As this will be your duty someday, it's time you started learning how to be a lord."

Shy of his eighth birthday, Romeo was pleased by this. He smiled shyly, sitting a little straighter in his own saddle. He wouldn't ever rival the Scaliger in height, but he'd probably at least be taller than his father. This in turn pleased Mariotto—children should be better, stronger, more able than their parents.

Then the pleasure went away, for them both. "Is Mother coming?"

It was a wary question. The boy sensed the tension and, as a natural pleaser, being caught in the middle was genuinely painful.

Mariotto's answer was abrupt. "No. This is a lord's duty. She has other concerns."

It was not a good answer, though it was a true one. But times past he'd have taken her back to their lands for this kind of journey. Times past he couldn't bear to be out of her company.

Times past he hadn't been sick just looking at her.

I must forgive her, a voice inside him insisted. But a second, more contrary voice said, *But for how long? How many times?*

That was the question. How often was he going to have to overlook her behaviour? Mariotto had long ago recognized his wife was self-centered.

But never had he truly seen what she was—a female Narcissus. Though it was not her own beauty she loved, though beautiful she was. No, she was enamoured with the drama of her life.

How ironic that it was the Palio that had shown him the truth. He had met her at a Palio fourteen years ago, wooed her and won her in that single night after he had emerged victorious. *Shamefully victorious,* he thought, recalling his trick that had sent his best friend toppling to the ground even as Mari had scaled the wall to cross the finishing line. But that best friend had been her betrothed. True, they had made no vows...

I did, though. Mari recalled the many oaths of friendship he had made. Of the thin knives that they'd had made. His own knife had shed his blood as he'd cut his palm and mingled his life with Antony's, making them blood-brothers.

That same knife murdered my father.

The anger of that thought passed swiftly enough. Antony had not done the deed. Even Mari acknowledged it, though in the heat of the moment he'd accused Antony of murder and more.

But it had felt so gloriously righteous. To accuse Antony of a deed far worse than his own was expiating, expunging the stain on Mari's honour that his behaviour with Gianozza had left.

That should have been a warning to me. I wanted it to be true. I wanted Antony to have been the one who murdered my father. Why? Because it would off-set my sins, make them shrink in comparison.

Which is ridiculous. A sin is a sin. Holding it against someone else's deeds may make them seem small, but that does not erase the sin. Only make it easier to live with.

And of course, there had always been the reward. He had his love. A great love, a love like out of an epic poem.

Only didn't all those end in tragedy? Either the story closed the moment the couple was united, or else the greatest lovers of history were remembered for their tragic lives rather than their love. Francesca da Rimini and Paulo. Pyramus and Thisbe. Lancelot and Guinevere. Orpheus and Euridice. Abelard and Heloise. Even Dante and Beatrice. *What lovers are ever remembered for joy?*

But friendship—friendship was remembered as rare, and lasting, extending beyond death. Achilles and Patroclus. Castor and Pollux. Damon and Pythias...

I sacrificed friendship in the name of love. After all, isn't love more admirable? Courtly Love, the love of chivalry, of perfection. That is supposed to be the best.

At once he saw the flaw. That sort of love was supposed to go unrequited. Unconsummated. It was meant as love from afar. *But I was weak. I acted. At first I thought it had brought more joy than sorrow, that I could call it Comedy. But now I see it is a long-playing Tragedy.*

One that could have been fixed. At the Palio, he and Antony had been partnered to run as a pair. At first awkward, then angry, then hilarious, then finally their natural friendship had won through. If only for a moment. They had won the race together. All was about to be mended.

And then Gianozza had intervened, playing the drama, forcing a knife into a wound that had just finally closed. Combined with the death of Antony's little son that night, while Mari's own son thrived, had proven too much. The feud had not ended, had not mended. True, it was not raging, as it had in the days of Mari's ancestors. There were no brawls in the streets. No one was dying.

But I could have had my friend back.

Mari had learned from his youthful mistake, could now see consequences to his actions. His wife had not. This petty feud was how she defined herself. More than wife, more than mother. She was the figure of desire, the cause of strife. Aphrodite. Helen of Troy. Guenivere.

And what does that make me? Lancelot? Am I simply the vessel for her affection? A leading character in the great romance that is her life? Did she ever truly love me?

"Father—are you angry with me?"

Shaken from his reverie, Mariotto fixed a smile on his face. "No! Of course not. No, actually I was thinking."

"What about?"

Mari chose not to share his qualms about Romeo's mother. Yet still he answered his son with the truth. "Friendship."

"What kind?"

Mari cocked his head. "What do you mean, what kind?"

"Doesn't Aristotle say there are different kinds of friendship?"

"You know, I think he does." Lip curling a little, Mari tried to recall. "Let's see. He says there's usefulness, pleasure, and..." His voice trailed away.

"Respect for character," supplied Romeo.

"Just so." Mari had not forgotten. "But it's not that friendship is limited to those things. If I remember, Aristotle says friendship grows out of those things, into something more."

"That's what the Bible says. *'Two are better than one,'*" parroted Romeo, quoting Ecclesiastes, " *'because they have a good reward for their labour. For if they fall, the one will lift up his fellow: but woe to him that is alone when he falleth; for he hath not another to help him up.'*"

"Woe to him indeed," said Mariotto, looking off towards the road ahead.

Romeo was silent for a time. Then he reached out and patted his father's knee. "I will be here, father. If you fall."

"Thank you, Romeo." There were times Mari worried for his son, worried that his wife was fanning the flames of that same love of love that so burned in her. But in this moment, he was touched. His son was one of the kindest souls he'd ever known. Clever, too. But unlike the young heir of Verona, he wasn't so clever he was his own worst enemy.

No, there was only one thing threatening Romeo's happiness. "Son, there's something I want you to remember. Sometimes it might feel that wanting is more exciting than having. But if we exalt desire, it can keep us from appreciating what we already have. Does that make sense?"

Romeo nodded. "Yes. I have you. And mother. And Benvolio. And Cesco, sometimes. That's enough—I shouldn't look for more friends."

Mari smiled ruefully. "I didn't mean that! It never hurts to make friends."

"But if you have too many friends, your soul is split into shards."

"What? Who told you that?"

"Aristotle. He says friendship is a single soul dwelling in two bodies."

That smote Mari to the heart. *That's what we were, Antony and I. And I severed that bond. I was the one who stabbed him, with a knife far sharper than the one that stabbed my father.*

I want to go back to how we were. I want to return to that friendship. A partner.

In that moment a word bubbled up from the depths of Mari's brain. No, not a word. A name. Illyria. What had Orsini said? *'An ideal, a mythical state, a place where one pines for the thing one wants most in the world.'* That was Illyria.

I want to go there.

But he recalled his own words just moments earlier. Desire would keep him from appreciating what he had. Like a son who was turning into a thoughtful and generous young man.

A son he would not have without his wife.

So, as he rode along towards his ancestral estates, Mariotto found a new reason to forgive Gianozza. Even to love her. Just as she did not love him for the man he was, but for the role he played in her story, he found himself able to love her for one role she had played in his life.

She had given him Romeo.

AUTHOR'S NOTE TO ILLYRIA LOST

Preparing this volume, I wanted to pen a second part to the earlier Illyria story. Originally I considered making a direct sequel, where Mariotto is drawn into a plot to murder the new pope. But it felt simultaneously too on-the-nose and too off-topic.

Instead I focused on Orsini's description of Illyria, and realized that in DOOM I had shown the blow-up between Mari and Gianozza, but not the aftermath. So many moving parts, and they were not the main focus of the story. Yet there was more to be said about Mari's revelation, if you can call it that. From loving and forgiving his wife (and himself) for all things, he has grown. The scales have fallen from his eyes. He has matured, where she has not.

I also have a single scene in DOOM between Romeo and his father. It's rather harsh, and may give the impression that Mari doesn't much like his son. That was not my intent. As we know from the play, Lord Montague is very concerned about his son. But he thinks good counsel is the cure to what ails Romeo—reason, to deal with emotion. Though similar in many ways, Mari does not understand his son. Or perhaps understands him too well.

As for the Mari/Gianozza relationship, what is there to say? He has one line to her in the play ("Come, madam, let's away."), and that's in her only scene, where she speaks only two lines. It is clearly open to wild interpretation. After years of doing the play over and over (and over) again, this is mine. It is not meant to be cold, or hating. But neither is it passionate. Not anymore. They are united by just one thing— their love for their son.

This falls in the midst of Chapter Thirty-Four of DOOM. In 1329, April 23rd was Easter Sunday. It begs the question, with all the dates to choose from, why set this tale that day? What does it matter?

Well, for starters, there's the metaphor of death and rebirth. But I would be lying if I gave that as my reason for picking that day as my setting.

Careful readers may note the repetition of certain dates. Among them is April 23rd, Shakespeare's birth and death days. Another is July 12th. That is the week during which the play *Romeo & Juliet* occurs. If my timeline is used, we'll reach those events in 1339. Based on the calendar of that year, the play starts on Sunday the 11th, Mercutio and Tybalt die on Monday the 12th, and the lovers die on Thursday the 15th.

April 23. July 12.

Shakespeare born on April 23rd. Mercutio dies on July 12th. So if I can ever steer events to one of these two days, I do.

I also have personal reasons for this. April 23rd is my wedding anniversary (entirely a coincidence, I swear—we are not those people). July 12th is my birthday. These dates are both of professional and personal significance then. I therefore pay them their due when I am able.

Heart's Ease

For Constance Cedras

PETER
Musicians, oh Musicians,
Hearts Ease, Hearts Ease,
O, and you will have me live, play Hearts Ease.

MUSICIAN
Why Hearts Ease?

PETER
O Musicians,
Because my heart it selfe plaies, my heart is full of woe.

—*Romeo & Juliet*
ACT IV SCENE V

CESCO WAS SAILING AWAY, FLEEING the disaster and despair in Verona. He had written a bitter valediction, declaring his intent to defy his stars. Fifteen years old, outlawed and penniless, with only his cousin Detto to aid and protect him. If ever Cesco needed Pietro, *this* was the moment.

But no ship on the quay was available, or else swift enough, to catch the vessel in question. So, swallowing all thought of awkwardness, Pietro left his companions and ran to the house of an acquaintance.

"Ser Alaghieri!" exclaimed Antonio Ansaldo as Pietro was ushered into his salon. "Or, as I must call you now, Count. Please, come in, my dear Count, and sit! My congratulations on the victory at Treviso, and my condolences for the death of your master. So swiftly may Fortune's Wheel turn. No one knows better than I."

Grateful for the warm welcome, Pietro did not sit. "Forgive me, but my business is urgent. Do you have a ship I may hire?"

"A ship? Of course! I have just invested in a new argosy. She is waiting for orders." He waved to a parcel of papers. "I was just pondering what new trading venture to embark upon."

"I must depart this moment," Pietro told Ansaldo. "Money is no object."

"You need no money here," replied the Venetian with a smile and a wave of his hand. "Well do I remember the kindness you showed me before the trial. And the discretion during it," he added meaningfully.

He was referring to the defence Pietro could have mounted in Shalakh's case against him. Ansaldo could have been acquitted for what he owed the Jew if he had admitted he had made the bargain out of love for his friend Bassanio. It was an odd law, unique in the world—a man was not guilty of a crime in Venice if it was committed for love.

Of course, were Ansaldo to admit his love for another man, he would swiftly find himself a pariah. He had preferred to risk death, perversely wiling to prove his love through sacrifice, than ever voice his true feelings.

Pietro had no interest in playing on that string of gratitude. He was annoyed with himself for even allowing it to enter his mind. And he was grateful he did not need to employ it. "Can it set sail tonight?"

"It will take some doing. I have no one to man the oars at present."

"How quickly can you hire some?"

"About two hours. Will that do?"

"I don't know. I must reach the *d'Oria*. It's urgent."

"The *d'Oria*?" Ansaldo frowned.

"What?" asked Pietro, his heart sinking fast.

"When did she sail?"

"At sunrise."

Ansaldo glanced out the window, looking at the position of the sun. He shook his head, his face a masque of regret. "I am so, so sorry. There is no hope."

"No—"

"I know that ship. I tried to buy her as she was built. But then I the Jew's lawsuit hit, and I was short of funds. Lamba Doria got in first. She's a flyer. Three-masts, and hull as clean as a Turkish shave. Unless she hits a storm or a shoal, there is no hope of catching her before she puts into port." Seeing Pietro's crestfallen face, Ansaldo reached out to clasp his arm. "I am so very, very sorry. I am willing to try."

Pietro shook his head. "No," he said heavily. "I am clearly not meant to follow. It is in my stars."

Ansaldo took it upon himself to console his guest. Not wanting to face the others, Pietro was willing—sometimes the company of someone you hardly know is easier than those with whom you are close.

Which is probably exactly what Cesco is thinking.

Pietro had the presence of mind to send his friends a note with his whereabouts, and tell them to find lodging for the night. Then he sat with Ansaldo, downing goblet after goblet of wine while sharing the public version of the news from Verona, though making it clear that Cesco was entirely guiltless of the many crimes of which he was accused—indeed, had confessed to.

"Though," added Pietro with a pained twist of his lips, "if he were tried in Venice, he could plead what you did not."

Ansaldo could have looked wary, but Pietro did not mention it to wound. The wounds were already present. "He could plead love, you mean."

"He fled, for love. And found that love denied him."

Ansaldo refilled Pietro's wine. "Then he has my profound sympathy, and eternal friendship."

Pietro's mouth curled at the corner. "He would resent the one and reject the other. He wants to be beholden to no one."

"Wisely, wisely," said Ansaldo, who had found himself beholden to a man willing to cut a pound of his flesh away.

They drank for a time, and talked of nothing. As Pietro's nose took in the scent of the water lapping below the windows, a memory came trickling back to him. "I wonder, Antonio, if I might ask a favour."

"Ask away."

"It is a strange one. There is a song, you see. Plucking at my brain. I should like to hear it played, tonight of all nights."

Ansaldo beamed like the sun off of water. "Of course. I shall send for musicians."

He was gone less than five minutes, during which Pietro gazed out the window at the buildings across the canal, wondering what life was like when one could simply take ship and depart, free of responsibility, of care. But of course, Cesco was free of neither.

And I? I am free to marry, now. I am free to practice law, to buy land, spend some of the vast fortune heaped upon me. I can have my own children, unfettered by prophecies, by lies and murderous plots. I am free in a way he never can be.

So why do I feel I am the one chained, and he is the one escaped?

Ansaldo re-entered, rubbing his hands together. "They are coming."

"Thank you. It is a whim—on my first visit to your fair city, more than fourteen years ago—fourteen years—I heard a sad song that has stayed with me. It was sung by Marco Polo's daughter."

"Polo's daughter? Which?"

"The eldest."

"Fantina? Oh, that's a sad story."

"Oh no," said Pietro, his shoulders slumping, his head canting to one side. "She's not ill?"

"No no," said Ansaldo. "Though sick at heart, I am sure. She married—unwisely, I suppose is the polite way to say it. Upon her father's death, her husband insisted on her portion of the Polo fortune—not her dowry, mind, but the independent part left to her by Polo—being transferred to his name. So her share of her father's jewels are now called the Bragadin gems, after her husband."

"So much sadness," murmured Pietro. "So much grasping. Pride, greed, wrath."

"Lechery, gluttony, sloth, and envy," added Ansaldo. "Are not those the weights upon the souls in your father's Purgatory? Ah! Here are the musicians, come to lighten the weights on our hearts."

They came, trailing bells and strings and flutes, eager yet defiant. *If Cesco* were here, he could outplay them, outsing them, and outface them.

Pride. Wrath. Lechery. Gluttony. Sloth. Envy. Cesco is weighed by them all. The only one he is clear of is Greed, and that is the one he is accused of, the reason he is exiled.

But not the reason he ran. No, he ran because the weight of the time proved too great for his young shoulders.

"Come, musicians, play! Play for the new Count of San Bonifacio!"

Hearing that, Pietro felt a shiver pass through him. He was still unused to the name, which he imagined hanging about him like a giant's robes. The title's former owner had been a large man, with a cheerful face and a bitter heart.

A bitter heart. That's what Pietro feared. For himself. For Cesco. Perhaps that was the curse laid on him by Pathino and Vinciguerra both. Perhaps the title came with a bitter heart. Or a broken one.

Seeing his guest's distraction, Ansaldo softly asked, "What shall they play?"

"Heart's Ease," said Pietro. "Have them play Heart's Ease."

Thus Ser Pietro Alaghieri, Count of San Bonifacio, ended that sad summer day filling his ears with the final verses of the old song of longing, of pining, of loneliness:

And thus they spent the silent night
In sweet delightful sport,
Till Phoebus, with his beams so bright,
From out the fiery port
Did blush to see the sweet content
In sable night so vainly spent
Betwixt these lovers two.
And then this gallant did persuade

That he might now be gone.
Sweetheart, quoth he, I am afraid
That I have stay'd too long.
And wilt thou then be gone? quoth she,
And wilt no longer stay with me?
Then welcome all my care and woe.
And then she took her lute in hand,

And thus began to play;
Her heart was faint, she could not stand,
But on her bed she lay:
And art thou gone, my love? quoth she,
Complain my lute, complain with me,
Until that he doth come again.

Until that he doth come again.

AUTHOR'S NOTE TO HEART'S EASE

This takes place moments after the end of DOOM. Venice is a recurring thread woven into the Star-Cross'd tale—Tharwat first appears in Venice (my own Moor of Venice, as it were); Dante dies because of Venice; Pietro grapples with hard truths while imprisoned there; Cangrande discovers his best friend and cousin both plotting against him through Venice; Cesco is literally blinded there, having his eyelids sewn shut as he is kidnapped; Detto is stabbed, though not fatally, while leaving Venice; and finally, when Cesco flees the known world for new faces, new challenges, new friends, new foes, he does so from Venice. Venice is the crucible, the trial by fire for my characters—ironic for a water city.

In DOOM we also see what happens to Shylock after *Merchant*. But not what happens to Antonio, the title character. I wanted to see him again, and perhaps make more of him in the future. I find him one of the saddest characters in Shakespeare. He is in love with his best friend, but cannot say so, instead going great lengths to prove a love that can never be declared. His first line is a lie—"In sooth, I know not why I am so sad." He knows. He just cannot say. Imagine a closeted gay man in the 1950s. Everyone knows, no one says. The sadness of not being who you are, combined with the sadness of someone you love marrying elsewhere.

Of course, 'Heart's Ease' is the song Peter asks the musicians to play after Juliet fakes her death. It's a very funny scene, but Peter himself is hurting badly. Again, eagle-eyed readers may note that a bastard of Poco's has been taken in by Capulletto as a servant. That child is named for Poco's brother, Capulletto's friend—Pietro.

So it felt entirely appropriate that both Peter and Pietro should be moved by the same piece of music, at once mournful and hopeful.

Heart's Ease.

DESPERATE PILOT

FOR ALEXANDRA LACOMBE

"Now let hot Etna cool in Sicily,
And be my heart an everburning hell!"

—Marcus
Titus Andronicus
Act III, Scene i

"Come bitter conduct, come unsavoury guide.
Thou desperate Pilot, now at once run on
The dashing Rocks thy Sea-sicke, wearie Barke."

—Romeo
Romeo & Juliet
Act V, Scene iii

CATANIA, SICILY
27 AUGUST 1329

THE SUN OF SUMMER BEAT RELENTLESSLY down upon the shining deck of the ship, heating the boards underfoot. It was unbearably hot, hotter than the youngest passenger could ever remember being in his life. His skin burned, his muscles ached, and he was full of life.

The seasickness that had plagued him the first few days had passed, and now he crossed the deck with an easy rolling gait, the rocking swell making his step feel momentarily weightless.

Keeping out of the path of the crew, Detto Nogarola leaned his forearms on the rail, looking out at their next port of call. The wood scalded his forearms, and he winced but did not pull back. Not in front of hardened sailors. At fourteen, appearances matter.

He focused on the approaching shore, and the buildings that hovered over the water, beneath the huge mountain in the background that smoked like a furnace. He didn't know the name Catania, but Etna he had heard of. Who hadn't? The volcano had erupted five times in the last hundred years, though not as dramatically as it had in the distant past. That it was smoking now was exciting. Detto wondered if it was wrong to hope for it to erupt while they were here. Probably.

A shadow moved beside him, and Detto pointed. "White smoke. Do you think Etna's chosen a new pope?"

A shrug. "Why not? Everyone else has." The bored voice conveyed no interest at all.

A rowboat came skimming across the water, bearing the pilot who would guide the cargo ship into Catania's port. Detto was now accustomed to the practice, having experienced it the week before in Brindisi. That was where they had first alighted, after an eventless voyage down the Italian coast. Detto had felt a pang as they'd spied the port of Ravenna, home to so many memories. Cesco (not Cesco!) had gazed without comment at the seaside town where he had spent eight happy childhood years. Where his adopted grandfather, the great poet Dante, was buried. Where he had lived a restless but joyful existence.

Before Verona. Before the Scaligeri. Before Mercutio.

Detto was still apt to slip, which irked him. The pair of them had played games with names often enough as children, donning new identities for days at a time. Lies had tripped lightly from their tongues, invented as they touched the air.

Yet now Detto found himself slipping, calling his cousin by his Christian nickname. But Cesco was Cesco no more. It was both an insult to forget, and a bitter reminder of the life they were fleeing.

Moreover, it was dangerous. Nearly a month since their flight, by now word would have spread across the land. Francesco della Scala was accused of patricide, heresy, and a dozen other lies. Enough to string them up in any country, should they be recognized.

As if tempting fate, they had done little to change their appearance. Both were now tanned, the elder moreso as he'd spent hours upon hours in the rigging, just staring into the sky, feeling the wind on his face. The effect was unfortunate, as far as disguises went. The scar from where Detto had been stabbed before Christmas was now a white beacon against his skin.

The same was true for Cesco (not Cesco!). The old scar above his eye was clearer now, as were the marks on his eyelids from where they had once been sewn shut. The scar from the lance he had taken in the thigh three years ago remained hidden except for when they swam. His most recent scars, the ones on his wrists, were covered by a pair of bracers that laced along the sides. Detto was grateful for the bracers. The last thing they needed was a painted sign pointing to Cesco's recent brush with self-slaughter.

Nonetheless, they had made some effort to alter their looks. Cesco (not Cesco!) had cut off his long, curling hair, a decision he'd regretted almost at once, as he was forced to don a cap to keep his scalp from burning raw under the sun. Both teens hailed from a more northerly clime, having only ever journeyed as far south as Rome. And everyone was saying this was the hottest August in recent memory.

Detto, meanwhile, had grown. Already muscular for his age, the constant employment of his arms and shoulders in new endeavors had added to his frame. Whereas his cousin was lean as ever, his muscles as tightly corded as the halyard used to run up the mainsail.

Such terminology was now coming easily to Detto's lips, while his cousin acted as though sailing was his lifelong career. Detto wondered if that would be the case. Would they become sailors? A few weeks past, he would have dreaded the thought. But a life at sea—the rhythm, the work, the simplicity of it—Detto could see the appeal.

He couldn't imagine his cousin crewing a merchant vessel like this. But a warship, or even a pirate ship—that was something that might be attractive. Physical danger spurred Cesco (not Cesco!) to be his best self, stripping away all trappings, hopes, doubts, regrets. That sort of thing had been sorely lacking these last weeks. Not even a rough summer squall to test their stomachs and balance.

Yet even on a warship, there would be tedium, long hours in which there was nothing to do but be alone with one's own thoughts. And there the real danger lay.

Hence Detto's perverse wish for adventure, danger, some madcap scheme, some frightful natural peril. That was when he decided what they would do when they went ashore. They would visit Mount Etna, gaze into the depths of the volcano. A manufactured danger, not a genuine one. But it would be danger nonetheless, a danger less dangerous than being left alone to think.

The pilot swarmed up the ladder with the natural ease of one who had lived his whole life moving from ship to ship. He was in his middle years, unshaven this week, with the first white showing in his chin whiskers. His hands were stubby but sure as he grasped the gap in the rail beside Detto and came aboard. He spared the two young men hardly a glance, heading straight for the tiller to guide the cargo ship safely into port.

Gazing landward, Detto made his statement of intent. "Cesco, I want—sorry, I don't know why I keep—nevermind. I want to see Etna."

Arching an eyebrow, his cousin waved at the mountain. "There it is. See?"

"Properly. When will we have another chance?"

A grunt. "Truth is truth." Cesco (not Cesco!) squinted at the smoking mountain. "That will take us a few days."

"Have someplace you need to be, do you?"

"The ship will be gone before we get back."

"So we take another. Or we explore Sicily. We might look up Don Pedro's father. Imagine Pedro's face when he sees us at court." Silence. "Benedick might be with him."

A venomous look. The objection didn't even have to be voiced. No ties to the past. No reminders. And Benedick did not need their ill-luck as he searched for new boon companions in the Aragonese court.

Still, Detto did not regret trying. He was determined to restore his cousin, if not to his old self, at least to some semblance of life. Swearing not to take his own life was not, Detto understood, an oath to live. It was mere existence. Like a spirit made flesh, but without any divine spark.

Keeping his voice light, Detto said, "What do you want to do, then, after Etna?"

There was the briefest of pauses, then an unexpected answer. "There's an astrologer buried near Milazzo. Tharwat's old student."

Astrology. An unwelcome topic. But at least here was a sign of interest. "Shall we pay our respects?"

"O, by all means. I'd like to kick the dirt over his grave, disturb his rest."

That clearly led nowhere, so Detto waved his hand at the city. "Tell me about Catania."

"What's to tell?" answered his cousin. "A town, a port, with a history. Everything has a history."

"What kind of history?" pressed Detto.

"Like any other." Cesco (not Cesco!) turned away to look at the pilot, who was had taken control of the steering now, guiding them safely up to the quay. "I wonder if that's what all Sicilians look like, or if he's an outlier."

Detto glanced over his shoulder at the man, who did not look particularly interesting—neither handsome nor unhandsome, neither tall nor short. His nose was a little narrow, his brow a little furrowed, though as much by practice as by nature. "What do you mean?"

"Sicily is a crossroad of the world. Romans, Greeks, Jews, Carthaginians, Arabs, Berbers, Moors, Spaniards, Normans, even Vikings I imagine. Pirates, conquerors, traders, pilgrims. All passing here and leaving their mark."

"Ah." If this was his way of answering Detto's question, so be it. "So what can you read in the pilot's features?"

A shrug, a turn back towards the water. "I was hoping for distinguishing features. Like the German influence on—" He broke off, then shook his head as if pestered by a gnat.

Detto knew he had been about to compare the many blonde-haired citizens of Verona, stemming from years of Germanic settlers coming down from the Alps. "We'll have to see the people to compare. Perhaps he's not a native."

"He must be, to know the shoals so well." Cesco (not Cesco!) paused, rubbing his forehead with his knuckles. "That should be a profession."

"What should?"

"A pilot for life. When you approach an unknown and dangerous shore, there should be someone to greet you and guide you safe to harbour. Someone to just take over control of your life until you're safely arrived."

It was tempting to start a religious debate. It had certainly worked before. But Detto settled for a simple truth. "You'd never submit to anyone else controlling you."

Twitches of opposing emotions flashed across his cousin's face: amusement, despair, anger, resignation. "Truth is truth. Come—let's order our things aboard." Seeing Detto's eager expression, he snorted. "Yes, by all means, let's face Vulcan's raging heart."

They had little in the way of belongings, and were able to debark before the cargo had started to unload. They hired a pair of mules and set out to find a guide. As they strolled towards the market, Detto took in the town.

It was not friendly. Some port towns, like Ravenna, were clean and well kept. Catania was the opposite. As they navigated the dirty streets, an agitated man staggered into the road brandishing a knife, shouting incoherent obscenities. Cesco (not Cesco!) and Detto paused, hands dropping to their swords. Whatever the man's intent, he did not care to provoke two armed fellows half his age. He staggered away, and an old man in the window above applauded them.

"How do you rate the people now?" Detto asked.

Cesco (not Cesco!) clicked his tongue. "A fair representation of humanity."

Yet the city had beauties and treasures. There was an Egyptian obelisk pilfered during Rome's rule, and the newly-built Castello Ursino, an imposing fortress that somehow looked more impressive and formidable than any of Verona's fortifications.

"It should," remarked his cousin when Detto said as much. "It was built by Frederick II, who knew the importance of functional defence."

In another square they paused by a massive elephant carved from volcanic rock. When Detto asked his cousin why he was chuckling, Cesco (not Cesco!) said, "Pure disappointment. This beast is rumoured to have been sculpted by Heliodorus. You know him? Heretic, idolater, and necromancer? No? Well, this would have been five hundred years ago. He tried to become bishop of Caetana—it was still Caetana then—and when he failed, he flew this elephant to Constantinople to complain. But it seems sadly earthbound to me. Another dream shattered."

This was his cousin's longest speech in a week. Pleased as he was by even this spark of interest, Detto couldn't help an incredulous laugh. "How do you remember all this?"

Cesco (not Cesco!) tugged their mule on. "I don't. I'm just making it up."

They passed the Roman Odeon, an amphitheatre (though it was nothing compared to Verona's), and several ruins of baths—Detto recognized them from the working ones he'd been to at home. Which he would have to stop thinking of as 'home'. He would never see it again.

Lingering at the construction site of a new church dedicated to San Francesco d'Assisi, which backed the *cavea* of the old Roman theatre, Cesco (not Cesco!) remarked, "So much of Rome remains. I keep waiting to turn a corner and find Sextus Pompey and his pirates."

Detto knew the allusion—Sextus Pompey had turned pirate after his father's defeat at Pharsalus—but not the details. "Was this his base?"

"He haunted it from time to time. There are coins with his likeness minted from here. I saw one in Ravenna, old Guido Novello's collection. I don't doubt if it's the source of his ill-luck."

Guido Novello had been their host in Ravenna, leaving the city only to take up the leadership of Bologna. He had deputed his brother the archbishop to rule Ravenna in his stead, but a distant relative had seized the opportunity, murdered the holy man, and taken over. To this day Novello was attempting to win back his rights, without success.

Detto watched his cousin finger the century-old coin hanging by a leather cord at his neck. It did not bear the likeness of Sextus Pompey. Instead, it bore that of Cesco's chosen namesake, the god Mercury. It had once belonged to a loyal hound, and later Cesco had given it with his heart. Only to have them both returned. At least one had been intact.

As had become his habit, Cesco (not Cesco!) kissed the coin, then let it drop. "Ill-fortuned, these relics of Rome. But if we mean to stay in Sicily, we might travel to Naulochus. Not that there'd be much to see. But that was the beginning of Octavian's transformation. First Sextus was defeated, then Antony, then Lepidus. Like a snake shedding skin. Leaving only the new name…"

That parallel was obvious enough. Yet talk of emperors made Detto wonder again of their eventual destination. Cesco (not Cesco!) would be welcomed at the imperial court. He had even once dreamed of usurping Ludwig, taking his throne.

But that was before.

As they came to market, Detto found himself taking in the people in a new way, trying to differentiate a Greek complexion from a Carthaginian chin or a Roman nose. He was startled to see their pilot of the morning here, so far from his trade. There must be other pilots, of course. Perhaps they worked in tandem.

The two young men found a willing guide, though they were disappointed to learn that the volcano had erupted only a few weeks before, and the smoke now rising was it calming, not stirring.

"Damn," said Detto. "I wanted a show. Was it bad?"

Their guide, Biaggio, shook his head. "The ground shakes, and some lava flows. We know to stay away, though some foolish children like to cook meat over it, or throw rocks into its path to watch them burn. But the eruption is past."

"I'd still like to see it." Detto glanced at Cesco, who shrugged his assent.

As it was still mid-afternoon, they decided to forego sleeping in the grubby town, but rather in a village higher up. Biaggio had family there, and could promise a warm meal at his mother's table.

Up in the hills, Biaggio pointed. "There, my friends. That is the house of my cousin. He keeps bees. You know of the bees? They are famous around the world. They live and thrive around Etna, making the sweetest honey you have ever tasted. The Hybla bees, they are called."

For some reason, Cesco (not Cesco!) looked grim. But he said nothing.

The food was even better than promised, a far better fare than they'd enjoyed onboard ship. Most of the evening was spent listening to Biaggio's mother prattle about the village and wax philosophic about living in the shadow of a volcano. "Waiting for death every hour!" She was clearly angling to be asked why she remained, and at last Detto obliged. She answered with indignation. "This is my *home!* What would I do somewhere else?"

"What indeed?" replied Cesco (not Cesco!).

They bedded down, and at first Detto found himself unable to sleep without the easy rocking of the ship. His cousin had never been a sound sleeper, plagued by nightmares all his life. Detto could hear the breathing, the unnatural stillness, and knew he was not alone in staring out the window at the night sky above the smoking volcano.

All at once there was a red glow. At first Detto thought it was a torch, but it seemed too far off, and too large. His skin began to prickle and his hair stood on end as he sat up, squinting into the darkness at the undulating crimson patch that glowed on Etna's side. "You're joking!"

Cesco (not Cesco!) had sat up as well, and was stifling an ironic chortle. "You can hardly complain now. You're going to get your show."

As if in answer, the earth shook. Not badly, merely oscillating their beds a few inches across the floor. They gripped the wooden frames of their little truckle-beds, gasping. Detto recalled a much worse earthquake, one that had at last united Cesco with the woman who would be his downfall. Not that it was her fault. But if not for that quake, they might never have become lovers, and she might not now be dead, and their lives might not be in tatters. Cesco might still be Cesco.

So it was with trepidation that he looked over to his cousin. Would the shaking ground take him back, or propel him forward?

By the light of the stars outside, Detto saw the answer at once. There was a pregnant pause, then both teens leapt up to hurriedly don boots, farsettos, belts, and swords. Strapped and shod, they then roused Biaggio for a midnight excursion up the mountain.

"It is not safe, *signore*," protested their guide, with less vehemence than he might have done if properly awake.

"If it erupts properly, will we be safe here?" countered Detto.

Biaggio shook his head. "The mules will balk."

"Then we'll go as far as they'll carry us, and continue on foot."

Biaggio looked up Etna's face, and wavered. The money was excellent, and needed. But a night-time climb of an erupting volcano was madness.

Oddly, his mother was in favour of his going. "What, should we not eat?"

And yet, once they were prepared and setting off, Biaggio's mother hissed grim warnings at their backs. "Biaggio! If they venture too far, leave them!

You must come back to your mother! Do not risk you life for these fools! They are courting death!"

"I have experience," grimaced Cesco (not Cesco!).

Mounted on mules, the trio started towards the infernal glow high on the hill. Behind them, one shadow retreated from the flickering light.

ACCUSTOMED TO ETNA'S STENCH, the mules journeyed further than anyone expected. The three humans had to improvise scarves around their faces and cover their eyes from the sulphurous stench that rose all around them. The mules were slow, and there was no hurrying them. The ground was steep and crumbling, liable to slip away underfoot. They had to be prepared to throw their weight forward at a moment's notice, should their mount start to slide.

"Should have hired goats," muttered Cesco (not Cesco!).

"Goats would have thrown us, signore," said Biaggio, sitting tensely atop his mule.

It was likely Detto's rapport with animals that kept the mules going for as long as they did. He had a natural affinity for beasts and fowl, and so was able to soothe his mount as it trudged through the night. With that animal not turning back, the others were stubborn enough to continue on as well.

But at last the mules would go no farther. Close to dawn, the earth gave a tremor that felt like Etna trying to shake them from her back, and the mules all threatened to flee. They had to dismount and haul on the leads to even get them to stay. They would climb no further.

Nor would their guide. Biaggio pleaded, "Please, *signores*. There is no telling what she will do!"

"Then wait here with them," snapped Cesco. He took two skins of water from his saddle and started to ascend on foot, Detto in his wake.

The sun had not yet crested the sea at their backs, but the sky was glowing red ahead of them. A false dawn of fire. The air raked their lungs and eyes, but they as they neared the summit excitement quelled their discomfort. Reaching the crest, they advanced slowly. The sun broke behind them, casting long shadows ahead of them along the reddish earth peppered with rocks so black they looked like shadows themselves. The very ground was steaming, sending gusts of choking fumes swirling into their path.

Then they were there, looking down into the heart of the inferno. A cauldron of raging heat, desperately boiling up into plumes that seemed to reach for the watchers high above.

Softly Cesco (not Cesco) began to recite:

"Ma ficca li occhi a valle, ché s'approccia   'But fix your eyes below, for we draw near
la Riviera del sangue in la qual bolle   the river of blood that scalds
qual che per violenza in altrui noccia."   those who by violence do injury to others.'

Detto knew the line, and the reference. And he thought of all the people who should be cast down into that glowing, growling chasm. So he was surprised when he heard his cousin ask, "Do we belong down there, do you think?"

Detto cuffed his eyes and stared. He had fought, both in sport and in battle. But he did not consider fighting violence. Violence was against the weak. The helpless. The innocent. "Of course not. You've not murdered."

"Haven't I?"

They stood for a time, gazing down into Etna's heart, Detto framing arguments and discarding them, Cesco lost in the labyrinth of his thoughts. The silence seemed full, with the roaring hiss deep beneath them.

When the earth shook again, they weren't prepared. There was no warning at all. Worse, this was far more violent than any previous quake. Detto staggered, kneeling and throwing his hands to the ground. But the shaking didn't subside, and their ears were suddenly filled with a roaring sound, the clash of stone giants, of the Titans of old. The sound of God as he first created the Heavens and the Earth.

Thrown off balance, Cesco pitched forward. Instead of dropping to his knees or catching himself, he threw his arms wide, as if to take flight...

...or else embrace the fall.

Lunging forward, Detto clutched his cousin by the sheathe of his sword. The move turned Cesco, twisted him halfway so that he was now leaning sideways over the swirling, smoking, scalding pit just inches past that edge.

Still Cesco did not right himself. He kept his knees locked, his eyes on the leaping fingers of lava that were more desperate than ever.

Detto swore at him furiously, adding, "You promised!"

Still looking down, Cesco began to lean away from destruction. Hauling hard, Detto was able to yank Cesco back from the edge, sending them both toppling across the hard ring around the crater.

There was another rending sound, and the whole of Etna shook, with clouds of dust and earth in the air, raining down on top of them like bursting, burning raincloud.

They both covered up until it had passed. Then, flat on his back, Detto kicked his cousin in the hip. "You say you defy the stars! That you won't be their puppet!"

Face blackened and scalded, Cesco (not Cesco) fumed. "You're the one who wanted to see Etna!"

"That's what we do! We run the knife's edge! But we don't go over!"

"I'm here, aren't I?" came the snarl as little droplets of fire rained around them. Cesco (not Cesco) swatted at his hand. "Ow!" Squinting at Detto through the smoke, he grinned, his mood turning like his chosen namesake's. "But I don't think 'here' is a good place to be. Shall we scarper?"

They scarpered, sliding down away from the summit. The noise seemed to have shifted, and a hundred yards away from the crater they were able to pause and look back. The glow of the volcano was receding, as if water draining from a bowl. The sulphurous fog and droplets of flame were both diminishing. Yet it seemed to be snowing. Flakes of ash drifted down through the air, some of them briefly sparking with one last flare of life.

"Ow!" Cesco (not Cesco) slapped his skin.

"Burned?" asked Detto.

"Stung," snarled his cousin, holding an angry bee in his hand. He stared at his fist as if he might close his grip. At last he released her, letting her fly off to die elsewhere. "Stung and sore, sweet no more."

From behind them there was a cry, more distant and more desperate, that made Detto turn. "What was that?"

"Biaggio, chasing the mules no doubt. We'll have a long walk back. Dusting ash from his hair, his cousin pointed towards a distant glow. "Something's happening that way. Shall we look?"

Less able to emerge from anger than his cousin, Detto merely grunted his assent and they began a sideways trek around Etna, towards where smaller rending sounds were continuing to echo.

Detto was determined not to be the first to speak. Surprisingly, he wasn't. "You think I'm still acting the puppet."

Unsure if his cousin wanted to talk or argue, Detto remained silent.

"Tell me," insisted Cesco (not Cesco). "How am I still a puppet?"

Detto decided the question was real. "By refusing to make a choice."

"I made a choice. I'm here."

"And after that, what have you decided? We didn't *choose* to go east or west. We went to the first ship that presented itself. Which left it to chance— in other words, the stars. Letting them pilot your destiny." Detto paused, then added, "And taking risks in the hope that one will kill you, that's not living."

"It's what we do, you said."

"Yes. It's what we do. But not why we do it."

"Someday we will go over. We will fall on the knife."

"I know," said Detto softly. "But not willingly. Not by choice. And not today."

A grin. "No. Not today." Under the falling ash, they trudged on.

Ten minutes later they spied what had happened. A large piece of the southeast face of the volcano had fallen away. Suddenly freed, the glowing orange, red, and black ooze was creeping down the length of Etna's face. They watched, thrilling, as the slow-moving river of death reached a spindly tree, which burst into flames.

Neither one spoke as they approached nearer than they should. It was hypnotic, power and evil and wonder all in one. They stood watching its progress, stepping back as it took a slow surge in their direction. The heat on their faces was incredible. Detto felt the temptation to stick a finger or a toe into the muck. If he felt it, how much worse must it be for Cesco (not Cesco!)?

His cousin answered this when he lifted a rock and sent it sailing into the lava flow. It landed with a plop—and then surged into flame as it was consumed.

That started them laughing, and suddenly the goal was to find more items to set ablaze. More rocks, a couple pieces of wood torn from a scrubby tree. If the air weren't so choking, they would have sacrificed their scarves and shirts. So the game became skipping rocks across the flow, as they would across water. They whooped and cheered as Detto got a rock to bounce three times, bursting into flames before it landed a final time.

Turning to search for another flat rock, Detto barely had time to react as a figure came hurtling towards them out of the ashfall. The knife reflected the patchy glow from the lava at his back. Detto evaded it, shouting and stumbling backwards—right towards the lava. Cesco caught him by the elbow, bracing him. But that meant his hands were occupied, and could not draw a weapon.

The figure came forward, knife threatening. His face was covered, but his clothes looked familiar. He pointed at Cesco's throat, where the scarf had fallen away. "That coin! Give it me!"

Cesco's voice was easy. "You're not going to kill us for an old Roman coin."

"Give it me!"

"What for?"

"Proof that you're dead! Won't be much left when Etna is finished with— no no! Stay together. Hands in sight."

Now firmly on his feet, Detto had tried to shift sideways. With only a knife, they could easily outflank him. Something about the stubby fingers gripping the knife's hilt connected, and Detto realized why the clothes were familiar. "You're the pilot."

Their attacker reached up and tugged the layers covering his face. It was indeed the pilot, whom they had seen in the market. Clearly he had been trailing them.

"Why could you not sleep in the house? Then it could have been easy. That boy needn't have died."

Detto saw Cesco stiffen and winced. He would take Biaggio's death personally. Another person dead just for coming into contact with the thread of Cesco's life.

Yet his voice was casual as he said, "I take it there's a bounty."

"A fortune. Francesco di Verona, traveling with his cousin. Descriptions and drawings. Arrived three days back. Lucky no one else was looking. Poor Biaggio. But he knows me, don't he. He'd've peached. Now give me the coin, then turn around."

Cesco opened his hands. "Come and take it."

Grinning back, the villain flipped his blade so he was holding it by the point. "Ah ah. I've a dead eye, son. The coin." He held out his free hand.

Cesco considered, then reached up to undo the thong about his throat. "Let Detto go."

"We'll see." Which meant no.

Cesco made a show of balling up the thong that held the coin, then raised his hand. He suddenly pitched the hand forward, and the pilot rocked back, struck by the skipping stone concealed until now in Cesco's palm.

Both young men bolted forward, but the tough old pilot was quick to swipe his knife again, reversing the grip and slashing even as he cuffed blood from his eye. Used to the tumbling fight on shipboard, he knocked Detto past him with an elbow to the ear, while stabbing for Cesco's throat. Twisting like an eel, Cesco caught the incoming hand at the wrist, staggering backwards as the pilot drove all his weight behind the tip of his blade.

Detto opened his mouth to shout, but already it was over. A twist and shove from Cesco and there wasn't even a moment to be afraid. As Detto dragged his cousin back, all that remained was to watch the results.

The desperate pilot staggered several feet into the oozing flow of lava, breaking the hardened crust that had cooled by touching the air. Flames burst to life all along his loose sailor's trousers. He attempted to turn, but one of his calves seemed to melt away. Sinking to his knees, he flailed with his hands, still brandishing the knife. He had time to scream before sound was choked from him, the flames having reached his face coverings. He flailed and writhed, burning everywhere, dying faster than he could understand. When at last he stopped, it was a mercy. All that remained was a patch of fire that was slowly swallowed by the liquid death that slid just feet away from them.

Detto turned to his cousin. "Cesco—"

Face lit like a figure from the Underworld, Cesco (not Cesco) turned to gaze at Detto, his dancing eyes reflecting the flowing molten stream beside them.

"Not today," said Mercutio.

AUTHOR'S NOTE TO DESPERATE PILOT

This story comes from one of those very happy accidents of research.

Plotting what happens after THE PRINCE'S DOOM, I was looking at the route Cesco and Detto's ship must take, and for a time thought I'd have them stop over in Palermo. But Catania is less well-known, and more directly on their route west from Brindisi.

I was reading up on the town, which stands in the shadow of Mount Etna, looking for historical quirks. The idea of using the volcano itself seemed absurd. Maybe they could hike up its face for fun, but actually having it erupt while they were there—that was too obvious, too on-the-nose, a bridge too far. Still, wanting to be thorough, I looked up the dates of Etna's eruptions, which are thankfully quite meticulously kept.

Etna didn't erupt once in 1329. It erupted twice. From June through August, there were two eruptions, sending lava flowing down the southeastern flank of Etna, destroying part of Acireale, and building the cone of Monterosso.

This is one of those times when all the strings come together. I had written a draft of this before penning THE HYBLA BEES—inspiration is not always chronological. As I worked on that one, I discovered that those famous bees were found on the slopes of Mount Etna. How much serendipity can one desire?

I wanted this story to exist partly to close out VARNISHED FACES, but also because the next book opens more than a year after the events of DOOM, with Mercutio and Detto firmly established in their new lives, with new intrigues all around them.

As much fun as that promises to be, I am forever drawn to the spaces between the known stories. I know what happens next. But this year, from August 1329 to July 1330, is a mystery to me. So I decided to emulate the lads by tossing a rock into the seething volcano of the times, just to see what happens.

A Poet's Nightmare
Part Three

"DON'T GO."
　　　"I don't—"
"Don't."
"— appreciate —"
"Don't!"
"— your tone."
Silence.
"It's not funny."
"It's a little funny. I'm dying. Allow me a laugh."
Coughing.
"I'll fetch Pietro."
A hand.
"In a moment. We shall not be alone again, you and I. Dear me, listen—I wheeze like a punctured bellows."

"I preferred you bellowing."

"And I'd prefer you punctured. A jest, boy. Just a jest. We do not have long. I have been thinking what to say to you."

"To me?"

"I know what to say to Pietro, and my dear Beatrice. I have penned my farewell to my wife, and another for my youngest son, should he not arrive in time. For the rest of my family, I will see them soon, and will need no words. My poor Giovanni. We said goodbye long ago, and now I will see him again." *A cough.* "You, boy. What shall I say to you?"

"Nothing needs saying."

"We've never lacked for words before."

"Best we part now, when we've run out of conversation."

"Ha!" *Coughing.* "I am not immortal."

"So much is clear."

"Nor are you, boy."

"Time will tell."

A snort. "Youth."

"Immortality."

"The same thing."

"Yet you are wrong. You're immortal."

"Oh? I feel my mortality slipping even now."

"Yet your name shall live forever. I'll see to that."

"Where I am going, I can take care of my own immortal soul. You see to yourself."

A tear. "You'll thank me one day, old man."

A smile. "You should live so long, boy."

—*Dante & Cesco*

FIN

ABOUT THE AUTHOR

David Blixt is an author and actor living in Chicago.

As an actor, David has made a career out of Shakespeare. An Artistic Associate of the Michigan Shakespeare Festival, he is also co-founder of A Crew Of Patches Theatre Company, a Shakespearean repertory based in Chicago. He has acted and done violence design for the Goodman Theatre, Chicago Shakespeare Theatre, Steppenwolf, the Shakespeare Theatre of Washington D.C., First Folio Shakespeare, among many others. For the last decade he has taught stage combat and theatre history at the Chicago High School For The Arts. In the course of his career, he has acted in, directed, and done violence design for over forty productions of *Romeo & Juliet*.

As a writer, his interests are far-flung. In his STAR-CROSS'D series he places the characters of Shakespeare's Italian plays in their historical setting, drawing in figures such as Dante, Giotto, and Petrarch to create an epic of warfare, ingrigue, and romance.

In his COLOSSUS series, David explores the first century conflict between Rome and Judea as he relates the fall of Jerusalem, the building of the Colosseum, and the coming of Christianity to Rome.

In HER MAJESTY'S WILL, Shakespeare himself becomes a character as David explores Shakespeare's "Lost Years," teaming the young Will with the dark and devious Kit Marlowe to hilarious effect. In 2017 this novel was adapted for the stage by David's longtime friend and fellow MSF Artistic Associate, Robert Kauzlaric.

In 2018, David released WHAT GIRLS ARE GOOD FOR, his first novel about pioneering reporter Nellie Bly. The following year, while working on the sequel, David discovered eleven lost novels by Bly herself, which he then edited and released to the public for the first time in 125 years.

David continues to write, act, and travel. He has ridden camels around the pyramids at Giza, been thrown out of the Vatican Museum and been blessed by John-Paul II, scaled the Roman ramp at Masada, crashed a hot-air balloon, leapt from cliffs on small Greek islands, dined with Counts and criminals, climbed to the top of Mount Sinai, and sat in the Prince's chair in Verona's palace. But David is happiest at his desk, weaving tales of brilliant people in dire and dramatic straits.

Living with his wife and two children, David describes himself as "actor, author, father, husband—in reverse order."

Learn more at www.davidblixt.com.

The Master of Verona

Cangrande della Scala is everything a man should be. Daring. Charming. Ruthless. To the poet Dante, he is the ideal Renaissance prince—until Dante's son discovers a secret that could be Cangrande's undoing.

Voice of the Falconer

Eight years after the tumultuous events of *The Master of Verona*, Pietro Alaghieri is living in exile in Ravenna, enduring the loss of his famous father while secretly raising Cesco, the bastard heir to Verona's prince, Cangrande della Scala.

Fortune's Fool

While the brilliant, wily young Cesco is schooled in his new duties, Pietro travels to Avignon to fight his excommunication and plead for Cesco's legitimacy, unaware that an old foe has been waiting for this chance to seize control of Verona for himself.

The Prince's Doom

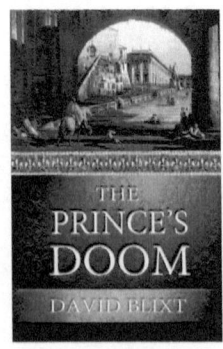

Verona has won its war with Padua, but lost its war with the stars. Heartbroken, Cesco turns his troubled brilliance to darker purposes, embracing a riotous lifestyle in order to challenge the lord of Verona, the Church, and the stars themselves.

VARNISHED FACES

Some stories are part of a grand narrative. Others are small, insular, intimate, yet no less deserving to be told. Taken together, these pieces form a tapestry of life, love, and longing in early Renaissance Italy.

ORIGIN OF THE FEUD

A collection of essays on Shakespeare's ROMEO & JULIET, exploring the nature of the show, revealing its history and inspirations, unlocking the hidden comedy in the famous tale of the star-crossed lovers.

COLOSSUS: STONE & STEEL

A Roman legion suffers a catastrophic defeat at the hands of a band of Hebrews. Knowing Emperor Nero's revenge will be swift, they must decide how to defend their land against the Roman invasion. For twin brothers, this means bringing the fight to the Romans.

COLOSSUS: THE FOUR EMPERORS

When Nero is impaled on his own artistry, the whole world is thrown into chaos. Titus Flavius Sabinus must navigate shifting allegiances and murderous alliances as his family tries to survive the Year of the Four Emperors.

HER MAJESTY'S WILL

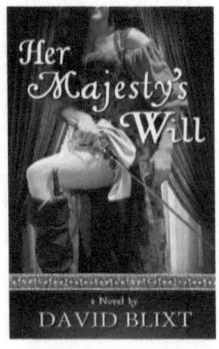

Swept up in the skirts of a mysterious stranger, Will Shakespeare becomes entangled in a deadly and hilarious misadventure as he accidentally uncovers an attempt to murder Queen Elizabeth herself.

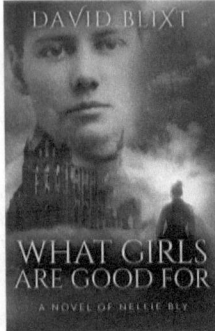

WHAT GIRLS ARE GOOD FOR

From the real-life events of Nellie Bly's life and reporting comes this tale of rage, determination, and triumph—all in the frame of a tiny Pennsylvania spitfire who refused to let the world tell her how to live her life, and changed the world instead.

CHARITY GIRL

Fresh from her escape from the madhouse on Blackwell's Island, Nellie Bly investigates the doctors who buy and sell babies in Victorian New York.

CLEVER GIRL

Inspired by a political speech inspires her, Nellie Bly undertakes her most daring undercover assignment since she escaped from Blackwell's Island: she's going to trap the most crooked man in politics, Edward R. Phelps, the self-styled "King" of the Albany lobby.

MORE FROM SORDELET INK!

WWW.SORDELETINK.COM

www.ingramcontent.com/pod-product-compliance
Lightning Source LLC
Chambersburg PA
CBHW020413180626
46812CB00003B/957

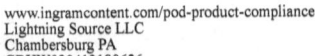